Changeling

"The second in Galenorn's D'Artigo Sisters series ratchets up the danger and romantic entanglements. Along with the quirky humor and characters readers have come to expect is a moving tale of a woman more comfortable in her cat skin than in her human form, looking to find her place in the world."
—*Booklist*

"Galenorn's thrilling supernatural series is gritty and dangerous, but it's the tumultuous relationships between all the various characters that give it depth and heart. Vivid, sexy, and mesmerizing, Galenorn's novel hits the paranormal sweet spot."
—*Romantic Times*

"I absolutely loved it!"
—*Fresh Fiction*

Witchling

"Reminiscent of Laurell K. Hamilton with a lighter touch . . . A delightful new series that simmers with fun and magic."
—Mary Jo Putney, *New York Times* bestselling author of *A Distant Magic*

"The first in an engrossing new series . . . A whimsical reminder of fantasy's importance in everyday life."
—*Publishers Weekly*

"*Witchling* is pure delight . . . A great heroine, designer gear, dead guys, and Seattle precipitation!"
—MaryJanice Davidson, *New York Times* bestselling author of *Swimming Without a Net*

"*Witchling* is one sexy, fantastic paranormal-mystery-romantic read."
—Terese Ramin, author of *Shotgun Honeymoon*

"A fun read, filled with surprise and enchantment."
—Linda Winstead Jones, author of *Raintree: Haunted*

continued . . .

Dragon Wytch

"Galenorn cleverly reveals her plot threads in the latest Otherworld offering . . . Action and sexy sensuality make this book hot to the touch." —*Romantic Times*

"All great stories must have great heroes and heroines. [*Dragon Wytch*] is no exception. In her books, you enter a world of wonder, danger, whimsy, suspense, sensuality, and action . . . This book is a great ride, and the destination is well worth the wait." —*Bitten By Books*

Darkling

"The most fulfilling journey of self-discovery to date in the Otherworld series . . . An eclectic blend that works well." —*Booklist*

"Galenorn does a remarkable job of delving into the psyches and fears of her characters. As this series matures, so do her heroines. The sex sizzles and the danger fascinates." —*Romantic Times*

"The story is nonstop action and has deep, dark plots that kept me up reading long past my bed time. Here be Dark Fantasy with a unique twist. YES!" —*Huntress Book Reviews*

"Pure fantasy enjoyment from start to finish. I adored the world that Yasmine Galenorn has crafted within the pages of this adventurous urban fantasy story. The characters come alive off the pages of the story with so many unique personalities . . . Yasmine Galenorn is a new author on my list of favorite authors." —*Night Owl Romance*

A Harvest of Bones

Yasmine Galenorn

BERKLEY PRIME CRIME, NEW YORK

THE BERKLEY PUBLISHING GROUP
Published by the Penguin Group
Penguin Group (USA) Inc.
375 Hudson Street, New York, New York 10014, USA

Penguin Group (Canada), 90 Eglinton Avenue East, Suite 700, Toronto, Ontario M4P 2Y3, Canada
(a division of Pearson Penguin Canada Inc.)
Penguin Books Ltd., 80 Strand, London WC2R 0RL, England
Penguin Group Ireland, 25 St. Stephen's Green, Dublin 2, Ireland (a division of Penguin Books Ltd.)
Penguin Group (Australia), 250 Camberwell Road, Camberwell, Victoria 3124, Australia
(a division of Pearson Australia Group Pty. Ltd.)
Penguin Books India Pvt. Ltd., 11 Community Centre, Panchsheel Park, New Delhi—110 017, India
Penguin Group (NZ), 67 Apollo Drive, Rosedale, North Shore 0632, New Zealand
(a division of Pearson New Zealand Ltd.)
Penguin Books (South Africa) (Pty.) Ltd., 24 Sturdee Avenue, Rosebank, Johannesburg 2196,
South Africa

Penguin Books Ltd., Registered Offices: 80 Strand, London WC2R 0RL, England

This is a work of fiction. Names, characters, places, and incidents either are the product of the author's imagination or are used fictitiously, and any resemblance to actual persons, living or dead, business establishments, events, or locales is entirely coincidental. The publisher does not have any control over and does not assume any responsibility for author or third-party websites or their content.

A HARVEST OF BONES

A Berkley Prime Crime Book / published by arrangement with the author

PRINTING HISTORY
First Berkley Prime Crime mass-market edition / December 2005

Copyright © 2005 by Yasmine Galenorn.
Cover illustration by Julia Green.
Cover design by Lesley Worrell.
Interior text design by Kristin del Rosario.

ISBN: 978-0-425-20726-0

BERKLEY® PRIME CRIME
Berkley Prime Crime Books are published by The Berkley Publishing Group,
a division of Penguin Group (USA) Inc.,
375 Hudson Street, New York, New York 10014.
BERKLEY® PRIME CRIME and the PRIME CRIME logo are trademarks of Penguin Group (USA) Inc.

PRINTED IN THE UNITED STATES OF AMERICA

10 9 8 7 6 5 4 3

Always and forever
to my beloved Samwise.
Our love abides and grows
Through both sorrow and joy.

And to all the orphaned cats and dogs,
Waiting in alleys, hiding in abandoned buildings,
Who are hoping against hope to find their "forever" home.

ACKNOWLEDGMENTS

Thank you to the usual crew: Linda Parker, Barbara Etlin, and Alexandra Ash, my beta readers on this one; Christine Zika, my editor; Meredith Bernstein, my agent, for believing in me.

Love and thanks to our cats for bringing such joy to our lives. When two of them were lost, I thought I'd go crazy. I want to thank the wonderful regulars on the Petsforum Cats Forum for helping me keep it together through two weeks of hell I never want to go through again.

Thanks to my wonderful Warpies for all their support. To my sister, Wanda. To Margie, Vicki, Siduri, Ceu, Carl, Theresa, Tiffany, and Brad—good friends all. Daniela, for being a dear and providing the German translations for me.

My readers—old and new. Without you, we authors would be lost.

And of course, Mielikki, Tapio, Rauni, and Ukko, my spiritual guardians, gods, and guides.

If you wish to contact me, you can through my website: www.galenorn.com.

I'd like to make a plea here: Spay and neuter your pets; support your local cat and dog rescue organizations. And please, if you can, offer a good home to an orphaned fur-baby. Consider opening your heart to those animals who are waiting for someone to take them home.

Lastly, remember: Sometimes when we harvest the fruits of our labors, we end up with more than we expect. Sometimes we must delve into old secrets in order to put them to rest. Sometimes love crosses all boundaries and barriers, no matter who or what tries to stop it. May you find love in your life, and may all your harvests be fruitful.

Bright blessings to all,
the Painted Panther
Yasmine Galenorn

But in her web she still delights
To weave the mirror's magic sights,
For often through the silent nights
A funeral, with plumes and lights
And music, went to Camelot;
Or when the Moon was overhead,
Came two young lovers lately wed,
"I am half sick of shadows," said
The Lady of Shalott.

ALFRED LORD TENNYSON
The Lady of Shalott

Love is not changed by Death,
And nothing is lost
And all in the end is harvest.

EDITH SITWELL

One

❖

From Brigit's Journal:

The house is remarkably big, and there are so many things to remember. I hope I do well. Mr. Edward rather frightens me, though the Missus is nice enough.

I didn't know school would be so expensive; they were very firm on that account—they don't accept charity cases and I've no resources or family to whom I can turn.

My only hope is to save up enough money to try again. I'm disappointed, of course, but at least this situation is better than starving. It won't be so bad. The time will pass quickly, and I'm used to the work—I've never been spoiled or without chores to do. And I'm sure that in a couple of years, I'll be able to carry out my original plans. I just have to bide my time, mind my manners, and do what is expected of me until then. At least they let me have a cat—bless them for that. My Mab is such a darling, and she'll be good company for me when I need to talk about my troubles. I learned long ago, best to turn to animals for that, they can't tell

yours secrets. Even a diary isn't safe from prying eyes.
But a cat will listen, and keep her silence for you.

"JEEZUZ!" AN ARGIOPE darted across my hand, off the branch I was holding. A second later, both tree limb and spider went flying. The striped orb weavers had grown fat on the last of the autumn insects; now their webs stretched in a parade through the tangle of brambles, silken strands shimmering under the feeble sunlight glinting through the buildup of clouds.

As long as they stayed where they belonged I could handle them, but we'd invaded their territory, put them on high alert, leading to more than one scare when I pulled a vine out of the way here or moved a branch there. Still, despite the thorns and arachnids and chilled sweat running down my forehead, I was having fun.

I still couldn't believe it. To my delight, Joe had actually gone and bought the lot next door to my house. Even though it resulted in weed-whacking duty for me, I was happy. When he began making noises about making things between us permanent I'd been nervous at first, not because I didn't love him, but because I'd been burned in the past—bad. But he was proving himself through his actions, and that was worth far more than a bunch of empty promises.

The early autumn had been mild with an Indian summer, but October came roaring in with a vengeance. A windstorm whipped through Chiqetaw, bringing with it gusts of sixty-five miles per hour, and rain had pounded down for days. All of western Washington was on flood watch—not unusual for this time of year, but still nerve-racking. Jimbo fretted because Goldbar Creek had crested a foot over height, flooding the back part of his woods where we'd found his friend Scar's body, and Harlow fussed about having to drive the long way into town in order to avoid a washout on the shortcut she and James usually took.

About halfway through the month, though, we finally hit a clear spot and the meteorologist promised us dry weather—give or take a few showers—just in time for my birthday, which was on Halloween. Considering that he worked at KLIK-TV, I had my doubts about the accuracy of the forecast, but hey, I could dream, couldn't I?

So when Joe suggested I take a week off to help him clear out his new property, I decided, why not? He needed the help and I needed a break. I'd just finished a grueling three-day stint at the store, catering to the Washington Tea Tasters Society during their annual conference. The event left the Chintz 'n China spotty on inventory, but with a tidy profit. So I placed enough orders for the holiday season, told Cinnamon the store was hers for the week, and promised to drop in every day or so to make sure things were running smoothly.

I stood back and took a deep breath, surveying the inroads we'd made on the mountains of blackberries. It had taken almost all day, but Joe and I'd managed to clear out the longest brambles, fighting our way through thorn and thistle. They were so thick and tall in places that we ended up pruning away at the ends until we could get close enough to clip the vines off at the ground. Then came the chore of digging them out, trying to get as many of the suckers as possible, along with the main root stem. I'd already punctured myself in a dozen places even though I was wearing heavy gardening gloves. At least I'd been smart enough to wear jeans and high-top boots, or my legs would be a bloody mess by now.

I stood back and stretched my neck to the right, wincing as the vertebrae popped. In just two months, the yoga classes I'd been taking had made a tremendous difference in my flexibility, but my body was still rebelling. I wasn't giving in, though. I'd been feeling on top of the world lately, fitting into clothes I'd tucked away three years ago, and I could make it through an afternoon of physical labor without getting winded now. Maybe one of these days I'd get a chance to really unleash my inner Lara Croft.

Joe pulled off his bandana and mopped his forehead. The thermometer read fifty-six degrees, but we were both sweating. "That's the third batch, and we aren't even halfway done," he said, gazing over the weed-strewn lot.

We'd carted away three loads of thorny blackberries.

Surrounded by thick, chest-high weeds, the lot buttressed up against my yard on the fourth, separated by a tall fence over which the brambles tenaciously crept. We discovered a driveway parallel to my own when we started cutting back the weeds, giving us the impression that perhaps a house had once stood on this lot. A few scrub trees dotted the yard, rising out of the brambles and weeds. Near the back, a tall yew—gnarled and knotted—towered out of the jungle, watching over the neighborhood, stark and solemn.

I calculated the amount of foliage left to clear before we'd be able to see the entirety of the lot. "I'm estimating at least another full day's work ahead of us," I said. "Then you can bring in a rototiller and dig up the roots."

"Sorry you agreed to help?" Joe asked, a grin on his face.

I planted a kiss on his cheek. "Nope, I may not like the spiders or the thorns, but I needed this break. Besides, this way, I won't have to hire somebody to cut these damned brambles back next year. They've been trying to creep over the fence ever since I moved in."

"I just thought that, you put in such a hard week, you

might be regretting all the work this is turning out to be."
He knelt down in the dirt near the leading edge of the re-
maining blackberries and dug away at the rich loam.
"Hey, look at this. What do you suppose it is?"

I cautiously picked my way through the thorny stubble
and squatted beside him. He was staring at what looked
like a layer of bricks jutting out from beneath the front
line of the bramble brigade.

"I don't know." The bricks continued beneath the
brambles and I used a stick to pry away the vines. "Patio,
maybe? Maybe we were right—maybe there was a house
under all this mess. Whatever it is, it seems to go back a
ways. Why don't we hack off another two or three feet of
berries to get a better look?"

He picked up the machete he was using and started
whacking at the vines while I gathered them up and tossed
them aside. After a few minutes, more of the brick became
visible. As we cleared another few feet, I began to realize
that what we thought was a patio actually led to a large
brick-lined hole in the ground. The afternoon light was
waning, and it was difficult to tell just how big the chamber was.

Joe lay down on his stomach and stuck his head over
the edge. "Hand me the flashlight."

I sorted through the tools until I found the high-beam
light. I placed it in his hand and he shone it down into the
inky void and scooted forward a bit. Worried that he'd
scoot himself right over the edge and plunge to whatever
might be waiting below, I knelt beside him and planted a
hand on his butt, holding onto his belt.

He glanced over his shoulder with an evil grin. "Want
to take a break?"

I smacked his ass. "Yes, but not right now. Get your
nose back in there and tell me what you see."

"Yes'm." He peered back into the hole and flicked the light from side to side. After a moment, he rolled back up again, looking confused. "That's a pretty big hole down there. Basement, maybe?" He shrugged. "Do you know if there was a house on this lot? When I bought it, the lawyer didn't mention anything about one. He just told me that Mrs. Finch said go ahead and start work on it whenever I wanted, because she didn't have any use for it."

Irena Finch, nee Irena Brunswick. One of the town's economic mavens. She ran in the same circle as Harlow, but she had old money. Once in a while, she showed up in my shop. I had a suspicion she belonged to the smelling-salts crowd—those women who used fainting as a form of manipulation, and who practiced the art of the guilt-trip with as much finesse as Trump practiced the art of the deal.

I frowned. I'd lived here going on three years, but had never heard anything relating to a house on the corner. "I have no idea. Until we uncovered the driveway, I thought it was just an empty lot that had never been used. I've never had any reason to ask. What did you see?"

He shrugged. "Hard to tell. The brambles are still covering most of it. They've draped down over the sides, and it looks like the longer vines grew over the top until they formed a canopy. Whatever the case, this has been covered up for a long, long time."

Curious, I jerked my thumb, motioning for him to move over. "I want a look."

He handed me the flashlight and I stretched out, poking my head over the edge. The next thing I knew, Joe had grabbed a firm hold onto my legs. Probably a good idea, considering my track record. In the past year, my skirmishes into mayhem and murder had landed me in the hospital twice. Though, to be fair to myself, during my last adventure, it had been Joe who'd ended up in a cast.

As I flickered the light around, I began to get a feeling for the immensity of the brick-lined lair. Joe was right. It looked like a basement, and I was pretty sure I caught a glimpse of a staircase descending from the other side, but any access—if it *was* a set of stairs—was still obscured by brambles. I caught my breath as the scent of bonfires and decay and mold settled into my lungs. A chill raced along my spine and I suddenly longed to be in my house, warm in front of the fireplace. I scooted forward as a sound caught my attention.

"What is it?" Joe asked.

"Shush. Let me listen."

I closed my eyes and reached out with all of my senses, listening to the creeping tendrils and soft fall of soil where we'd dislodged the roots near the edge. There—a movement of the wind through the leaves, something shuffling through the foliage? A small animal stalking its prey through the bushes?

Perhaps. Then, a lone caw of a crow echoed and once again, a sound that didn't belong. Soft and low, like a woman sobbing. As I tried to pinpoint where it was coming from, a cold gust of wind shot through the tangle and slapped me in the face. A single shriek echoed in my ears, and then, all was silent.

"What the hell?" Shaken, I rolled away from the edge. I stumbled to my feet. Joe was staring at me, a bewildered look on his face.

"What happened?" He slipped an arm around my waist. "Are you okay?"

I tried to gather my wits. "Didn't you hear that? The scream?"

He shook his head. "No, I didn't hear a thing."

"But it was so loud that my ears are still ringing." How could he have missed it? Unless it had been my imagination.

"Em, honey, I didn't hear a thing except you grunting. There couldn't be anybody down there. Look, there's no way we can even think of getting into that hole without tearing ourselves to shreds on the thorns. Maybe you're just tired."

I muttered something and stared at the brambles. I was sure I heard something, but if it was as loud as it sounded, surely Joe would have heard it, too. "Well, maybe so. But I have a nasty feeling about it, and I want to go home. Now. I need a hot shower and some light."

Quizzically, he turned back to the basement of bricks, then wrapped his arms around me. "Hon, it's just the foundation of an old house. There's nobody down there. We have to clear out the brambles at some point. Don't get upset, please. With all the storms and stress, everybody's been on edge lately."

I took a deep breath. "You're probably right, but I could have sworn I heard someone scream, Joe."

"I know, I know."

"We'd better rope this off so nobody goes tripping in and breaks their neck," I said.

As Joe and I strung a rope around the area, tying it to several bushes, he glanced at the sky. "Come on, time to get inside. The light's almost gone and the temperature's dropping. The weatherman's wrong, there's another storm on the horizon."

I didn't have the heart to tell him I had the feeling that the storm had already broken and was bringing with it more than a downpour of autumn rain. In silence, we gathered up our tools and placed them under the tarp. I took one last look at the sky as we headed back to the house.

All Hallows Eve was on the way, all right. I could feel it in the air.

I'M EMERALD O'BRIEN, the owner of the Chintz 'n China Tea Room, and I'm also the town witch. I gave up fighting the title long ago, because it fits, and the majority of folks in Chiqetaw use it as an endearment rather than a putdown. My two children are my life's hope and joy. Miranda's a fourteen-year-old genius who wants to go race around the stars someday, and Kipling—or Kip, as we call him—is my nine-year-old son who's forever getting himself into one scrape or another. He's a good kid, but I swear, half the silver hairs on my head are thanks to him.

Chiqetaw is a small town east of Bellingham, Washington, tucked away off Highway 9. My best friend Murray convinced me to pack my family up and move here after I divorced my ex—a nasty affair that left a deep, abiding desire for revenge in my heart. But ever since I fell in love with Joe, who's hunky and buff in every sense of the word, and who has a heart as big as his biceps, I don't give a rat's ass what Roy does. As long as he treats his children right, a task he's never proven good at, he could turn into a drag queen and head for Las Vegas, for all I care.

All in all, Chiqetaw has been good for us, even though it's proven a test to my sanity at times. About a year ago the universe took it upon itself to plant a cosmic badge on my chest and, like it or not, I found myself drafted. Whether moving to Chiqetaw was the catalyst, or I moved here because of some predetermined destiny, I don't know, but the area turned out to be a psychic powerhouse, and it swept me up in its vortex.

In the past year I've faced down astral beasties, mortal

murders, monsters out of myth and legend, and broken an ancient Chinese curse. Half the time, I feel like I've been dumped into a movie produced by some maniac Hollywood director. Think Lara Croft, Buffy the Vampire Slayer, and Jessica Fletcher, all rolled into one.

Trouble is, I don't fit *any* of the uniforms. *Emerald O'Brien, thirty-six—all right, almost thirty-seven—year-old tea shop owner and tarot reader.* Nope, just doesn't track with the same pizzazz. Kick butt? Highly doubtful, considering my couch-potato past and my never-ending sweet tooth. Invincible heroine by birth? Not really. I've learned the hard way that my psychic powers don't imbue me with any mystical invulnerability. Detective extraordinaire? Not once have I *ever* expressed the desire to be a famous sleuth.

All the same, the universe handed me the role of karmic facilitator and if there's one thing I've learned over the years, it's that we can't escape our fate. I tried and failed. So now when the universe delivers a dossier to my doorstep, I take a deep breath, clench my teeth, and accept the mission.

SINCE IT WAS Friday, the kids were still at school when we tromped through the backyard to my brand-new porch. Joe, along with my best friend Murray and her boyfriend Jimbo, spent the second week in September building a small enclosed porch onto the back of the house, so now we had a place to remove our muddy shoes and overcoats before entering my far-from-spotless kitchen.

I flopped down on the bench and pulled off my sneakers, setting them on the shoe-stand. As I slipped out of my windbreaker and hung it on a hook, I had the oddest feeling that someone was watching me. I glanced over my shoulder but nobody was there. Must just be the day, I thought.

"Come on, time to get washed up. Horvald's coming to dinner tonight and we're not feeding him spaghetti." I slipped through the door. Joe followed.

Joe was actually a better cook than I was. Or rather, he enjoyed it more. At first that bothered me, but pretty soon I realized what a find he was, and so when it came to company or special dinners, I let him take charge in the kitchen, contenting myself with the job of assistant.

He laughed. "No spaghetti—but first, come here."

As I looked up into his eyes, I felt myself falling again. Falling into his gaze, into his arms, into what had quickly become a deep and dangerous love. Dangerous because I hated showing any sign of vulnerability, dangerous because if something happened, this one would hurt in a way that I hadn't felt since Roy and I broke up.

He pulled me to him and planted a long, leisurely kiss on my lips. "Let's get washed up, woman!" he said, and grabbed me by the hand. We hustled upstairs to the bedroom.

"Do you have a clean shirt?" I asked.

He pulled one out of the drawer I'd cleared for him in my dresser. "Yeah, I replenished my stash yesterday. So, you want to hit the shower first? I've got to call the station and make sure everything's running smoothly."

As I stood under the steaming water, scrubbing away the dirt, my thoughts kept slipping back to the hole in the ground. Joe was probably right, it had to be the foundation or basement from an old house. Whatever it was, I didn't like the energy. I had the oddest sensation that we'd awakened something when we exposed it to the light. Even under the pulsing hot water, a line of goose bumps rippled across my arm.

I toweled off, then wrapped myself in my terrycloth bathrobe before padding back to the bedroom. Joe was flipping through one of my *Time for Tea* magazines. He hastily tossed it on the bed when I came in.

I grinned. "Thinking of going into competition with me, Files?"

He snorted. "Just trying to get some ideas for a birthday present."

"Aha! Caught you. Try perfume, jewelry, maybe a gift certificate for a spa day." I'd been learning to enjoy little luxuries rather than focus on the practical all the time. "Everything okay at the station?"

He nodded, looking satisfied. "Yeah, Roger's on top of stuff as usual. So far, it's been a dead shift—which is just fine with me. Means nobody's in trouble." Joe was the captain of Chiqetaw's medical rescue unit. Ultimately, he was responsible for all of the EMTs, and they couldn't have chosen a more conscientious leader. The men's safety came first and, even on his days off, he never let a shift go by without checking in.

As he stripped off his clothes I caught my breath, once again aware of how beautiful he was—my own Norse god come to sweep me away. He caught me looking and winked. Blushing, I shrugged, and he grabbed a fresh towel and headed into the shower.

I slipped onto the bench at my vanity. I'd cultivated a beauty ritual over the years, a daily pampering except on my grungiest of days when I was too tired to care. Opium dusting powder under my breasts, on my inner elbows, behind my knees. Matching lotion on arms and legs. Then deodorant, face cream, and finally, a spritz of Opium eau de toilette.

I examined my closet. What to wear on a cool autumn evening? With the changing season, I'd revamped my wardrobe. Maybe my relationship with Joe had rekindled my interest in clothing, or maybe Harlow had won and I'd turned into a girly girl, but whatever the cause, I'd begged her to go shopping with me.

She'd jumped at the chance. She was suffering from new-mother claustrophobia, and since her nanny was more reliable than Old Faithful, we spent an entire afternoon haunting the shops in Bellingham, heating up my credit card on calf-length rayon skirts and camisoles and crisp linen shirts. I'd even bought a new pair of suede knee-high boots that looked great with just about everything.

I slipped on my favorite bra and panties, shimmied into a flowing plum skirt and matching V-neck sweater, then hooked my gold chain belt around my newly resculpted waist. Yep, yoga had been good to me. I'd never be stick thin—wasn't built for it and didn't want to be. But at least I could fasten my jeans without sucking in my gut.

"I'm headed downstairs," I called into the bathroom, and Joe let out a garbled "okay."

I reached the foyer just as the front door opened and a gust of wind blew Kip and Miranda through the door. As I looked at them, I couldn't help but think about how fast they were growing up. This year, after-school activities ate up their early evenings and neither one made it home till close to six most weeknights.

Miranda was tutoring others in science and math, while being tutored in English. Kip had computer club, and he'd just started gymnastics, for which he showed a surprising aptitude. Since I was usually at the shop until six, I'd taken comfort in the fact that they were being supervised while I was at work. Miranda might be fourteen, but I'd learned the hard way that even a small, friendly town like Chiqetaw held more than its fair share of dark secrets.

"Mom! Hey, you look pretty tonight. What's the occasion?" Randa grinned at me as she dropped her backpack on the bench in the foyer and shrugged out of her coat.

I waited until they were both sans jackets and motioned them over for a hug. I managed to get in a quick peck on the cheek before they slipped away, out from under my wing. Yeah, they were growing up all right.

"How was school? Cause any trouble today?"

Randa rolled her eyes. "Come on, Mom, you've asked that every day since we started school this year. It's getting old."

"I stand corrected, but I still want an answer. What did you two do today?" I nodded toward the hall. "Come help me get dinner ready. Mr. Ledbetter's coming to dinner."

"Yay!" Kip said. He liked Horvald, who treated both of my kids like grandchildren. "What's for dinner?"

"Joe's grilling steaks on the porch."

They followed me into the kitchen, where Kip scrambled up on the counter and pulled the cookie jar down from the cupboard. I held up two fingers and he nodded, handing Miranda two cookies and taking two for himself. Then, because he knew me all too well, he handed me a couple of Oreos. I winked at him and he laughed and put the jar away.

Randa hopped on the counter, swinging her legs as she nibbled on a cookie. "I had to meet with Gunner again today. Why are you making me go? Mrs. García de Lopez says my grade is borderline. If I study, I can probably bring up it up on my own."

I tapped her knee. "No whining, Miss. You know perfectly well that, left on your own, you'd ignore it until it's too late. I know exactly what you think about the English language when it's not being used to describe a star system."

She sighed, but I saw the spark of a grin back there. I had her number and she knew it.

At the beginning of the school year, Randa had joined a brand-new program for gifted teens who went to the Chiqetaw Middle School. Within two weeks, my brilliant daughter had promptly nosedived in English, receiving a high D on the first two quizzes. Given her past performance, stellar except for English and P.E., where she'd always managed at least a C, her advisor called me. Mrs. García de Lopez suggested either letting her work it out on her own, or requesting a tutor before the problem got any worse.

Much to Randa's dismay, I'd chosen the latter. When she whined, I firmly reminded her that she'd gotten what she hoped for—more challenging schoolwork—and now that she belonged to an advanced group of students, she'd better get used to the extra effort. In *all* subjects, not just her favorites.

"How's Gunner working out, by the way? Is he any good?"

A flush raced up her cheeks and she ducked her head. "Yeah, though he could lighten up a bit," she mumbled. "He doesn't think anything matters except English. He's really talented. The teacher thinks he can make it as a writer."

Um hmm . . . the red face, the mumbling. My little girl was getting her first crush, though I wasn't about to say anything. Fourteen is a volatile age and I didn't want to embarrass her, especially in front of her brother, who would use juicy information like that to his best advantage.

I turned my attention to Kip, who launched into an explanation of the Trojan horse—he was learning Greek and Roman history this year. Half-listening, I pulled the steaks out of the fridge. Joe had placed them in a Ziploc bag, added port, ground black pepper, basil olive oil, and a little Worcestershire sauce earlier in the day, and set them to marinate. They smelled heavenly. A quick rummage through the cupboard uncovered a platter on which to arrange them after they finished grilling.

"Would you please start on the potatoes?" I asked Randa.

"How many?" she asked, without complaint. Randa had recently learned how to cook and had developed an unexpected liking for simpler tasks, especially considering how she'd kicked and screamed her way through home economics the first year.

"Enough to fill the red bowl. If you'll peel and dice them, I'll boil and mash. And then, if you would fix a salad, I'd appreciate it."

With a nod, she headed into the pantry as Joe popped into the kitchen. I winked at him. "Hurry up, Files. We're doing your work for you!"

Kip and Randa waved a friendly hello. Miranda accepted our relationship in stride. She liked Joe, and never complained about him hanging around. And Kip . . . Kip was overjoyed, what with having another man around the house to listen to him, throw a few balls, help with model cars. Joe won his heart when he'd challenged him at a few video games.

Joe managed to walk a fine line, never interfering with my parenting, but neither would he allow himself to be a doormat, for which I was grateful. I might have the last word with the kids, but they always treated him with respect.

While Joe and Kip grilled up the steaks, I mashed the potatoes and Randa put the finishing touches on the salad. The French bread was ready to go in the oven, and Joe would make a gravy out of the marinade. Horvald had promised to bring an apple pie from Davida's Choco-hol Bakery, so dessert was taken care of.

Promptly at seven, the doorbell rang and Horvald wandered in, pie in one hand, bouquet of mums in the other.

"The last from my garden," he said, holding out the flowers. The retired security guard had a thumb as green as my name, and kept me in freshly cut flowers all summer long. Horvald also kept an eye on us, which was comforting considering some of the mishaps we'd gone through. He was more like a grandpa than a neighbor.

Randa swept by, gracefully scooping the pie from his hands, and scurried into the kitchen. I snagged an empty vase from the living room and we followed her. As I arranged the flowers in the vase, Horvald sat back, watching.

"The four of you make quite the team, don't you?" He wasn't joking.

I glanced at Joe and Kip, who were carrying in the platter of steaks. The smell wafted ahead of them, convincing my stomach that, yes, food was on the way and the danger of starvation would be staved off for yet another day.

With a gentle nod, I returned Horvald's gaze and smiled. "Yeah, I guess we do." We gathered around the big old kitchen table where, for a moment, the only sound was that of stainless on china and the busy cutting of meat.

After we were all settled into our meal, I turned to Horvald. "How long are you going to be gone?" I asked. He and Ida—my babysitter extraordinaire and a fine retired schoolteacher—had become an item earlier in the year.

"Just for a few days. We'll be back in time for your birthday, though. Ida and I are driving down to the Salish

Lodge & Spa at Snoqualmie Falls. We leave tomorrow morning, bright and early."

"Cool, we'll keep an eye on your houses for you," I said.

Joe suddenly set down his fork and turned to Horvald. "You've lived around here a long time, haven't you? You must have seen the changes that have gone on in this neighborhood."

"I've lived in Chiqetaw all my life," Horvald said. "Why?"

I immediately caught Joe's drift. "I suppose you've noticed that we're clearing out the lot next door. We haven't told many people yet, but Joe put money down on it a couple months ago and the owner said we could start in on it whenever we wanted. We're tearing out all the brambles so we can see what we have to work with."

"You thinking of putting a house there?" Horvald asked. I could sense he was brimming with questions.

Joe shrugged. "Maybe. The thing is, today we cleared out a patch in the middle of the lot and found what looks to be an old foundation. A basement of some sorts. And we found what looks like it might have been a driveway at one time. Do you know if there was ever a house on that lot?"

"Way cool!" Kip jumped up and started for the back door.

I caught him by the arm. "Just where do you think you're going, kiddo?"

He turned to look at me, his expression falling. "I guess I should've asked first, huh?"

"I guess you should have. Sit down and finish your dinner. I don't want you or Randa mucking about over there, especially after dark. You could fall in and hurt yourself. Capiche?"

After he gave me a muted "okay," I turned back to Horvald.

"So, was there a house? Something feels odd about the place." I didn't want to come out in front of the kids and say that I'd been spooked. Maybe Horvald could shed some light on the situation. Before he could answer, a crash of thunder broke through the sky and rain cascaded down in sheets. Yep, the KLIK-TV weatherman was just as effective as their star reporter, Cathy Sutton.

"So, you found the old Brunswick house? Or rather, what's left of it." Horvald mopped up the last of his gravy with a piece of French bread. He patted his stomach and politely covered his mouth as he burped. "Wonderful dinner. You know, I haven't thought about that family in years. It's a shame, everything that happened to them."

Randa and Kip leaned forward, all ears.

I glanced at them and cleared my throat. "No tragedies, I hope?" Irena Finch hadn't mentioned she ever lived on my street when she came to my shop.

He shook his head. "Not if you're talking lives lost, or anything like that. But the house . . . oh, she was a beauty. A mansion, three stories high, not including the basement. It towered over the other houses around here. I didn't live where I do now. In fact, your lot, my lot, everything down to the highway was woodland back then. The Brunswicks lived at the end of the road. Sixteen-nineteen Hyacinth Street. They were rich, and their son Brent was the captain of the high school football team. Irena Finch is his sister."

"Yes, she's the one selling me the lot. Or rather, her lawyer is. I've never met the woman myself. She inherited the land, I gather," Joe said.

"She married Thomas Finch, who comes from one of the oldest families in Chiqetaw. Real blueblood, you know," Horvald said, touching his nose. "Anyway, the Brunswick house burned to the ground."

"Wow," Kip said, captivated. "Did anybody die?"

I repressed a smile. My son, all right. Kipling the Morbid.

"Not that I know of," Horvald said, lowering his voice as he leaned toward Kip, whose eyes were growing wider by the minute. "But one Halloween night, a fork of lightning hit the house during a thunderstorm. The wood was dry and the rain wasn't strong enough to put out the flames. Nobody was home, and by the time the fire department got there, the blaze was totally out of control."

"Jeez," I said. "That's harsh. But at least nobody was hurt."

"No, but the fire destroyed everything they owned. They had insurance, of course, but it was still bad."

"When did it happen?" Joe asked.

Horvald squinted, thinking. "Oh, it had to have been back in 1955 or so. The Brunswicks decided not to rebuild. The twins were about twenty, I think. Brent had left for Europe about a month before the fire. I don't know whether he ever came back. Irena got married right around that time and I think Edward and Lauren Brunswick moved back to New York after their daughter's wedding. I'd forgotten all about that family until now." He turned to Joe. "So you really bought the lot?"

"Yep. I'm going to be your neighbor." Joe started clearing the table but I asked the kids to take over.

As Horvald headed for the living room, I rested one hand on his arm. "Are you sure you're telling me everything you know about the house?"

He gave me a strange look. "Why? Is something wrong?"

I glanced out the back window over at the darkened lot.

Nothing was visible except the inkiness of the night and swirling leaves in the wind. "No, I guess not. No reason." But the sound of a woman crying stuck in my mind for the rest of the evening, and I couldn't shake the feeling that something was wrong, and that we'd awakened something better left asleep.

Two

·❖·

From Brigit's Journal:

I don't know what I'd do without my Mab. She keeps me laughing when I don't think I can take life here any longer, and she keeps me company on nights when I'm alone. I've never had a puss before, and I'm grateful the Missus allows it. Of course, Mab catches the mice, so she earns her keep.

America has been quite the experience. I thought coming here would mean leaving my old life behind, but it's almost as if the past haunts me. I think about sweet William a lot, but time has healed a lot of those wounds. I wonder, if I were to go home, would they reopen, bring back the tears? I suppose I'll never know. All I know is that this land is strange and yet, familiar. In fact, this very house and yard remind me of Glenagary's Rock. I wouldn't be surprised to find a barrow if I hunted through the woods long enough.

Speaking of Glenagary's Rock, I had quite the scare a few mornings ago. I was out in the backyard hanging clothes when a gust of wind swirled around me, catch-

*ing up my skirt. I thought something was watching me,
but when I turned around, there was only the tree there,
blowing in the wind.*

*I don't like that tree—it gives me nightmares, and I
can't help but wish Mr. Edward would chop it down.
Silliness, I suppose. It's a perfectly fine tree. Mary
Kathryn would say I'm letting my imagination run
away with me. Still, I try to avoid the backyard at night.
I thought I saw lights out there once, but it was probably just the moonlight.*

I WOKE FROM disturbing dreams that I couldn't remember, with a vague sense that something was out of
place. Joe was lying beside me, curled up against my back.
I turned to stare at his tangle of strawberry blond hair.

My sweetheart. He might be ten years younger than I,
but he exuded wisdom, confidence, and compassion. Even
though his job terrified me—I was always afraid he was
going to get burned or fall through a floor trying to rescue
somebody—I knew it was his passion. The job was the
perfect match for him. And he was the perfect match for
me.

Careful to avoid waking him, I slipped from beneath
the covers and padded to the window. Overcast, but no
rain yet. If we were lucky, it would hold off long enough
to finish clearing the lot today. Murray and Jimbo had
promised to drop by and give us a hand, though I had the
feeling that Murray had more on her mind than yanking
out blackberries. Since coming out in the open about her
relationship with the renegade biker, she was having a
hard time with some of the guys on the force. They didn't
cotton to a head of detectives who was, in their opinion,

sleeping with the enemy. And she wasn't about to give up either her job or her newfound love.

I opened the window and took a long whiff of the chill morning air. The scent of wood smoke filtered in, and the thought occurred to me that maybe we'd better get a chimney sweep over before next week. We didn't use the fireplace often, but when we did, I wanted to feel safe. Right now I could go for a crackling fire, curled up in a leather chair with an afghan to toss across my legs.

As I stared into the backyard, the lot next door was barely visible over the top of the fence. Joe and I had discussed pulling the fence down, but we wanted to wait until we cleared out the years of vegetation. Plans were that the lot would become an extension of my property, when we finally made the move to join households. We wanted to plant gardens, create a little pond, maybe a gazebo. While not officially engaged, Joe and I had an understanding. This one was for keeps, regardless of I-do's or golden rings.

I realized I was shivering and shut the window. As I dug through my closet, hunting for my grunge clothes, Joe stirred.

"Honey? What time is it?" he asked, squinting at the nightstand.

"Nine. If you want to get the rest of the lot cleared, you'd better get up and eat. I'd like to get started before noon. I've decided I'm not going to clean the shop since I'm on vacation; Cinnamon and Lana can handle it." Every Saturday morning, rain or shine, the kids and I trooped down to the Chintz 'n China and went to work, dusting, sweeping, polishing until it sparkled. But I was giving myself full latitude on my time off.

The kids deserved a break, too, especially Kip, who had spent the first three Sundays of October at the Bread

& Butter House, serving dinner to the poorer residents of Chiqetaw. He'd pulled a stupid stunt in August, and I hoped the lesson would teach him a little bit about generosity and honesty.

Joe reached out for me and I crawled across the covers, still in my bathrobe, and settled into his arms. As we leaned back against the headboard, he played with my hair. "Emerald, are you okay with the fact that I bought the lot? I don't want to move too fast, and you haven't said much over the past week about it. I was hoping that you haven't changed your mind."

I rested my head on his shoulder. "You took me by surprise, but yeah, I'm happy. I just . . . for some reason, I'm just feeling uncomfortable today. Like I woke up on the wrong side of the bed or something."

"What's wrong?"

But I couldn't answer. Yesterday I'd been pleased as punch, but today I didn't want to go outside, especially next door, where we still faced a mountain of foliage. The thought of staying home, making soup and biscuits, maybe watching an old movie or two, was far more appealing than mucking around in the cold.

I shook my head. "I don't know. Maybe I'm just tired. I had nightmares last night. I guess they threw me off." My dreams were often turbulent, and Joe had more than once woken me out of the clutches of some evil menace waiting to gobble me up.

He pushed me into sitting position and began to rub my shoulders, massaging the knots that had formed there during the night. "What were they about this time? Not Roy, I hope?"

Ever since I'd let Joe into my life, I'd been having nightmares in which Roy tried to step in and destroy the happiness I had. While I wouldn't put the thought past my ex-from-hell, I wasn't about to court trouble by dwelling on it.

"Honestly? I don't know. Can't remember them, so let's just leave it at that." I shrugged, then forced myself to climb out from the protection of the thick comforter. "I guess we'd better get moving. The kids will want breakfast and my stomach's rumbling, too." Planting a kiss on his forehead, I slipped into a sweatshirt and jeans as he tumbled out of bed. He slapped my butt as he reached for his clothes. I shooed his hand away.

"Scram, fly! I'll go start the show. Hurry up though, I want you to make me eggs." Joe cooked up the best scrambled eggs I'd ever tasted. "You want coffee?"

He nodded. "Always, but not that mud you drink. It's so thick you could stand a spoon in it."

"Fine then, miss the best part of the day!" With an exaggerated sniff, I stuck my nose in the air and headed for the door, stopping short when I stubbed my toe on the dresser. I gave him an evil glare as he repressed a snicker, and headed downstairs.

After poking through the fridge, I finally decided on cinnamon rolls, fried ham and scrambled eggs, and fresh-squeezed orange juice for breakfast. As I was taking the rolls out of the package and arranging them on a baking pan, Randa trudged in, rubbing her eyes.

"Good morning, sweetie," I said, then gave her a longer look. She often spent her evenings out on the roof, sky watching, but it had rained like crazy last night. She looked like she'd been dragged through the wringer. "You didn't go out in the storm last night, did you?"

She shook her head. "Nah, but I had a weird dream. I woke up in the middle of the night, and it was hard to get back to sleep."

It would seem that nightmares had been the fare for the evening.

"Need any help?" she asked. "Should I start your espresso?"

"You know the way to your mother's heart, child." I gave her a quick kiss as she passed by, on her way to the machine that brought me heaven on earth. While she filled the mesh cup with four shots' worth of ground beans, I tucked the rolls in the oven and sliced up the ham, getting it ready for the skillet. Joe joined us and took over the spatula, scrambling the eggs while I mixed cocoa and Coffee-mate into the black gold that kept me running like a well-tuned machine.

Kip, smelling food, bounced into the kitchen.

"Feed the cats, please, before breakfast," I said.

He nodded and took off into the pantry, calling Samantha and her three kittens. Our family's felines were rescues from the animal shelter. The kittens had pretty much grown up, though I had the suspicion that Nigel was in for another spurt. He was on his way to sixteen pounds and counting. Before there were any unexpected blessings, I'd taken them to the vet and had them all fixed. The troop of furbles had wormed their way into our hearts, each one becoming an integral part of our family.

A moment later, Kip returned, looking confused.

"What's the matter, honey? Are we out of cat food?"

"Nah, but Samantha isn't by her dish. She's always there."

I frowned. Samantha never missed a meal. She looked like a fuzzy round calico bear. Though not as big as her son, she was no slouch in the belly department, with a paunch big enough to make any cat proud.

"Maybe she's still asleep," I said. "The seasons are changing and that can affect cats' appetites and their need for sleep. Don't worry about it, she'll eat when she's ready." He nodded and helped Miranda set the table. As Joe and I dished up breakfast, I asked them, "What are your plans for the day?"

Randa shrugged. "Library. I've got a lot of homework and I need to do some research."

I nodded. "And you?" I asked Kip.

He sighed. "I thought I might go with Randa, if she doesn't mind."

I stared at him, as did Randa. The library? Kipling?

He must have noticed the startled looks because he added, "I need to check out a book on basic HTML for the computer club. We're learnin' how to write code and our advisor told us to get a book on it. They cost like forty dollars or more and I thought you wouldn't want to buy it for me."

Randa gave him a skeptical look. "Yeah, right. You're probably trying to learn how to become a hacker, aren't you? Well, if you want to go with me, you can help me do the dishes this morning. The library doesn't open until eleven, so we've got a couple hours before we need to leave."

When Kip had first signed up for the summer computer camp offered by the Chiqetaw Community Center, I'd been amazed by how willingly he learned the material. Now he was applying that knowledge in school, for which I was grateful. However, I'd had the same sneaking suspicion that Randa voiced, though I wasn't about to say so aloud. Chances being what they were, if Kip could manage to get himself in trouble, he would. My son's sense of judgment was notoriously poor and he wasn't too swift in the think-first category. I comforted myself with the thought that at least he was taking an interest in school.

"Tell you what. See if you can find it at the library. If

you can't, check the used bookstores. Then, if you still can't find a copy of it, I'll order it from Barnes & Noble, on condition that you stay in the computer club until at least spring break. Okay?"

"Okey-dokey." He gave me a happy nod and turned back to his breakfast.

"By the way, if either of you decides to run off after the library, be sure to call and leave me a message. Where, why, and when you'll be home. And Kip, remember: No going over to Sly's. You know the rules."

Unless it was during schooltime, he'd been banned from hanging out with Sly, his best friend. I hated playing bad cop, but a couple of months ago the troubled youth had encouraged Kip to take part in what was essentially a scam. That had been the last straw. After giving Sly chance after chance, I finally had to face facts. The kid wasn't going to change, his parents didn't care, and I couldn't count on my son's common sense. So I'd limited the amount of time they were allowed to spend together.

Sly's mother had been no help when I'd approached her about the attempted scam, telling me to "mind your own fucking business and take care of your own damned kid."

As sorry as I felt for the youngster, I had to put my son first. Kip had finally resigned himself to my decision, but he was prone to forgetting whatever he didn't want to remember, so I reinforced the reminder at least once a week.

He grimaced, but said nothing; both he and Miranda knew my stance on whining. "Can I—"

"May I."

"May I have more eggs?"

Joe pushed himself back from the table and bowed. "Of course, *Monsieur* Kipling. Any other requests? Chef Joseph at your service."

Randa and Kip giggled while I stared at my plate, deciding whether I had room left for any more. The caffeine was working through my system and I was starting to wake up. A little rumble told me that I could stand another serving of scrambled eggs. "I'm with Kip. Bring it on, babe."

Joe snorted. "Your pleasure is my pleasure, *Madame*. Randa? You want anything else?"

She shook her head. "Nah, I'm going to go finish my chores before we head off to the library. Kip, don't forget—you're helping me with the dishes."

He nodded, his mouth full of cinnamon roll.

By the time the dishes were done and the kids out the door, it was almost eleven. Murray and Jimbo pulled into the driveway. They'd brought both their trucks so we could haul away the debris faster.

Anna Murray, my oldest friend, had been my roommate at the University of Washington before she moved to Chiqetaw to accept a position on the police force. I'd married Roy and stayed in Seattle, my one huge mistake in life. Although, without Roy, I wouldn't have Randa and Kip, so life with him hadn't been a total loss—it had netted me the two most important people in the world. After we broke up, Murray encouraged me to move to Chiqetaw and start my own business. I never looked back.

Mur had recently been promoted to the post of head of detectives. Tall, regal, Native American, she was buxom, with long, straight black hair that she wore caught back in a braid, and she possessed a grace I could never hope to match.

Jimbo, her boyfriend, was an old biker who built a life for himself out by Miner's Lake, where he trapped small animals for fur, raised bees for honey, and picked up odd jobs here and there working on cars. They made an unlikely pair. He was a rebel, she was dedicated to keeping order, and yet somehow, they'd found love in the midst of their differences.

In fact, they'd started out on opposite sides of the law, when Jimbo threw a brick through my front room window early in the year. He'd later decided to play the good guy. I owed him big, even though he insisted the debt had been paid in full.

Mur gave me a hug and thumbed me toward her truck. "We brought some heavy tools to yank out the rest of those vines," she said, hauling out what looked like a giant-sized set of pruning shears.

"Well, there's been a development in our excavation. Did you know there used to be a house on that lot?"

"What? Really? Did you find something?"

"Yep." We told them about the basement and, their interest piqued. We all trooped over to the lot, where Joe took down the ropes we'd put up to discourage sightseers from falling in.

Murray stared into the part of the chamber that we could see and turned to me, a puzzled look on her face. "Well, isn't that a kicker? I never would have guessed. Those brambles are more tenacious than I thought—they make the perfect cover. And Horvald said there was a house here?"

"Yep. A three-story mansion, I gather. He said it burned to the ground from a lightning strike, almost fifty years ago on Halloween night."

Jimbo shook his head. "Leave it to you, O'Brien, to stumble over a house burnt down by lightning. On Halloween, yet. You can't help finding hoodoo even when you aren't looking for it, can you?"

"Hey, I was born on Halloween, so don't go knocking

my birthday!" I laughed as we spread out and started chopping away.

About an hour into our work, we came to a second edge of the basement and had to haul out the mess we'd already cut away. While Joe and Jimbo kept making inroads on the thicket, Murray and I loaded armfuls of the thorny brush into the pickup beds. I was grateful for the thick jacket I'd decided to wear; the thorns snagged at it, but never managed to break through to my skin.

After a few moments, Mur stopped and leaned against the side of her truck. "Em, can we talk for a second?"

"Sure." Grateful for a break, I propped myself on the back bumper and stretched. "What's up?"

She let out a big sigh. "I don't know what to do. The guys are being an ass about Jimmy. And the Chief didn't come right out and say so, but he hinted that I deserve whatever flack I get if I continue to see 'that scum,' as he put it."

Youch. Harsh. Usually Tad Bonner fought on Murray's side, rather than attacking her. The turnaround wasn't good news. "Have you told Jimbo about this?"

She shook her head. "No, and I'm not going to. I don't want him punching out my boss, and I don't want him to feel like he's compromising my job. I'm so frazzled. I'm afraid this is the ammunition they've been looking for to get me fired."

"Surely Deacon and Greg aren't saying anything?" I couldn't believe the two nicest guys on the force would turn against her.

"No," she said, sighing. "Deacon and Greg and Sandy are great about this, even if they do think I'm out of my mind. But the guys who got passed over for promotion when Bonner appointed me head of detectives are talking behind my back, trying to stir up trouble."

I didn't know what to say. There wasn't much I *could* say. I put my arm around her shoulder. "They just need some time to get to know him, to see he's not the bad news they think he is. It'll be okay."

I was talking out of sheer bravado, but what else was I supposed to do? Tell her I thought she might end up having to choose between her career and the one man who had ever made her happy? Nope, wasn't even gonna go there. She needed to keep a positive outlook and, whatever she chose to do, she had to make this decision on her own.

We were about to return to work when Randa came pedaling up on her bike. Surprised that she was home so early, I asked, "Is anything wrong?"

She shook her head. "No, but I need to ask you something." With an apologetic glance at Murray, she added, "Alone."

I walked her over to the sidewalk. "Where's your brother?"

"I dunno, he left before I did. Probably over at Tommy's. He said he'd call and leave you a message."

"Okay. Well, ask away."

"May I go to a movie tomorrow afternoon? I need to know now."

Randa wasn't a big movie buff, so her request struck me as odd, but I figured that her best friend Lori had talked her into going. Lori was the one person in the world who could take Miranda's mind off star clusters and nebulas. "What's the movie?"

"*Alien Warlord.*"

I glanced up at her, confused. *Alien Warlord*? Not sure I'd heard right, I said, "That isn't exactly the type of movie you usually like. You sure you want to go? What's the rating?"

She scuffed her foot on the ground. "PG-13. And yeah, well, see, the thing is normally I wouldn't go see it, but Gunner asked me to go with him. And I . . . kinda . . . want to."

Stupefied, my mouth dropped open. Gunner? Her English tutor who she'd been bad-mouthing for the past two weeks? I'd barely gotten over the fact she actually had a friend her age—Lori Thomas was Randa's only real girl-friend. Now she wanted to date?

I managed to close my mouth before a bug flew in it.

"So, you want to go?" Act nonchalant, I thought. That was the key. I didn't want to scare her off from the idea, even though the thought of her dating simultaneously overjoyed and terrified me.

She nodded. "Yeah, I guess I do. He's nice enough, even if he is all hung up on English and writing."

Gunner was actually quite the nice young man. I'd met him and he was polite and respectful. And he was in the same grade, so that wasn't a problem. "Okay then, if it's a matinee, sure. You can go."

She blushed, but looked pleased as she glanced around the lot. "Wow, you guys really have been working hard. I'll kind of miss the berries, though. They were fun to pick. Do you need any help?"

I could tell she was hoping I'd say no and decided to give her a break. After all, it wasn't every day a girl was asked out on her first date, and I knew she'd want to go and call Lori and discuss the matter thoroughly.

"Nah, you scoot and enjoy the rest of the day. Do me a favor, though. Make sure that the ground beef is thawed. If it isn't, put the package in a Ziploc bag and close it tight, then set it in a big bowl of cold water. We're having spaghetti for dinner. And check to make sure Kip left a message. If he didn't, come tell me."

She nodded, gave me a quick peck on the cheek, and pushed her bike over to the house. As I started in on another tenacious root, Mur gave me a quizzical look. She sidled over as I grinned at her.

"My daughter's been asked out on her first date."

"A date? Good grief, is the sky falling?" She laughed and I joined in. Mur understood Randa better than anybody except me.

"Come here! Look at this!" Joe's excited cry startled us into silence. We hurried over to see what they'd found.

The men had ripped away a big patch of brush, exposing the full scope of the basement. It was about twenty-by-thirty feet and had probably underscored a good third of the house. As the light filtered down into the chamber, softly illuminating the dark corners, a chill of excitement raced up my back. Chances were, nobody had seen this basement for almost fifty years. I felt like an archaeologist, uncovering hidden secrets from the past.

Old timbers, charred and rotten, littered the floor, which rested a good fifteen feet below us. The entire basement was covered with thick layers of mulch. A concrete stairway led down into the room, but we couldn't reach the steps due to the tendrils and vines that still blocked our path.

My heart quickened as I stared at the mammoth chamber. "Oh my God, this is huge. Horvald said the house was a mansion, but I had no idea."

During the winter months, even when the leaves died down, the brambles had been so thick and woody they'd managed to cover the lot, along with all traces of the desolate remains.

Murray stepped away from the edge. "Em, I don't like it. Something feels wrong down there."

As I gazed down at the charred beams, a rush of wind

swept past, and once again I thought I could hear a faint moan. Licking my lips, I forced myself to look away. "I know what you mean. I thought I heard someone cry out last night when we first found it. A woman, screaming."

Jimbo shook his head and set down his pruning shears. He'd adopted a quiet respect for our abilities, and since his grandma was a hoodoo woman, he always took our warnings seriously. "What say we lay off for today and let you two figure out what needs to be done, if anything?"

Joe shrugged. "I don't have a problem with that. We can make an early dinner." He glanced at his watch. "Whoa, it's almost five. The light will be gone in another hour anyway. We did a lot of work today and it won't take long for Em and me to finish it up over the next couple days."

As we trooped back to the house, I glanced over my shoulder. Once again, the uncanny sensation that we were being watched tickled the back of my neck. Yeah, something was there, all right, but I had no idea what. But, whatever it was, we'd need to cleanse the area. That much I was sure of. Fifty years burial under a tangle of briars was enough to produce an energy all its own, even if nothing bad had happened there.

Once we were back at the house, Murray and I took over the kitchen. As I boiled water for the noodles, Murray fried up the ground beef and added a couple of jars of pre-made spaghetti sauce. We were winging it with deli coleslaw, pre-buttered French bread that we had only to slip into the oven, and a chocolate cake from the bakery.

Randa wandered in, carrying her science book. "Oh yeah, you wanted to know. Kip left a message. He was over at Tommy's but said he'd be home by five so he should be here any minute."

"Thanks, hon. Set the table, please." Grumbling, she

put down her book. As she opened the cupboard for plates and glasses, I turned to Murray. "Last night, when Joe and I first found the foundation, I got the queasiest feeling. Like I was staring over the edge of a cliff and about to lose my footing."

Murray stirred a can of diced tomatoes into the sauce. "Em, I'm not sure what happened, but there's a lot of residue energy tucked away under those vines." She glanced up at me. "You know if Jimmy was worried enough to stop working, then he felt something even though he'd never say so. He's not as head-blind as he thinks."

That was one thing we'd discovered about the burly biker over the past few months. Jimbo might not admit to having any psychic abilities but we'd seen them flare up in him. Sporadic and unbidden, the power was there.

"Yeah. I know," I said, suddenly feeling tired. I set the coleslaw on the table, then looked around the kitchen. "Looks like we're ready. Kip can eat when he gets in, so go ahead and call everybody to the table."

Just then, Kip came racing through the back door. He took one look at dinner, yelled "Spaghetti!" dropped his backpack on the floor, and ran to the bathroom to wash up. Jimbo and Joe lumbered in, while Miranda helped me slice up the bread. As we settled down to eat, Kip frowned, excused himself and peeked into the pantry. He came back, a worried look on his face.

"Mom, Samantha isn't there! Nigel, Noël, and Nebula are all eating, but Sammy's still not home. I haven't seen her since last night."

That didn't sound like Samantha. She was a little piglet, racing to the food dish every morning and evening. Missing one meal was plausible. Two set me on alert. I wiped my mouth with my napkin.

"Excuse me, folks, but I'm going to help Kip have a look around the house."

Randa dropped her napkin on the table. "I'll help, too."

Samantha liked to curl up in closets so we started there, digging through every closet, including the one in the storage room. After a few minutes, Joe, Jimbo, and Murray joined us and we scoured the house, calling for Samantha, peeking under every piece of furniture and into every nook and cranny. Twenty minutes later, we gathered back in the kitchen, sans cat. By now, both Randa and Kip had tears in their eyes. I put my arms around their shoulders.

"She's probably outside, kiddos," I said, keeping my voice even, though inside I was worried. Samantha seldom went any farther than the front porch, with one or two exceptions. "Tell you what, let's finish up dinner and then we'll all go out and have a look."

"But it's almost dark," Kip said, his lip quivering.

"I know that, but we can call around the yard. Maybe she got in the shed last night. I think I locked it, but maybe I didn't. And you can go over and check Horvald's yard. Once she ran across the street after a squirrel and ended up tearing up his spearmint. She'll turn up, honey. She's a smart cat."

I could tell he didn't believe me, but he acquiesced. We finally got back to the table, where we finished our dinner.

As I finished my dinner, I could feel the beginnings of a headache. Yesterday everything had been fine, but now I couldn't shake the feeling that we'd just stumbled into a dark forest that had closed in around us. Even Jimbo and Murray looked strained. The rest of the meal passed in silence, with no one saying more than "Would you pass the bread" or "More water, please."

Three

⟡

From Brigit's Journal:

I'm so upset! Miss Irena's spreading rumors about me—she called me a cheap tart and told everyone that I come from a broken home. My parents may be dead, but they loved each other till their deaths and I simply won't stand for her lies. But what can I do? I've never said a word against her, or complained about the extra work she causes, or the slights or snubs when she thinks I'm not looking.

If only my parents had lived. I miss them dreadfully. It's only been a couple of years. I think I could have taken my sweet William's loss, if they'd been around to support me. Some days, I miss them all so much, and the land of my birth more than anything. Why, oh why, did I come here? And now, there's so much at stake. I feel like a rabbit trapped in a magician's hat. If only I had the chance to start over. If only my father hadn't fallen asleep in that chair with his cigar, none of this would have happened. I'd still be home, safe.

All I feel is a sense of bleak desperation, and I won-
der if we'll ever be happy. Or will it all crumble, and
will I go home to Mary Kathryn in shame? There are
times when I think that might be best. I think I'll look
into ticket prices tomorrow on my day off. Perhaps this
is the only way.

I thought we were going to have it out in the open
last week, but at the last moment, fear took hold and we
kept silent. My life seems to be made of silent moments,
and like the Lady of Shalott, I silently watch from my
tower as the world goes on loving and living.

"WHY DON'T YOU take off and search the neighborhood?" I shooed the kids toward the door before they could
start clearing the table. "We'll take care of this, and when
we're done, I'll come out to help."

"Thanks, Mom!" Kip gave me a brief hug, then he and
Randa rifled through the supply cupboard in the pantry for
a couple of flashlights and took off out the back door. I
peeked through the window over the sink, watching their
bobbing lights as they began searching through the backyard. As I turned back, a thought crossed my mind.

"Mur, do you know anybody who works at the animal
shelter? I thought I might give them a call. Maybe they
picked up Sammy today." I hated that place. When I went
to choose a cat for our family, I wanted to cry. It tore me
up something awful to see the rows of cages sitting there,
scared and lonely babes peeking out of each one. I
couldn't give them all a home, but I'd taken Samantha and
her kittens, and at least I'd saved four lives. Even though
it would make finding her much quicker, I prayed she
wasn't locked behind cold bars again.

Mur shook her head. "They're on short staff, so you'll

have to wait until morning to go check it out, and maybe until Monday. She's wearing a collar and tags, right?"

I nodded.

"They'd call you if they found her. Our shelter is pretty good, compared to the ones in the bigger cities. I'll bet you she just snagged herself a nice place to hide and is curled up there, waiting until everybody's good and scared before she saunters home. Definitely give them a call if she doesn't show up tonight, but I don't think it's going to be necessary."

I gave her a thin smile. Murray had two large boas and they never got out of their cages unless she took them out. She'd never owned a cat in her life. But I didn't say anything. She was trying to cheer me up, and that's what friends are supposed to do.

"You're probably right, but I'm worried all the same." I glanced out the window into the darkness beyond. "It's going to be cold out there tonight." As I poured the spaghetti sauce into a container and snapped the lid on, Joe and Jimbo came back into the kitchen.

Jimbo was carrying Mur's jacket. "I hate to leave with the kids so upset," he said. "But Anna and I have a few errands to run before the evening's over." He gave me a peck on the cheek, a habit he'd recently adopted. I could see the worried twist to his mouth peeking out from the brush that he called a mustache.

At least he'd gotten rid of the fashion faux pas I'd recommended earlier in the year. His cornrowed biker's beard had definitely not transformed him into a "ten." Thanks to Murray's influence, Jimbo had recently shaved off the Deadhead-Rasta look, and now his beard was neatly clipped near his chin and his hair smoothed back into a long ponytail. He still looked rough and tumble, but hey—he looked *good* rough and tumble. I reached up and patted his cheek.

"You're a sweetheart. And so are you," I said, turning to Mur.

She sighed. "Damn it, I wish we could stay and lend a hand, but I have to stop at the station and make sure the men haven't done something stupid again." Murray glanced at Jimbo, obviously torn, then turned back to me. "I didn't tell you this because it's just so demeaning, but on Thursday, somebody—I still don't know who—got into my computer and E-mailed an X-rated picture to the chief from my account. Supposedly from me!"

I winced. "Holy hell, that sucks rocks. How X-rated?" You just didn't E-mail the chief of police porn.

She grimaced. "More than you want to know. Think overly endowed young man, with a big-breasted woman on her knees in front of him, and you get the idea. The woman was wearing a skimpy Pocahontas costume and I have the sneaking suspicion that whoever sent it was trying to suggest to Bonner that I wanted to reenact the scene."

I stared at her, unable to comprehend that someone on the police force would actually go to such lengths just because they didn't like Murray's boyfriend. Unless it was one of the men passed over for promotion who was bucking for her job. Either way, it was lowdown, dirty, and stupid to boot. Anybody willing to take a chance on incurring Murray's anger had to be either insane or . . . no, just insane. Murray could be a dangerous enemy; everybody knew she had a temper.

"Why didn't you say anything?"

She frowned. "I was hoping to find out who did it, but I don't think I'm going to. I've changed my password, but it's become obvious that I'm no longer just fighting for an equal chance on the force. I have enemies there."

Jimbo grunted. "If I ever catch the S.O.B. there won't be anything left of him. Nobody treats a woman like that and gets away with it."

I stifled a snort and thought about reminding him that earlier in the year he'd made an obnoxiously rude pass at me while drunk. And *then* had gone on to throw a crudely inscribed brick through my living room window. But I decided not to bother. Jimbo had changed, all for the better. I turned back to Murray.

"Keep me informed. This is just sick."

"Oh yeah. I'm not giving up. If I can find the asshole who did it, he'll pay. Trust me on that." As she shrugged into her jacket, a brown suede affair with fringe on the sleeves, she added, "Call me later and let me know if Sammy's shown up, okay?"

Joe and I walked them to the door. I stared out into the night. "Sure thing. Say, would you please take a look beneath your trucks and their hoods before you leave? Cats like to hang out in the stupidest places."

"Chin up, O'Brien, you'll find her," Jimbo said, waving as they clattered down the porch steps to the driveway.

I turned back to find Joe digging through the closet. "Where do you keep the extra flashlights again? We should help the kids look for the cat."

As I started to speak, his cell phone rang. He answered it while I headed back to the pantry where I kept a half-dozen flashlights. I was making sure the batteries were fresh as Joe came running in.

"Em, there's a fire over on Hamilton Drive. People are hurt and they need the medic unit. The entire station's been called out—this is a big one and it doesn't look good." He grabbed his jacket. "I'm going to be late. I might be gone all night."

I handed him his backpack, fear puddling in my stomach. "How bad?"

He rubbed his head, pushing back the strawberry blond curls that tendriled down over his brow. "Big Bad. We may need volunteers. Every truck in Chiqetaw is on the way. Apparently the Delta Mae apartment building has been engulfed by flames. There are fifty units in that building, five floors' worth, and the fire's out of control."

I leaned back against the wall, closing my eyes. "Those poor people." Then, realizing that every minute he stayed here kept him safe but put others at risk, I yanked open the door. "Go! And be careful, please. Call me when you get a chance."

He gave me a grateful smile. "You know how much I love you, don't you?"

Fighting back tears, I nodded. "I love you too. Just take care of yourself, Joseph Files." I hastily planted a kiss on his cheek and he raced toward his truck. My heart skipped a beat when he stopped long enough to take a quick peek beneath it, then shot out of the driveway on his way to the station. There were so many reasons I loved this man.

As I stood on the front porch, shivering, the kids came running up the street, both pale and with deer-in-the-headlights looks in their eyes.

"What? What is it?" I hurried them inside and shut the door, latching it firmly. "What happened?"

"M-m-m-mom . . . in the lot next d-d-door . . ." Kip only stuttered when he was frightened or terribly upset.

I leaned down and put my hands on his shoulders, bracing him firmly. "Kipling, honey? Take a deep breath—shush. Breathe." Randa was glancing back at the door. "What happened?" I asked quietly, hoping to hell that some pervert hadn't moved into the neighborhood. Or maybe, they'd found Samantha dead on the road.

Her voice quivering, Randa slid down onto the bench in the foyer. "Kip saw something next door. In the lot."

"You saw something? Something as in what?"

She shook her head. "I didn't see it, but Kip did."

"Lights," Kip broke in. "I saw lights. Round balls of light in the air."

I was taken aback, I hadn't expected to hear anything in that vein. Slipping on my jacket, I said, "Maybe somebody's prowling around over there with a flashlight."

Randa shook her head. "Not somebody, mom. Something."

I gave him a long look. "You didn't see anybody?"

"No, just the lights. They're all different colors."

Bewildered—we didn't have fireflies in the area and it wasn't the season for them anyway—I took a deep breath. "Okay, stay here. I'm going to go have a look. By the way, Joe had to go out on a fire. If something happens, call Murray."

I grabbed one of the flashlights and headed next door. Most likely somebody was just out walking his dog for the night, and had startled the kids, but I wanted to make sure that nobody was mucking around the foundation. I could easily see someone deciding to ignore the warning ropes. All it would take was one misstep and bingo—a broken neck from a nasty fall.

The night was crisp, but judging from the clouds, the mist would rise before morning. In Chiqetaw, the streetlights were reminiscent of the gas lanterns that adorned street corners years ago before electricity and mercury vapor hit the mainstream. Modern in use, but vintage in looks, they gave the town a homey, cozy feel.

As I neared the lot, the hairs on my arms and the back

of my neck began to bristle. Something was out there all right. I turned off my flashlight and slowed. As I rounded the fence that separated my house from Joe's new land, the clouds parted briefly, letting a bare glimmer of starshine through. The moon was near dark, of no use in lighting my way.

I squinted, searching the vague shapes and shadows, when a flicker of light caught my attention. Faint—so faint I could barely keep it in sight. One step at a time, I closed in, taking care not to go careening into the basement myself. The lights were a good twenty yards beyond the foundation, still out of reach, hovering in the last tangle of brambles we hadn't managed to clear yet. As I moved closer, they came into focus. Whoa, Nelly. Kip had nailed it. Dancing lights, all right.

The glowing orbs were about the size of a large grapefruit and they darted through the air, shimmering shades of pink and greens, pale yellow, and blue so bright it was almost white. Enchanted, I watched as they swooped and dove around the lot.

One of the orbs suddenly approached me, hovering at arm's length. It was almost a perfect sphere, and energy crackled from it. I reached out again, probing for a sense of what it was, but the orb darted away. Then, almost imperceptibly, it began to move forward again until it was hovering right in front of my face. My eyes ached from the light as I held my breath, waiting to see what it would do.

It circled me slowly, radiating behind my head, and then settled back in front of me. As we stood there in a comfortable standoff, I reached out again with my thoughts and asked, "Who are you? What do you want?"

Almost instantaneously, every light in the lot flickered

and vanished, and a low wail rose from the basement, chilling me to the core. Holy hell, what was down there?

Shaking, I nervously approached the edge of the foundation and peered beyond the ropes, over the edge. There, against the layers of mulch in the basement, a thick pillar of fog had risen. Perhaps it was the autumn mists that came with the damp, chill nights in western Washington. Or maybe, my mind whispered, maybe it was something else, something trapped down there.

Whatever it was, I decided I'd had enough. Time to head home while I was still in one piece. I'd deal with this mystery in the morning, during the daylight. As I opened the front door, a distant wail of fire engines reminded me that Joe was out on duty, in danger, and once again, I had to acknowledge that this world could be a most unsettling place in which to live.

The kids were waiting. I slipped off my jacket and handed it to Miranda, asking if she'd hang it in the closet, then set the flashlight on the table. Both Kip and Randa looked at me expectantly.

"Did you see them?" Kip asked, and I had the feeling he was both afraid I'd say yes, and afraid I'd say no.

I nodded. "Yeah, I saw them. You weren't imagining anything."

"Why didn't I see them, then? And what are they?" Randa asked. She stopped, swallowed, and added, "Mom, are they ghosts?"

I considered my wording carefully. Randa was better about the supernatural than she'd been a year ago, but she still spooked easily, and while I knew she'd inherited some of my abilities, she had chosen another route in life, even at her young age. Kip, on the other hand, was so open that he shone like a beacon, and it was all I could do to protect him and teach him to ward off anything big and nasty.

"I don't think so, honey. I don't know what they are, but until I can find out, you guys stay away from there. Okay? I don't want you hurt."

They nodded, Randa a little quicker than Kip. "All right. Tomorrow morning, you can run over to some of our neighbors and ask them if they've seen Samantha. I'll bet you anything that she's hiding. She'll come waltzing in before you know it."

Even as I said it, my gut churned. I was kidding them, as well as myself. We'd been all over the house and she was nowhere to be seen. I swallowed back my tears for the kids' sake and watched as they trooped up the stairs, faces glum.

DURING THE RESTLESS night, I got one break, or at least it seemed that way on the surface. Joe phoned to let me know that he was okay and the fire was out. He'd be staying at the station the rest of the night to finish up reports.

"Was anybody hurt bad?"

He kept his voice low. "Eight. Four serious burns and four minor. Randa knows the son of the couple that are in critical condition, actually—Gunner Lindemeyer's parents."

Oh God. Gunner? I leaned back against the bed, pressing my eyes closed. "Please tell me that the boy wasn't hurt too bad."

Joe sighed. "He was lucky. He woke up in time to get out but couldn't reach his parents' bedroom to wake them. The flames were too thick and the fire started in their apartment. We managed to rescue them, but they're in pretty bad shape. To make matters worse, the family didn't have any working smoke alarms—the batteries were all dead. I hate it when people don't bother to check their alarms to see if they're working."

I swallowed a rising swell of panic. "That's horrible. Do you think they'll live?" Somebody was going to have to break the news to Randa and I knew it would be best coming from me.

"Maybe. They're pretty bad off. If they do live, they'll need numerous surgeries to deal with the scars. Gunner's mother's better off than his father; I'd say she's got the best chance. Gunner suffered from some smoke inhalation, but he's going to be okay. The kid's just lucky he woke up and called 911. He could have slept through it."

Joe's voice cracked. I wanted to take him in my arms, and soothe him. This part of the job was hard on him, I knew that from watching firsthand. Working on the medic unit brought him in contact with so much pain.

"So when are you going to break the news to Randa?" he asked.

I blew my nose. "Probably first thing in the morning. They were supposed to go out to the movies together but that's not going to happen now. It would have been her first date." I glanced at the clock. 2:00 A.M. I sighed. "I just keep thinking of that poor boy. Does he have a place to stay?"

"Yeah, his aunt picked him up. He's pretty shaken up."

"I imagine. Man, this is shaping up to be a lousy week." We talked a little more and then I hung up and went downstairs to make myself a cup of tea. As I heated the water, I heard a rustling on the stairs and turned to see Randa, peeking into the kitchen.

"Mom? What are you doing up? Is something wrong?"

My heart fell. I could still send her back to bed and tell

her in the morning, but forestalling the news wouldn't make it any easier.

"Making tea. I just talked to Joe. Why are you up?"

She frowned at the table. "I woke up and thought somebody was standing next to my bed. But when I sat up, there was nobody there."

Great, so the astral world was alive and kicking.

"Well, come sit down. I want to talk to you for a minute."

I poured water over the bags in my pumpkin-shaped teapot. A delicate whiff of lemon rose up. My favorite tea had, at one time, been Moroccan Mint, but this summer it had been usurped by a new love—the London Fruit & Herb Company's Lemon-Lime Zest tea. The flavor was delicate, comforting. And within a few minutes, Randa would need all the comfort she could get. As reserved as she could seem, my little girl had a soft heart for her friends and family. I arranged a handful of gingersnaps on a plate and carried the tea tray over to the table. As I slid in beside her, she leaned her head on my shoulder and I kissed her hair.

"So you had a visitor?" Though I planned on telling her about Gunner's parents, I wanted to take care of matters at home first. "Did you see who it was? Were you scared?"

She glanced at me. "You aren't going to tell me it was just a dream?"

I gave her a gentle smile. "I could, but I don't think it was. There's a lot going on right now on the astral and we're nearing All Hallows Eve. The spirits are a lot more active this time of year."

"All Hallows Eve. Halloween. Your birthday," she said, grabbing a cookie and nibbling on it.

"Yes, my birthday." I shared my birthday with Nanna, my maternal grandmother, whose spirit still showed up every now and then to reassure me or help me get out of one scrape or another.

Nanna had taught me the family traditions. I learned them at her knee, and one of my most beloved rituals stemmed from an ancient western European celebration that had counterparts in many cultures throughout the world. Samhain, pronounced "Sow-ween," was the festival of the dead—a time during which people honored their ancestors. Halloween was a direct, though secular, descendant of that celebration.

When I was young, after the Halloween parties were over, Nanna would take me to her room. My mother would come along sometimes, though she never showed much of an interest in what Nanna wanted to teach her. There, we would set up a small altar with candles and family photographs, and on the table in front of the pictures, we placed plates of food for the dead and wished them good journeys, wherever they might be headed. Then Nanna would read the tarot to divine what was going to happen during the coming year. As I grew older, I joined her in the practice.

Once I married Roy, I had to make sure he was asleep before I'd sneak outside and sit on the porch. Bundled up in a thick jacket, I'd read the cards and talk to my ancestors. Nanna often showed up on these nights, patting my knee to let me know that I was doing the best that I could under the circumstances, and that my best was good enough.

But the year that Roy and I split, I dragged out Nanna's box, set up the altar, and began to teach the children their family heritage. Randa participated, though at first she'd been vaguely uncomfortable. But Kip loved the traditions, and they had become his favorite parts of Halloween.

Randa played with her cookie, finally setting it down

to pick up her tea. She stared solemnly at the cup. "Mom, can we add pictures of friends to the ancestor altar during Halloween? Or strangers? Maybe something we drew instead of a photograph?"

Where had *that* come from? I thought about it, then nodded. "Well, if they're dead and you want to remember them, I don't see why not. Who were you thinking of?" I couldn't imagine who she'd want to add.

Randa's gaze flickered up to meet mine and I saw a few tears staining her lashes. "The lady who was standing by my bed. I feel really sorry for her. She didn't scare me. She just seemed lonely. Like nobody remembers her."

My stomach knotted as I stared at Miranda. My little girl wasn't so little anymore. Fourteen, going on forty. Last year, this time, she'd been terrified out of her wits by ghosts. This year, she was feeling sorry for them.

"I think maybe I'd better have a look in your room before I answer your question." I wanted to run up there and demand to know who was prowling through my daughter's room, but I forced myself to slow down. Right now, I needed to tell her about Gunner's folks. "Let's set your visitor aside for a moment. I have some news I need to tell you."

She gave me a quizzical look. "Yeah? What's up?"

I crossed around the table and embraced her, pulling her into my arms. "I'm so sorry, honey. Gunner's parents were seriously injured in a fire tonight—Joe told me when he called. They're in the hospital with third-degree burns and we're not sure they're going to make it. Gunner will be okay. He suffered from some minor smoke inhalation but he's going to be all right."

Her look of bewilderment turned into one of horror. "Oh no, that's awful! They're really nice people. Are you

sure Gunner's okay?" Her shoulders began to shake and I
held her as tight as I could and kissed her on the forehead.

"He'll be fine. But this is going to be very hard for him.
Even if his parents recover, it's going to be an uphill battle for a while. He's going to need all the friends he's got."
As I smoothed the hair away from her face, she bit her lip
and nodded. "Life isn't fair, honey. That's one sad fact we
both know."

After a few minutes, she wiped her nose with a tissue
and took a sip of her tea. "What happened? Was it an accident?"

I let out my breath slowly and steadied myself. She
didn't need gory details, but she'd hear about it from
school or in the paper so I might as well tell her now. I
told her as much as Joe had told me, leaving out the gruesome parts. After we drank our tea, I escorted her back to
her bed and tucked her in. I tuned in, but couldn't sense
anybody or anything in the room. Randa caught my hand
before I could leave.

"Mom, would you plug in a night-light in my room
tonight?"

I smiled. "Sure thing. There's one in the hall bathroom,
I'll get it now." When I returned with the tabby-cat night-
light and plugged it in, she was sitting up in bed.

"When's the last time you checked the smoke detec-
tors?" she asked.

"Joe checked them two weeks ago. They're working
fine." I ruffled her hair and she didn't protest. "Anything
else?"

She shrugged and slid back under the covers. Nebula
crawled up onto Randa and mewed. Randa snuggled her
in her arms and rubbed her nose in the cat's belly. "She
misses her mom. So do I. Is Samantha okay?"

As I closed the door, I said, "I'm sure she's fine, hon.

She'll be home before we know it." I wished I didn't feel like a liar.

On my way back to my bedroom, I stopped on a whim and turned to look over my shoulder. There, in front of Randa's door, stood a woman. Around twenty years old, she was lovely, with long red hair cascading down her back. A tucked-waist dress fell to her calves, and she wore sturdy shoes. As I gazed at her, wondering what she wanted, the spirit's eyes grew wide with surprise and she threw up her hands, as if warding off a blow, and screamed.

Even though I covered my ears, I knew that her voice had echoed only within my mind. As the scream reverberated, she vanished from the hall. I raced over to where she'd stood but felt only a cool shaft of air that vanished as I touched it. Closing my eyes, I reached out. No presence, no animosity, no real energy save for the hairs bristling on my arms.

Confused and tired, I crawled back into bed, resting against the headboard. If things kept up this way, maybe I'd skip my birthday this year.

Four

❖

From Brigit's Journal:

I know my choices haven't been the wisest. I also know that sometimes people think I'm naive, and that I trust too much. My friend Margaret tells me so. I haven't confided to Maggie everything that's happened, but she knows about William and thinks this is all about my missing him. So I let her think what she will. I don't even dare write the truth in this journal—what if the Missus found it? Or worse, Mr. Edward or Miss Irena? I'd be in so much trouble. So I stick to half-truths and shadows. I am so sick of shadows.

If only I could put my heart away—lock up my feelings and go through life like some of the other girls do. Angela, for example. She was due to get married last year and then her beau ran off with someone else. She never cried, not once. And she seems fine—she has her work, and she's saving a nest egg for a little house, someday. But I wonder, when she's alone, does she cry? I never ask. There are some moments into which you do not pry. It seems like so long ago I lost my heart. I won-

der if I'll ever find it again. And will it be whole, or bro-
ken forever?

I WOKE TO see Samantha dart across the bottom of the
bed and off. "Sammy! Where have you been?" Pushing
back the covers, I leapt out of bed but when I looked
around for the cat, she was nowhere to be seen. Puzzled, I
knelt down and peeked beneath the heavy frame. Nothing.

A thorough search of my bedroom yielded no sign of
her, and the door to the hall was closed. A dream? I shivered, hoping it was nothing more ominous. I'd seen plenty
of animal spirits over the years, and I prayed that Samantha hadn't crossed over the Bridge to the other side.

As I stared at myself in the mirror, I began to acknowledge to myself just how worried I was about her. I
had to keep up appearances for the kids' sake, but in the
privacy of my room, images of cars and big dogs and
miserable pathetic humans who preyed on the inno-
cent—both two- and four-legged—ran through my mind.
Samantha relied on us, trusted us to take care of her. I'd
let her down. Somehow, someway, I'd failed.

A glance at the clock forced me to get myself in gear. I
wiped my eyes and jumped in the shower. Joe would be
coming over in an hour or so; I needed to be in good spirits for him, considering all he'd had to cope with last
night. Thank God I had Murray and Harlow to talk to
when I needed a little comfort.

As I lathered up, I leaned my forehead against the tile
and let the water stream over my shoulders, willing it to
remove some of the knots that had formed in my muscles.
Our yoga class was in hiatus for two weeks while our
teacher was away on vacation and though I tried to get in

a workout at home, it wasn't the same as having somebody guide me through the motions.

When Randa dragged herself down to breakfast, one look told me she hadn't slept very well. Kip glanced at her, then me, frowning. He must have sensed something was up because he waited until I was stirring the oatmeal and sidled over to me.

"Mom, what's wrong with Randa?" he whispered.

My kids asked tough questions, but I operated under the belief that the straight approach was usually best. I never lied to them unless I had an important reason. Sheltering them from the world's ills wouldn't help them, though I did tone down some of the darker aspects of existence when we got into discussions about crime and death and anger. If they could trust me to tell them the truth, then they might trust me with what went on in their lives.

"Honey, Gunner's parents were hurt really bad in a fire last night. Joe was there. He called me so I could tell Randa before she heard about it from somebody else." I gave him a tired smile.

Kip's eyes grew wide. "Her tutor?"

I nodded. "That's the one."

For once, he didn't press. He quietly set the table, even though it was Randa's chore. When he went to feed the cats, I heard sniffling in the pantry and followed him. His eyes were wet as he filled four dishes.

"I want Sammy back," he said, and my heart broke as his voice cracked. I sighed and wrapped my arms around him, rocking gently. He leaned his head against me and I softly kissed his hair.

"So do I, baby. So do I. We'll look for her again today." I contemplated telling them about seeing Samantha, but since it had been either a dream or a vision, I decided to hold off. They wanted her home in the flesh.

I dished out the oatmeal and poured orange juice, then made my mocha. I needed that black gold today, so brewed four shots of espresso and dosed it liberally with Coffee-mate, cocoa, and peppermint syrup.

Breakfast was a subdued affair. Kip hurried through his meal, and I knew he wanted to be outside, hunting for Samantha. I excused both of them from their chores, on the condition that they stay out of the lot next door. After stacking our plates in the dishwasher, I steeled myself for another trip over to the twilight zone.

As I picked my way across the lot, it was hard to imagine that I'd really seen the bright orbs darting and dashing around. Except, by now, I knew better than to question anything I'd seen firsthand. I'd learned *that* lesson the hard way over the past year.

As I got close to the basement, I tried to imagine what the house had looked like. Horvald's description had been vivid—but what it conjured up was the silhouette of a haunted house against a full moon, with lightning striking the weathervane. I decided that I'd been watching too many horror movies. I skirted the wheelbarrows we'd used to carry brambles to the truck and headed over to the basement, cautiously stepped over the tape, careful to avoid slipping. One misstep and it would be over the edge with me, and possibly a broken neck, broken arm, broken leg . . . a lovely thought I had no intention of trying out.

As I peeked into the dank hole, it was easy enough to see the thick layer of leaf mulch that filled the basement. Thick, charred timbers lay half-buried where they'd fallen. The fire must have been horrific, to sweep through and gut the house before the firemen could stop it. Of course, back then, technology still hadn't come into play in a big way, and the firemen may have had a harder time fighting the flames.

As a noise startled me, I glanced up. A fuzzy calico face was peeking at me from a patch of nearby brambles.

"Samantha!" Holding my breath, I crawled back over the rope and slowly began to inch my way in her direction, but three steps away, she turned and hightailed it into the thick of the bushes. "No!"

I whistled for her, called "Here kitty, kitty, kitty . . . here Samantha!" until my voice was hoarse, but there was no way I could follow her into the tangle without getting ripped to shreds by the thorns. Frustrated and shaken, I turned on my heel and marched back over to the house.

As I yanked off my jacket, Joe peeked through the door, startling me. I threw myself in his arms and gave him a long kiss. Every time he was out on a bad call, I reacted this way, but he took it in stride, letting me hold him until I was certain he was okay.

"Hey, it's okay. I'm home. Em? Em? What's going on?"

"I thought I saw Samantha next door, but I couldn't catch her," I said, taking his hand as I led him into the living room. "I don't know if I really saw her, or if it was wishful thinking. Anyway, it's been crazy around here." I told him about the Randa and the ghost outside her door. "I don't think the spirit's up to any harm. In fact, I'm not even sure she saw me, or if she's a spirit at all. There wasn't much actual energy there."

He frowned. "If it wasn't a ghost, what was it?"

I shrugged. "Could be a specter or a haunting . . . could be my tired eyes playing tricks on me."

"Not likely. So what else is going on? You've got that 'things-aren't-quite-right' look plastered across your face."

I glanced at my reflection in the mirror over the fireplace. He was right. Unfortunately, I also noticed the new surge of silver sprinkles in my hair, and right now I felt old, especially with my birthday coming up. Maybe I would visit Harlow's favorite salon and treat myself to a color job. Pampering would be good for my birthday. And what better way to pamper than a spa day?

I'd learned to happily live with my curves—although they were more toned now thanks to the yoga—and I had finally accepted that I'd never be an inch over five-five. My growth spurt ended over twenty years ago. But my hair and a facial—now, that might just be the ticket to help me feel rejuvenated for the coming autumn.

"Honey? Honey?"

Startled, I realized that I'd been staring at myself in the mirror for over two minutes. I gave Joe a quick peck on the cheek. "Don't worry, I was just drifting. Listen, about the lot you bought . . ."

"What about it?"

"We have a problem with dancing lights." When he looked at me, puzzled, I spelled it out for him.

Joe dropped back against the sofa, shaking his head. "At least you haven't found any dead bodies yet."

"What are you talking about?"

"Emerald," he said, and I could see the beginnings of a grin, "Since I've known you, you've stumbled over two murdered bikers and a dead romance writer and her daughter. You've been cursed by dragons, and together, we saw a big, potentially nasty legend come to life. Face it, you're a trouble magnet." He tried to cover his butt by kissing me soundly. A damn fine kiss at that; a full-lay-back-run-hands-through-my-hair-breath-stealing kiss.

After I managed to regain my composure from the unexpected but welcome ravishment, I shook my head and crossed my feet into a semi-lotus position. I hadn't mastered the full one yet, but I was working on it.

"Cad. Plying me with romance!" I bopped him over the head with a pillow resting behind my back and he laughed, grabbing it from me and tossing it across the room.

"You're not getting away with that so easy, lady." He reached out and drew one finger gently along my cheek, gazing at me through heavily lidded eyes that could see inside every corner of my being. "Pay up. I want your body."

Desire flickered in my breasts and the pit of my stomach, but I pushed it aside, just for the moment. "I'm serious, Joe. This is weird shit."

He sighed. "So tell me, what do we need to do? Is it dangerous?"

I mulled over the question. I could try to clean the lot, but without knowing what was going on, it probably wouldn't take. Cleansing required at least a working knowledge of what entities or creatures I might be dealing with and I hesitated to go in there waving my Florida water and charms until I knew what I was up against.

"I don't know. I haven't got the faintest idea of what's going on. Nor do I know who—or what—our visitor last night was. I think we need to do some research to find out just what kind of people the Brunswicks were. Meanwhile, be careful over there. Okay? I'm keeping the kids away until I know more about it."

He yawned and stretched. "That's probably the best we can do for now. Do you think your lady last night is connected to the lights you saw?"

I shrugged. "I have no idea. We're nearing All Hallows Eve. The dead walk during this time of year. Spirits rise to visit their loved ones, and the veil between worlds grows thin."

Joe regarded me solemnly. "You're really the one who needs to be careful, you know. I'm not head-blind, but I don't get hit by as much as you do. Promise me you'll watch yourself?"

He was serious, and for that I was grateful. Usually the men who'd entered my life ran when it came to matters like this, but Joe accepted the entire spirit world as part and parcel of my life. At the same time, he was cautious, not letting testosterone get in the way of clear thinking.

As I reached over and gave him a soft kiss on the cheek, the door opened and Kip ran inside. He took one look at me, shook his head, and ran upstairs. I wasn't about to get his hopes up by telling him about the groggy vision of Samantha on my bed or in the lot next door—too much possibility the sightings had been born out of my own desire rather than from reality.

"He's hurting. I hope we find her soon, or our whole family's going to be heartbroken, me included."

Joe cuddled me with one arm. "Don't forget about me, hon. I think the world of Sam and her kittens. Now, I'm going to go finish tearing out the last of those brambles so we can get down in that basement and find out what's going on." He stood up and headed toward the door.

I caught him by the arm before he went out. "Be careful. As I said, I don't know what we're dealing with. Just . . . take care of yourself."

With a nod, he slipped on his jacket and work gloves and headed next door. As I toyed around with the remote, trying to decide whether to go help Joe or hunt down Randa and see how she was doing, the phone rang. I picked it up and a familiar voice echoed on the other end of the line.

"Emerald? This is Maeve. I got to thinking about your birthday this morning and had the feeling that I needed to call you."

A feeling of relief swept over me, and I realized that I

wanted to talk to her, too. "Maeve, I'm so glad you called. Listen, can we meet for tea?" She agreed to rendezvous with me at my shop in half an hour and I hung up and grabbed my keys. I should check in with Cinnamon and Lana anyway. Might as well head out early.

After letting Kip know where I was off to, I slipped through the hedge to peek in on Joe, who had built up a sweat. The beads of perspiration glistened on his skin. I fought the desire to rip off my clothes right then and there.

"I'm taking off for the shop. I'll be gone an hour, maybe ninety minutes. You can reach me on my cell if you need me, and Kip knows to come over and get you in case something happens."

He pulled out a bandana from his back pocket and wiped his nose. The chill air was making it run. "What do you want to do about dinner tonight?"

"I'll pick up some takeout on the way home," I called over my shoulder as I hurried down the drive, back to my yard where I climbed into my Mountaineer.

As I put the car into reverse and pulled out of the driveway I could see Randa, out on the roof, staring over the railing I'd had installed when we first moved in so she could sky-watch the night away in safety. She lifted one hand in half-salute when I blew a kiss at her, looking forlorn. As I tooled off down the street, I murmured a quiet prayer to the universe. The only thing I really wanted for my birthday was a little extra time so I could devote it to everybody who needed my attention. Some days, there was never enough of me to go around.

IN THE ALMOST three years that I'd been running the Chintz 'n China Tea Room, it had changed. Not only had I updated the paint job and the shelf liners, but I'd upgraded my tearoom furniture after a thief trashed everything that wasn't bolted down during a major act of vandalism earlier in the year. After a brief bout with self-pity and anger, I dug in, refurbished the shop, restocked with better inventory, and installed a security alarm system.

We were set for autumn, with displays of Brown Betty teapots and delicate porcelain pots in the shape of pumpkins and onions. The windows were filled with silk autumn leaves and elk antler sheds that Jimbo had found out in the woods. Earthen brown baskets rested, filled to the brim with tea and crackers and honey. Bobble-head jack-o'-lanterns nestled side by side with beautiful witches dangling on crescent moons. I had even managed to find long garlands of apple-shaped lights and bordered the windows with them.

The display tables and every piece of china in the place sparkled, and my heart swelled. I loved my store and treasured both Lana and Cinnamon, who always followed through, uncomplaining. As I glanced around the room, I saw Cinnamon finishing up with Purdy Anderson, a colorful and influential member of Chiqetaw's matronly society.

"How are my two favorite ladies today?" I slipped up to the counter next to Purdy, who patted my arm.

"I'm so glad to see you, Emerald. You realize we miss you here, but I hope you're enjoying your vacation."

I just gave her a warm smile and nodded. Purdy was a notorious gossip and I knew better than to say anything I didn't want spread all over town. She picked up her shopping bags and wandered out of the store. Cinnamon sighed and rubbed her head.

"Hey, Emerald. Things are fine, before you ask. The weekend's been busy. A lot of foot traffic and a lot of sales. The weather seems to be driving people indoors."

I glanced in the tearoom. Maeve was waiting for me at a table in the corner. The rest of the alcove was packed.

"That's good news. We can always use the extra money. Looks nice in here, by the way. I'm going to go chat with Maeve for a bit. Cinnamon? Is something wrong?" I saw the sparkle of a tear in one eye and she looked strained, like she'd been holding her breath. "What's going on?"

She sniffed, then blew her nose with a tissue. "Oh, Emerald, I just found out that my boyfriend is getting out of jail early."

I blinked, not certain what to say. Her boyfriend was a rock-bottom jerk who had managed to get himself tossed in the slammer several times. My opinion of him was about as low as it could get. The man had three children to take care of, yet he had decided the best way to do that was to rob a convenience store. When Cinnamon first came to work for me, he was on trial and I'd wanted to go over to the jail and smack him upside the head.

Cinnamon lived with her mother, who watched her babies while she worked her butt off for me and went to night school to get her degree in accounting. I just wished the girl would come to her senses and see the jerk for what he really was: a lazy bum who would only drag her and the children down.

"How do you feel about that?"

"I miss him, and the boys barely know him. It's just that . . . today he called. He said he can't afford to live with us."

"Halfway house?" I asked.

She shook her head. "No, he says he doesn't have the money to pay for a place for me and the kids. He said if I want to live with him, I'll have to front the apartment myself. Emerald, what am I going to do?"

Maeve was waiting for me, but I didn't want to leave Cinnamon hanging. "What does your mother say about all of this?" I had met Mrs. Juarez several times and had a pretty good idea of what she thought of the boyfriend issue.

Cinnamon broke into a pale smile. "Ma thinks he's bad news. I thought by moving in with him I could take some of the burden off of her, but she says she'd rather have the kids and me stay with her while I finish up school than try to make it a go with David."

I took a deep breath and let it out slowly. "Your mother's a pretty smart cookie. I know you love David, but babe, this dude has been nothing but bad news since you met him. He has three kids and yet goes out and pulls a stupid stunt and gets himself busted? If he really cared about you and the kids, he would have gotten a job at Bigwell's instead of ripping them off. And for what? Fifty dollars? Do you really want that kind of influence affecting your children? He's more of a sperm donor than a father."

She shifted from one foot to the other. "That's what my mother said. I guess I have some thinking to do."

The shop bells tinkled and she glanced over at the door. "I'd better get back to work. You just know Amanda Withers is going to ask me about every single item in the shop." Cinnamon giggled and I flashed her a wide grin. Amanda was a pain in the ass, but the woman spent so much money in the Chintz 'n China that neither one of us really meant it when we complained about her.

"Dry your tears and go help her. We'll talk about this later. I promise. You don't have to decide anything today."

As she bustled off, I headed into the tearoom, poured myself a cup of apple spice tea, and dished up a slice of rhubarb pie. I settled at Maeve's table and she glanced up, giving me one of her efficient, yet friendly smiles.

"Emerald!" She folded her magazine and put it aside. I saw that it was something to do about llamas or knitting or maybe both. She saw my glance and held it up. *Modern Llama.*

"I guess they have a magazine for every interest," I said, biting into my pie. In my opinion sugar was one of the primary building blocks to life and I hadn't had my quota for the day. Time to catch up. I was also jonesing for more mocha. Starbucks was definitely on the itinerary when I headed home. I swallowed a mouthful of tea in hopes of fooling my caffeine cravings.

Maeve gave me an approving look. "I like a woman who isn't afraid to eat. Too many prissy-misses out there today. You look tired, my dear. There are dark circles under your eyes. What *have* you been doing with yourself?"

One thing I could count on with Maeve: She would say exactly what was on her mind. No pussyfooting around for her, and I rather liked it that way.

I frowned. "Maeve, some strange stuff has been going on. I'm not sure what the hell's happening, to tell you the truth."

"Not another murder, I hope?"

I shook my head. "No, not another murder. I think the lot next door is haunted, but I have no idea by what. And our cat's missing. And Miranda's new boyfriend—her first—just got caught in that awful fire. He'll be okay, but his parents are in critical condition."

"Fire can be so destructive. I hope the boy weathers this, and I hope his parents recover." She paused for a moment, staring at her hands. "Your cat will come home. Members of the feline population have a remarkable resilence. I'm sure she'll be back. As to the lot next door, I know you all too well to take what you say at face value. What's going on? If it were just any little spook, you'd know what to do and probably wouldn't even mention it."

"You've got me there." I told her about the dancing lights. She listened to my story all the way through without speaking, but I could sense that she was taking in every word, reading between the lines.

"It sounds like you have yourself a swarm of faeries. *Ignis Fatuus*, to be precise. Or corpse candles, as they are called in some areas. Surprising, within the confines of a town. But then again," she added, appraising me with a gentle smile, "perhaps not, given your nature."

"Corpse candles? That can't be good. I've never heard of them, or of the *Ignis Fatuus*." I believed in faeries, though not in the way a lot of people looked at them—as cute Victorian stylized cherubs. No, I knew enough about the history of the fae folk to pay them some serious respect and caution. But I'd never heard of *Ignis Fatuus* or corpse candles. A shiver ran down my spine as I turned the names over in my head.

"In common parlance, my dear, you have a field full of Will o' the Wisps. And you'd best tread carefully, because they usually mean business." She leaned forward so no one else could hear us. "These creatures are nothing to mess with, Emerald. Don't let your children go over there."

I swallowed the last bite of pie, my throat suddenly dry. Maeve was deadly serious, with emphasis on the word *deadly*. "What are they, then? Balls of light or energy, right?"

"They tend to take that shape, yes. Balls of light, dancing lights, energy orbs. Nobody really knows for sure. Science laughs off the existence of creatures like this, insisting on some idiotic notion that they're swamp gas or methane jets alight. But trust me, they're real and they're not at all human in nature. At least now, if they ever were." Her eyes flashed. Maeve might insist that she didn't have the Sight, but she had knowledge. And knowledge was power.

"I can tell they're of supernatural origin," I said, sipping my tea. "What do you think they are? Nature spirits? Astral beasties?"

She sighed, toying with her cup. "There are several legends. One says that corpse candles are spirits of the dead barred entrance to paradise, yet not cast into hell. Another insists they're faeries bent on destruction. Whatever the case, they're associated with moors and graveyards. In fact, there's a whole new set of ghost hunters out there looking to capture what they call 'spirit orbs' on camera. They have no idea what they're messing about with. These creatures aren't kindly souls waiting to guide others."

Spirits of the dead caught between heaven and hell? I wasn't a religious woman. In fact my beliefs about the afterlife centered around a vague notion of reincarnation, though I wasn't even sure about how that was supposed to work. But I was certain that our souls lived on after death. I'd learned that the hard way, through ghosts and ghoulies, as well as through Nanna's gentle visits.

"Could they be trapped in the Otherworld, unable to move on?"

Maeve caught my gaze and held it. "That's a commonly held thought. And it may be the answer. I can't tell you for sure, but I do know that, be they faerie or spirit, they congregate around sites where there's been great trauma and tragedy. And sometimes, they lead mortals to their death. Unlike the *Bean Sidhe*—the banshee. Will o' the Wisps don't warn of death so much as bring it with them."

I played with my cup, relieved that I'd told the kids to stay out of the lot. I'd have to reinforce my warning. "What can I do to clear them out? We must have stirred them up when we began excavating the brambles."

She looked alarmed. "Oh no, you can't just clear them out. There must be a reason why they're there. Until you find out, I don't recommend having anything to do with them. You could endanger your family."

Even as she said it, I knew she was right. There was nothing I could do until I found out what they wanted. And that wasn't going to be easy. I thanked her for her time and reminded her about my birthday party, then headed toward the door.

Cinnamon was busy with another customer as I left, waving. The afternoon had slipped away and dusk was crowding in. Daylight was in short supply here in cloud country during the autumn months, and I pulled my jacket snugly around my waist as I hopped into my car. My mood shifted suddenly, falling into depression as I started the engine and pulled out of my parking space. Life couldn't go along without a hitch, could it? There was always some snag, some danger in wait. Forcing myself to focus on the road, I navigated my way through the short lines we called rush hour traffic in Chiqetaw.

Joe was waiting for me when I got home, sitting at the kitchen table with a troubled look on his face. I tossed my purse on the table and sat down next to him. He was nursing a tall bottle of cola and looked like he needed another.

"What's wrong, honey? Didn't you get the steps cleared?"

"Oh yeah, they're clear now. I haven't been down to check out the basement yet, but that's not what's wrong."

He shook his head. "I got a call from my lawyer about half-an-hour ago. He told me to stop work on the lot, that I may not be able to go through with the sale after all. He said the owner wants to back out of the deal."

"What? Why?" Yet another glitch.

With a shrug, he said, "I don't know, Em. He'll have more information tomorrow. Until then, I don't know what's going to happen."

I stood behind him and wrapped my arms around his shoulders, resting my head on his. He was warm in my embrace, warm and loving and breathing quietly. Not angry, not fuming, just confused. Joe was so different from Roy, my ex, that it was hard for me to believe he was for real, but he was, and he was here in my kitchen.

"Don't worry," I said. "If it comes down to it, we really don't need the space. It would be nice, but it won't be the end of the world if the deal doesn't work out."

"Yeah, I guess so," he said, stirring a little out of his funk. "How'd it go down at the shop?"

"Nerve-racking." I was about to tell him about my conversation with Maeve when the kids broke through the back door.

"Mom! Mom! We saw Samantha. We think we know where she is!" Randa's eyes were bright, her cheeks flushed from the chill and from running. Kip, behind her, nodded, so excited he could only stumble over his words.

"You did? Where?" It was about time this family had a bit of good luck.

Randa and Kip both stopped short and Randa winced. "You're going to be mad when we tell you."

That was usually Kip's line. "What have you been up to? Where were you?" And then I knew. "Oh no, you weren't next door, were you?"

She slowly nodded. "Yeah. But Mom, we saw her run

in there and we had to follow. She ran down into the base-ment—and . . ."

"And you followed?" Heaven help me, they'd never make it to twenty. "You went down in that basement after I told you not to?" I took a step forward, furious. "Do you realize how dangerous that is?"

She sniffled. "I know, but we saw Samantha! She's down there, I think she's stuck in a secret room. We saw her run down the steps and when we followed her, she dis-appeared. But we heard her crying. Mom, she could be hurt."

The looks on their faces stopped the explosion that I felt rising. They were worried and afraid. Of course they were going to follow her down into the depths of hell to save her.

"Okay, listen to me. This is not over. But we'll go have a look. The two of you stay here, do you understand me? There are dangerous energies running loose over there and I won't have you hurt, even for Samantha's sake."

They nodded. Joe had already grabbed the flashlights and now, with a curious look at me that said he wanted the whole story as soon as we had the chance, we trooped over to the lot next door to save Sammy.

Five

From Brigit's Journal:

It was a difficult morning. I'd finished feeding Mab
her bowl of milk, and was trying on my good dress for
Mass this morning when I realized the zipper barely
closed anymore. It's not going to be long before everybody notices. Mother Mary, what should I do? I'm no
closer to a decision than I was a month ago, and I'm getting little help in the matter. I must admit, weakness of
spirit was not a fault I'd expected to find in my love, but
there's no denying it. Whatever 'tis done, will be at my
bidding, and my bidding alone.

There's the evening supper bell. Goodnight, diary,
and thank you for listening. I have no one else here, in
this land of strangers. Sometimes, I feel like I've no
friends at all, though I know I'm stupid to think so. But
when you can't bring yourself to tell your friends what
secrets you're hiding, then are they really friends? I
don't know.

*   *   *

AS JOE AND I made our way through the rubble of debris still littering the empty lot, the hairs on my arms began to stand at attention and I brought up short, reaching out to touch him on the shoulder. Just ahead, the lights were dancing furiously, bobbing and weaving around the back end of the foundation.

Joe inhaled sharply and stopped in his tracks. "What the hell—"

"You see them, then?"

"Faintly—they look like little twinkles to me, like Christmas lights. They're pretty."

"Trust me, those twinkles are a lot bigger than you're seeing them, and a lot more dangerous than Christmas lights. I was going to tell you about my conversation with Maeve when the kids rushed in. Joe, those things are Will o' the Wisps, and they're dangerous. Don't listen to them, don't follow them, don't try to interact with them." I swallowed the lump rising in my throat. Over the years, I'd dealt with some strange beasties and spirits, but had little to do with the faerie realm. If Maeve was right, then that's where these critters originated; faeries somehow connected with the dead, of another world and yet touching ours.

"Will o' the Wisps? I remember those from playing Dungeons & Dragons. They weren't very nice in the game, either." He took a step closer to me and felt for my hand. I squeezed, then let go and moved forward.

"This is no game, Joe. These beings have been known to lead people to their death. So keep an eye on me, and if I say 'move,' then move. Fast."

He nodded as I began to inch forward, all too aware that the glowing orbs had noticed our approach. A few of the brightly colored spheres began to float toward us. I held my breath as one—brilliant green—hovered near my face, right in front of my eyes, flickering, shimmering, pulsating. Attracted like a moth to a flame, wanting nothing more than to reach out and touch it, I forced myself to look to the side, not allowing myself to become fixated on the energy.

"Are you okay?" Joe whispered. "What are they doing?"

"Yeah, I'm all right. They're probing us. Come on, let's head down to the basement. Watch your step." I sidled around the globe and cautiously approached the edge of the stairs. Made of concrete, they had survived the fire and fifty years of weathering. In the beam of my flashlight, I could see where patches of grass and roots had broken through the cement and cracked the gray stone. Overall they looked safe enough. If there was a railing, it had long ago splintered away or perhaps burned up in the fire, but the stairs buttressed one wall of the brick-lined basement.

I put my foot on the first step, then breathed a little easier as it rested firmly beneath my weight with no complaints or crumbling. My light flickered on the mulch at the bottom, thick and untouched for fifty years save for the trail Kip and Miranda had left through it. Fighting the urge to run back and paddle both their butts for disobeying me, I gathered my courage and began to descend into the darkness.

The silence thickened. Joe followed a few steps behind, but it felt as if he were a million miles away as the gloom enveloped me, closing in the windswept night. Mist rose from the mulch, a low blanket of rolling fog, and my stomach tightened as I drew closer to the bottom. As we continued our descent, the energy shifted and the dancing lights swooped down around us, darting and twisting.

Should I try to reach out? Touch them? Communicate? The minute I considered it, I backed away from the thought. If I opened myself up, they'd use that wedge to their advantage. No, best to keep my thoughts to myself.

My foot touched the mulch and sank up to the ankle in leaf debris, and I tried to avoid thinking of what might be hiding in the muck. I steeled myself with the memory that I'd crawled on my belly through compost and bugs before to save my son. At least this time my feet were firmly planted on the ground. As Joe joined me, the look on his face was loud and clear: He still hadn't gotten used to playing in the Otherworld, but he was making a valiant attempt.

The Will o' the Wisps seemed to take a bead on him and his eyes lit up with apprehension as they drew near. I could feel their energy, tentacles reaching out to tease, to call him closer.

I touched his arm. "Hey, come back."

Startled, he jerked around to stare at me, looking confused for a second. "Huh? Oh . . . yeah."

"What are they saying to you?"

He ducked his head and I could see the worry in his eyes. "I'm not sure, all I see are twinkles of lights. But now that I think about it, I heard a low whispering in the background. Emerald, I don't like this. These things scare me."

"They lure mortals in. Maeve warned me about them. Just try to keep a clear head. Come on, let's see about finding Samantha. Maybe I really did see her down here—maybe it wasn't a hallucination."

I took his hand and led him deeper into the basement. In the dark, with only our flashlights and the dancing orbs illuminating the night, there was no real way of telling what the place looked like now—or had looked like when the house was intact. As we neared the place where Miranda had said they'd heard Samantha, I began to trace the walls with my light. And . . . there, yes—the outline of a door. Rounded at the top, hardwood that was charred but not fully burnt. The door had an iron lock, and as the kids had said, it was locked. Firmly.

"I can't open the damn thing. Can you?" I stepped back to let Joe in to give it a try. The lights were buzzing us now, whirling like pinwheels. Oh yeah, something was up, all right.

Joe dug his feet into the mulch and tried to push it open. Nothing. He motioned for me to stand back. "I'm going to shoulder bust it."

"Just be careful."

He inhaled deeply, blew the air out of his lungs, then lunged at the door with his shoulder. I heard a nasty "crack" as he bounced back, cursing a blue streak. One of the Will o' the Wisps broke off and buzzed his shoulder. A bright flash illuminated the basement and Joe yelped and dropped to his knees.

"Babe, are you okay? What happened?" I knelt beside him, flashing the light in his eyes, which just made him swear louder. "Oops! Sorry."

He winced as I encircled his waist with my arm and helped him stand. "Jeez, that thing stung me! And the door must be made of ironwood." He stretched his neck to one side, then the other. The lights swirled around us and—not thinking—I turned on them.

"Back off, you buggers!" Even as I shouted, I realized that perhaps this wasn't exactly keeping the low profile that I'd suggested earlier. But they retreated. "That's better. Just chill out."

Joe snorted through his pain. "You know, I love you. You're such a firebrand." He grimaced again. "My shoulder feels like it's been stung. There's no chance I can get through that door with brute force, Em. But before we leave, why don't you listen at it first; see if you can hear Sammy?"

I reluctantly left his side and slogged my way through the leafy debris until I was next to the door. I pressed my ear against the wood, straining to hear any sound that might be on the other side. As the night settled around my shoulders, I heard the faint shuffle of movement. A step? A cough? A meow? There, yes, the faint meowing of a cat coming from the other side of the door.

"I think I hear her," I called softly over my shoulder. "Sammy? Samantha?" I waited, listening, and once again, heard a soft cry.

Joe frowned as I hurried back to his side. "If she's there, she had to find a way in, but I don't see how. Maybe there's an underground opening or some vent we haven't seen. That's entirely possible, you know? Some of these old houses had basements that weren't finished. I wish I could pick the lock, but I'm not very adept at that sort of thing. How about you?"

"What? You think I can pick locks? How about safe-cracking, while we're at it?" I shook my head, wondering just what other skills Joe thought I had up my sleeve. "Not one of my multitude of talents, babe. But Murray might be able to help us out. Or a locksmith."

Joe nixed the latter thought. "I can't bring a locksmith on this property until I talk to my lawyer. Remember? I may not actually own this place. Technically, we're breaking and entering right now, though I imagine we could talk our way out of it. Whatever we do, we have to be discreet."

"I don't see why—nobody's been in this basement since the house burned down." At his firm but patient look, I caved. "Okay, no locksmith. But let's call Murray, please? If Sammy is in there, I'll be damned if I'm going to leave her. Irena Finch can kiss my ass on that one."

He nodded. "Okay, let's get the hell out of here. This place gives me the creeps and I'm hurting like a son of a gun."

I let him go first. Who knew what the Will o' the Wisps might do to an injured man trying to climb a flight of stairs in the dark? I wondered if they were like bees, who swarmed when their attack pheromones hit the air. But they left us alone. As we ascended I glanced over my shoulder, back at the door that waited, silently locked against time. Mist rose into a pillar, swirling as the lights fluttered around it, and I could almost see a figure dancing within the flowing streams of fog. With a shiver, I turned and hurried up the stairs, back to the welcoming light streaming from my kitchen window.

THE KIDS WERE hovering by the door. I hushed them before they could overwhelm us with questions. "We need to make a few phone calls, and Joe needs a bandage."

They recognized my tone and obeyed without question. When we had stripped off our coats on the back porch and burst through into the kitchen, I turned to Randa.

"Kettle on, please. We need tea. Orange Spice would be lovely."

She gave me a quick nod, filled the kettle and set it to heating. "What teapot do you want to use, Mom?"

I winked at her. "Your choice. And thank you, sweetie. Kip, bring me some bandages and the antibiotic ointment from the medicine cabinet, would you?" He dashed through the arch leading to the living room.

I forced Joe to sit down at the table. "Shirt off, mister. Right now."

He grinned. "Shouldn't we wait until the kids are asleep?" he murmured under his breath. I glared at him, trying to staunch a smile that welled up in spite of myself.

"You know what I mean. Off with it."

I saw the look of pain that crossed his face as he lifted his arms over his head. Shit, what the hell had he done? As he stripped off his shirt, I examined his right shoulder. A dark bruise covered the side of his upper arm from where he'd shoulder-butted the door, along with several lacerations that looked like they might have come from a jellyfish stinger. Well, hell. Not good.

Kip came running in with the phone. "Mom, did you find any trace of—" he asked, breathless, but he stopped abruptly as he caught sight of Joe's new body art. "Whoa . . . what happened to you?"

Joe glanced down at his arm, cautiously lifting and turning it so he could get a good look at the bruises and the lacerations. He blanched, looking slightly queasy. "Ugh. That looks nasty."

I coughed. "Yeah, I'd say so. Randa, bring me the aloe out of the fridge, please. Kip, we may have heard Sammy over there, but can't be sure. We're going to try to get into that room, but I want you and Randa to make me a promise on your word of honor. I mean it. You break the promise, you're in deep shit. Understand?"

As Randa handed me the bottle of cold gel, she caught my gaze and I saw a flicker run through her eyes. "Mom, what's going on over there?"

I shook my head. "I don't know yet. Which is one of the reasons I want you and Kip to promise me this: Neither one of you—together or alone—are to set foot in that lot again until I give you permission. I mean it. Not even if you see Samantha. I miss her too, but there are dangers over there. Those lights, for example. From what I can find out so far, they've been known to lure people into harm's way. I'm talking about end-up-in-the-hospital trouble."

Kip plopped down in a chair, his aura flaring. "And Sammy is over there with them."

I sighed and placed the aloe on the counter, then knelt to stare into my son's face. Tears were hiding behind those big brown eyes. "Sweetie, we'll do our best to bring her home. It may take a day, or maybe a week, but we'll keep looking until we find her. You have to trust me. You have to let me and Joe do the work. Will o' the Wisps have been known to kill people by hypnotizing them and leading them into trouble. I can't let you take the chance. Not even to save Samantha. Do you understand?"

He sniffed and dashed his sleeve across his eyes, trying so hard to maintain control, to avoid breaking down in front of us. "Okay."

I reached out, intending to give him a hug, but he slipped out of my embrace and ran off. I could hear his feet as he thumped up the stairs in defeat. Not anger, like when I'd banned his friend Sly from the house, but disappointment. Randa stared at the floor for a moment, then, without a word, followed Kip upstairs. I wasn't sure I wanted to know what she was thinking.

I finished smoothing aloe across Joe's bruises, silently ruminating on what we were going to do.

Joe seemed to sense my mood. He stared out the window. This had to be hard for him too. He'd been so excited when he told me that he'd bought that lot. We'd actually started making long-term plans, something I never thought I'd do again with anybody. I put the aloe back in the fridge and dialed Murray's number, calling her at work first. If I remembered right, she was on duty this evening. She answered on the second ring.

"Hey babe, listen, things have taken another turn." I filled her in on the day's events. "We need to get into that room, to see if Sammy's in there." I avoided mentioning that Joe wasn't sure about his ownership of the property. What she didn't know, she couldn't object to.

I could hear her tapping her pencil on the desk. "Em, I wish I could get out there tonight, but I can't. But . . ." She lowered her voice. "If you really need somebody to break into the room, call my house. Jimmy's there and I happen to know for a fact that he can pick a lock."

"He told you that?" I asked, grinning for the first time that evening.

"Nah, it's in his rap sheet." She coughed. "Anyway, give him a call. Maybe he can come over. Otherwise, you'll have to wait until tomorrow morning if you want me to show up."

I put in a quick call to Jimbo and went through the whole story again. All it took was a "Can you help?" and he was out the door and on his way over.

"You know, Jimbo has proven himself to be one hell of a guy," I told Joe. "He dropped everything without a question and he's headed over here right now." I started to wrap my arms around Joe's shoulders, but stopped when I remembered his bruises, and kissed him instead. "I'm so glad you two finally became friends. Especially with Murray dating him."

Joe flashed me a look of love and patience and exasperation all rolled into one. "Em, I have to tell you, it was hard for me to forgive him for what he did to you. The man threw a brick through your window with a nasty word written on it. He hit on you at a restaurant and you had to head-butt him into submission, for cripes sake."

"He apologized, and he paid for the window. And most important, he helped me when I had no other place to turn. That kind of friendship you can't buy."

I had never whitewashed the way Jimbo behaved toward me when we first met, but I'd let it go, learning to value the diamond-in-the-rough biker who'd been thrust into my life. And now that he and my best friend were in love and struggling to make their way in a world that didn't want to accept their union, I wasn't going to nitpick over actions that no longer held any meaning for me. Joe had made a valiant effort to become friends with Jimbo and it had worked. They found more in common than they expected to find.

Less than ten minutes after I'd called, Jimbo was standing on my doorstep, all six-foot-three, two-hundred-twenty pounds of him. He winked. "I'm all set, O'Brien. Let's get this show on the road."

The lights were nowhere to be seen as we passed by the hedgerow but the moment we approached the basement stairs, they flickered into view again. Joe warily glanced around. "What the hell is going on? I can't see anything, but I can feel something here."

"There are faeries out here," I said. "Dangerous ones. Just follow my instructions, even if you can't see them, because I can."

"Do what she says," Joe told Jimbo. "Those things bite. I know."

Jimbo's granny was a hoodoo woman, and that's how he viewed me. God only knows what he called Mur. The nimbus of his aura glittered with protective energy. Oh yeah, Jimbo had his guard up, even though he didn't realize it.

"Shit." He glanced nervously at his shoulder. I could

see an orb dancing around him. "There's something there, right?"

"You have good instincts."

"Well, how do I make them leave me alone?" He batted at the air, like he might try to ward off a bee. "You said these things are out of some sort of fairy tale? Like Snow White?"

"Not out of a fairy tale. We think they're a type of faerie," I said. "Will o' the Wisps, also known as corpse candles."

"I don't like that name," Jimbo grumbled.

"Neither do I, but it's fitting because they're supposed to be connected with the dead. Dangerous critters if you don't take care. Just ignore them and I'll tell you if you need to do something or move out of the way." I pointed toward the basement. "The door's down there." I held up the light and pointed the beam toward the bottom of the stairs. I could tell Jimbo was spooked; his energy flared as I took the front, leading the way down into the darkened maw. Jimbo followed and Joe flanked the end.

I sucked in my breath. Put me in front of a thug or a mugger and I'd run away faster than you could say "scram." Drop an eight-legged beastie on me, and my screams would bust your eardrums. But spirits and their ilk? While I preferred to avoid tangling with them, at least I usually had some idea of how to cope with such situations.

We slogged through the mulch to the sounds of our breathing, the foliage shifting beneath our feet as the faint buzz of the Will o' the Wisps danced through the basement. As we came to the door, I stepped aside to give Jimbo room to work, holding the flashlight on the lock.

He glanced at me, one eyebrow raised. "Old lock," was all he said as he pulled out a small tool kit and flipped open the lid. Asking Joe to hold the pouch, he selected a thin tool that looked something like a dentist's pick and knelt down to gain better access. I kept an eye on the lights, which were hovering in a semi-circle around us, having ceased their continual movement. Did they mind us intruding? Were they here to warn us off, or encourage us onward?

Shivering, I pulled my jacket tighter around my shoulders.

"O'Brien, hold it steady, would you?"

I straightened the light so that it was shining on the door again. Jimbo played with the lock a few more moments, then jiggled the door handle and, with a low creak, it slowly swung inward. A gentle breeze rushed past, as if the room inside had awakened, taking its first breath in almost fifty years. I glanced at the men; both silently awaited my cue. This was my territory and neither one seemed eager to interfere.

Taking a deep breath, I stepped into the darkness. As I entered the room, a soft whisper echoed past, and thin fingers of a breeze raced through my hair, lifting it gently before rushing by. The wind, I told myself. Only the wind. I took another step, swinging my light from side to side as I tried to illuminate as much of the room as possible.

To my right, I could make out a bed—a small cot against the wall, with a nightstand beside it. To the left, there appeared to be a writing desk and a chest of drawers. I took another step forward, my breath coming in shallow gulps. The energy here was thick, dank, and dark, in hiding from the world for half a century's cold slumber. Cold as frost on the window, cold as bones in the earth.

Jimbo stepped back, letting Joe slip in ahead of him. With the addition of Joe's light, we were better able to see what we were dealing with. This had once been a bedroom, that much was obvious, though it looked sparse and utilitarian for such an influential and well-placed family. The bed frame was rusted, iron-wrought, and simple. The clothes and mattress had decayed enough to be disgusting, but not enough to hide a simple floral pattern. I exhaled as I reached out and touched the cloth.

When my fingers grazed the material, it was as if I was touching a shroud. The feeling of death and decay and of long nights waiting in the cold. I shuddered and Joe rested his hand on my shoulder, steadying me. I blinked, turned, and found myself staring into Joe's eyes.

"Em? Em? Are you all right?"

I nodded, "I picked up something from the cloth—psychometry. Nothing specific, just a feeling of loss and death."

Jimbo wrangled a flashlight out of his jacket and entered the room, starting the hunt for Samantha. "O'Brien, sometimes you scare the piss out of me. Let's find your cat and get out of here. I think it's time to blow the joint."

Despite my nervousness, I laughed. "Babe, you are a breath of fresh air. But save the dynamite. I had quite enough of your lovely explosions, and I'm not helping you blow up any more of my china. Don't worry, we'll make it home in one piece, Will o' the Wisps or not."

We began searching for Sammy, calling for her. I thought I heard a cry under the bed but when Jimbo got down on his knees to look, there was no one there. I was poking around near the nightstand when I noticed a framed picture on the wooden table. A lovely young woman stared at me, frozen on film in a single moment of time. She was willowy, with long red curls, and she held a tortoiseshell who looked a lot like our Sammy. A dreamy, lost look filled the woman's eyes, and as I stared at the photo, I recognized her. I'd seen her the night before—outside Randa's room.

Goose bumps rose along my skin. Whoever she was, she'd been visiting in my house. I tucked the picture in my pocket.

"Look at this!" Joe held up a faded journal. The pages were damp, but most of the writing was still readable. He held the flashlight steady while I examined the diary. The front flap identified the owner as "Brigit." As I gingerly accepted it, the same flow of energy tingled through my fingers that I'd felt from the picture and the cloth. *Brigit.*

My red-haired ghost had been a woman named Brigit who had been staying with the Brunswick family. Whether she was a relative or a friend, I couldn't tell. I slid the journal in my pocket next to the photograph.

Jimbo hauled a suitcase out from the closet, along with a few dilapidated dresses. Functional but not pretty. "Tag on the luggage says that this belonged to Brigit O'Reilly. Looks like she came from a place called Glengarriff, Ireland."

I decided to wait before telling them that Brigit was my ghost from last night. After all, she hadn't been antagonistic, and I wanted to get a better feel for what we'd discovered before I threw another iron in the fire.

"I don't see Samantha anywhere," I said as we made a last sweep around the room. "Do you?"

Both Jimbo and Joe shook their heads. As we took one last look around the perimeter of the room, Joe flashed his light over the back wall. I gasped. It was covered with murals; the paintings had faded but were still in relatively good condition. Though they were difficult to make out in the dim light, I could see a castle, white and rising into the sky, and a parade of knights on horseback headed toward the fortress. We closed in, concentrating our flashlight beams to better take in the panorama of murals.

"Camelot," Joe whispered.

"Camel what?" Jimbo said.

"Not camel. Camelot, King Arthur's court. This has to be Camelot," Joe said. "Look, a castle made of gleaming white, and knights in shining armor?"

A splash of color caught my eye and I stepped closer to examine the vista sweeping across the wall. A woman dressed in green with long copper hair watched the procession of knights out of a window. She stood in a tower set off from the castle and by her side rested a loom, loaded with a half-finished tapestry. A tear trickled down one cheek.

I took yet a closer look at the woman in the painting. *Brigit.* The woman was Brigit. One of the knights, the only one looking up toward her tower, had to be Lancelot. Fragments of a poem, long ago learned and beloved, began to dance through my head. "And sometimes through the mirror blue, the knights come riding two and two. She hath no loyal Knight and true, the Lady of Shalott."

Joe stood behind me, his hands on my shoulders and whispered, " 'There she weaves by night and day, a magic web with colours gay. She has heard a whisper say, a curse is on her if she stay to look down to Camelot.' "

I withdrew the photograph from my pocket. There was no mistaking it—the painting on the wall matched Brigit, the red-haired dreamer who had left behind a suitcase, a few dresses, and a journal of handwritten poetry. "Could she be one of the Brunswicks' cousins?"

Joe shook his head. "I have no idea—" He stopped and glanced over his shoulder, paling as he did so. "Em, turn around. Slowly. We have company."

I slowly edged my way around. The doorway to the

open basement was swarming with the corpse candles. "Oh shit. We need to get out of here. Now. Sammy isn't here. Let's go. Shut the door on the way out."

"What is it?" Jimbo said.

"How do we get through them?" Jimbo asked. "To me, it's just a bunch of pretty lights, but I know you're seeing something else."

I bit my lip, trying to decide if it was safe to just walk through the swarm. "We're going to have to just brave it. Don't listen to anything you might hear and whatever you do, don't stop once we're on the move. I'll try to distract them so you two can get out without being bombarded."

I took a hesitant step forward, then a stronger one and headed for the door. The lights were buzzing louder; the damned things were agitated. With a deep breath, I plunged into their midst. A swirl of desire hit me, beckoning me to drop everything and give chase under the darkening moon. I forced myself to shake it off. I had to distract them away from Joe and Jimbo. As I pushed out the door, the majority of lights followed me. I kept my eyes focused on the sky, on a glimpse of a tree limb.

"We're out! Get your butt over here, O'Brien!" Jimbo's call echoed in my ears and the lights went zipping every which way. I shook my head and fastened my gaze on the men, slogging as fast as I could in their direction, scattering mist and mulch and debris as I went. As I neared the steps where Joe anxiously waited for me, Jimbo had reached topside and turned around, poised to return if I should need him.

Just then, a scream pierced the air and I covered my ears.

Joe grabbed my arm. "Come on, Em—move!"

"Did you hear her? Did you hear the scream?" I stumbled up the stairs, Joe dragging me along by the arm.

"I didn't hear anything and I'm not going back down to check."

I glanced over my shoulder at the basement, which was now filled with a buzzing nest of Will o' the Wisps, darting through the mist that had risen thick over the mulch. "Holy hell, we sure stirred them up. Come on, let's get out of here before they come after us!"

As we raced back to my house, my mind was ablaze with questions. Where was Samantha? And what about the mysterious Brigit? Why was her spirit visiting me, and what about her cat, who had long ago been a mirror reflection of my own Samantha? And why had she fled, all those years ago, leaving behind her belongings in a room guarded by knights and tall towers and poetry?

Six

> *"He holds my hand, a gentle touch,*
> *Our love we cannot show,*
> *But still it lingers in our hearts,*
> *Though part we must, I know."*

THE MINUTE WE trooped into the house, the kids surrounded us, clamoring for information about Samantha. I hated having to tell them that we hadn't found her yet, but there was nothing else I could do. Obviously shaken, Randa disappeared into the living room. Kip let out a big sigh. As he passed the pantry, Nigel came out and rubbed against his leg, meowing loudly. Kip swung around, eyes blazing.

"Nigel wants his mom! He's upset, and so are Noël and Nebula. An' so am I! What are we gonna do?" He sounded so desolate I wanted to cry, but what was I supposed to tell him? There was nothing I could say to remedy the situation.

Nebula was prowling the kitchen along with her brother. I scooped her up and scratched her behind the ears. "Today's Sunday. Tomorrow I'll go to the animal shelter and see if Sammy's there. If she isn't, we can make fliers after you get home from school and hand them out all around the neighborhood. We can offer a reward."

His lip trembled. "Do you think she was hit by a car?"

I sighed and plopped Nebula into Joe's arms. "Come on. I'll see what I can find out." Though I was hesitant to do it—God knows what I might find out—I headed into the living room, followed by Kip, Joe, and Jimbo. Randa was curled up in the rocking chair with a notebook. She glanced up from the page as I dug through my rolltop desk until I found an ornate gold key on a black ribbon.

"What are you doing?" she asked.

"I'm going to find out anything I can about Sammy." I opened the new étagère I'd bought to replace the one that had been destroyed in a robbery during the spring. While the insurance had paid off on my losses and I'd managed to replace most of the crystal that had been stolen, my Faberge egg collection was gone forever.

Next to a tiny crystal unicorn that had survived the damage sat an exquisite jade dragon—small enough to fit in my hand.

"O'Brien, you ever getting rid of that thing?" Jimbo gave it a cursory once-over but his gaze didn't linger. The dragon had been cursed and he'd seen it in action. In fact, the curse had first brought Jimbo into my life.

I shrugged. "I'm thinking of selling it to a museum. I could put the money away for the kids' college education. I guess I still have it because deep down I keep hoping that one of Daniel's relatives will surface. I don't know if I can ever forget his haunted face."

"Ain't gonna happen," Jimbo said. "That family is defunct."

"He's right." Joe peeked over my shoulder. "There's nobody left to give it to, Em."

I knew they were right but Daniel had died because of the statue, and I still couldn't let go of the last residual guilt that lingered like ghosts in the wind. I knew his death hadn't been my fault, but there was a tiny quiver of doubt still lurking in the recesses of my mind.

However, right now I had more important things to lose sleep over. I reached in and pulled out a crystal ball. A gift from Maeve, the antique orb weighed heavily in my hands. I cradled it, carrying it over to the sofa where I sat cross-legged in the middle. Joe and Jimbo took their respective seats in the rocker and recliner. I motioned for Kip to sit on the floor left of me, and for Randa to sit on my right.

I looked over at Joe and Jimbo, then settled back against the cushions. As I dropped into trance, the room fell away from my consciousness, slowly at first, then faster. I took three deep breaths and, on the third, summoned Samantha's spirit. "Show me where you are."

A whisper of energy grazed my cheek, and then another, and I could see a shadowy place, where the moon rose high in the sky, full and round. Trees, barren and black, marched across the horizon in a stark silhouette and crisp autumn leaves dappled the landscape. Cautious, I glanced around, hoping for a landmark, but nothing resonated as familiar. As I tried to decipher what I was seeing, Samantha crept out from beneath a dark patch of shrubbery.

"Sammy! Are you alive?"

She gazed at me with those liquid emerald eyes, and I knew that she lived. She was very much alive and afraid.

I called her, gently this time, and she began to make her way in my direction, but a flicker of lights zoomed between us, and another cat—this one ghostly and distant—raced by. Skittish, Samantha whirled around and vanished back into the shadows.

"Sammy! Come here . . . come to Mama . . ." I waited, straining to see any movement, to hear any sound. Nothing stirred and I knew I'd lost the connection. Frustrated, I opened my eyes and set the crystal aside.

"Samantha's alive. I can't pinpoint her energy in terms of where she's hiding. But I saw her and she recognized me. She's afraid, though, and possibly lost." I took hold of Kip and Randa's hands and squeezed. "Trust me, we'll do whatever it takes to find her. I miss her too. For now, you'll have to go on faith that she's okay."

"She didn't look hurt?" Kip asked, his voice quivering.

"No, honey. She didn't seem hurt to me."

Comforted, if only a little, they kissed me and took off upstairs to get ready for bed. I slipped the crystal ball back into the étagère and locked the door.

Jimbo headed into the kitchen. "Hey, how about some of that mint tea you always make for me?" Joe and I were about to follow when we heard him let out a shout. "O'Brien! Get your butt in here!"

We rushed in to find Jimbo's face plastered to the door window. "What? What is it?"

"There's some broad out in your backyard in her nightie."

I motioned for him to step aside and peered out into the darkness, but all I could see was a trail of mist. "Where?"

"She was right there! I saw her in the backyard, near your shed." Jimbo paled as he leaned against the window, searching frantically. "Where'd she go? I know I saw her! What the hell is going on?"

I patted his arm. "I believe you. Let me go see what I can find out—"

"I'll go with you," Joe said. "If somebody's prowling around out back, I don't want you out there alone."

Bless his protective heart! But Joe wouldn't be of any help at this point—I was walking into a playground where the rules went far beyond fists and testosterone-laden threats. "Sweetie, this isn't anything you can protect me from. I know who she is. At least, who she *was*."

"Does this have anything to do with the spirit that showed up last night?" he asked.

Jimbo perked up. "Spirit? What spirit? You mean I saw a ghost?"

I nodded. "I'll tell you about it as soon as I come back. I need to go now if I hope to pinpoint anything. While I'm out back, put the kettle on. Joe, you know where the tea is."

I grabbed a sweater from the back of a chair, and slid on a pair of loafers. Shivering in the chill night air, I headed toward the shed in my backyard. As I neared the building, I could feel a ripple in the air. The trees beyond the shed were barely visible in the black of the night, but I found myself drawn to the giant oak that towered in the corner of my yard, draping over into the lot next door. Pulled like a butterfly toward nectar, I moved forward one step at a time.

Brilliant flashes flickered through my mind. The Will o' the Wisps? And then they were there, hovering above the fence as if they wanted to cross into my world but couldn't. They bobbed near the oak, weaving their peculiar dance. As I watched them I could sense something else—*someone*, perhaps? The mist gathered into a whirlwind, and for a moment, a face was visible in the white tendrils that twisted together. A woman's voice echoed out of the fog.

"Come back to me—come back. Where are you? I miss you!"

"Brigit? Is that you? Brigit O'Reilly?" I spoke softly, trying to avoid registering any alarm. The scent of fear provoked both wild animals and wild spirits. And then, with a sob as low and quiet as my heartbeat, the mist vanished and the Will o' the Wisps withdrew behind the fence.

I stared at the retreating lights, buffeted by feelings of bittersweet loss and a wistfulness for something that might have been but now would never be. Everything familiar had been ripped asunder. Tears streaming down my cheeks, I turned and headed for the house, where Joe and Jimbo waited anxiously.

"I was about to come out there when I saw you turn away," Joe said. "Em, what's going on?"

I blinked as the light from the kitchen brought me back to reality. Motioning for Joe to pour me a cup of tea, I sat down and absently munched on a cookie. Chocolate was definitely one of the most important food groups and I'd been sorely lacking in that department the past couple of days. I swallowed my Oreo and told Jimbo about the spirit outside of Randa's room.

"So, is she the woman Jimbo saw out back?" Joe asked.

I nodded. "I think so." I hustled out to the porch, where I sorted through the pockets of my jacket until I found the picture of Brigit, along with her journal. "Recognize these?"

"Those are from the room—" Joe stopped and took a closer look at the photo. "Was that her?"

"Yeah, and she's the spirit I saw upstairs, and she was

out back just now. And don't forget the painting in the secret room. Brigit looks just like the woman in the mural."

"So we're dealing with the ghost of a young woman from Ireland. She lived in the basement of a prominent family in town and something happened because otherwise—well—her spirit wouldn't be hanging around, would it?" Joe looked perplexed.

"Not unless it was the only place that ever felt like home to her—then she might return there. But the screams lead me to think otherwise."

I thumbed through the journal, squinting to read the faded writing. Brigit had possessed a delicate hand, tiny and precise. The entries were meticulously penned, with poetry interspersed throughout the volume. The poems weren't particularly good; she didn't really have much talent, but they sounded straight from her heart. Several spoke of a village near the sea, and it was obvious she missed her home. Others, though, were fraught with unfulfilled love.

"She was in love," I said. "She was in love with someone and afraid it wasn't going to work out."

Jimbo grunted. "Don't even go there, O'Brien. All too familiar."

I glanced up at him. The big lug was totally smitten with my best friend, and wasn't afraid to admit it, but I knew he worried about how the relationship was affecting her career. As I flipped through the journal, two folded sheets of paper dropped onto the table. "What's this?"

I set the book down and gently opened the crinkled onionskin paper. On it, in a firm hand that didn't match the writing in the journal, was another poem. This one, I recognized.

"*The Lady of Shalott*?" Images of the walls in the secret room flickered through my mind. "I think we're right about the mural—it refers to the *Lady of Shalott*. With Brigit playing the lead. But who was her Lancelot?"

Joe shook his head. "Someone she left behind in Ireland, perhaps? Maybe she had to leave her boyfriend behind. Maybe he died."

There was no sign of a signature, and no way of telling who had copied out the famous ode to unrequited love. I felt the same wave of sadness I had out back. I quickly replaced the poem in the journal, setting it aside.

"Tomorrow I'm calling Harlow," I said. "If anybody can find out about the Brunswicks for us, she can." My other best friend, Harl, was the doyenne of the social circles in Chiqetaw. "Until then . . . I just don't know."

Jimbo glanced at the clock. "I need to get a move on. Anna will be off work in an hour and I want to have dinner waiting for her."

"Your special fried chicken?" I asked with a grin. The biker was an excellent cook, only one of his many surprises.

He leaned down and planted a quick kiss on my cheek. "Just don't let those critters out there get you, woman. Anna would never forgive me." With a wave at Joe, he headed out the kitchen door and I watched through the window as he hightailed it around the side of the house to the driveway, where he hopped on his chopper and revved out onto the street.

Joe and I locked up, armed the security system, and headed upstairs. I peeked in on Kip; he was sleeping like a baby, but when I opened Randa's door, she was sitting by her window, staring out forlornly onto the roof. I slid down beside her on the floor.

"What's the matter, honey? Sad because it's too cold to stargaze tonight?" She always grew irritable in the autumn and winter when the rains impeded her access to the skies.

She bit her lip and hung her head. "No, not really."

I leaned closer. "Is it about Samantha?"

She nodded briefly. "Yeah, and Gunner's folks. I talked to him today. I called to tell him I'm sorry."

"How are they doing?" I encircled her shoulders with my arm and she rested her head against me.

"They're holding on—it's too early to tell, but they haven't gotten any worse. Gunner is really upset. Tomorrow I'd like to drop by his aunt's after school. Is that okay? He won't be back in class for a few days."

My selfish little girl was thinking about someone else for a change, and I was more than happy to see the compassionate side of her rear its pretty head. "I think that's a great idea. Remind me to give you some money and you can take a bouquet with you." I noticed the notebook in her lap. "Homework? I thought you finished it on Friday night."

Blushing brightly, she hugged the paper to her chest. "I did. This . . . is something else."

Though I knew I should keep my mouth shut—when I was a teen, I'd hated it when my parents intruded on my privacy—I made a tactical error. "So what is it?"

Randa pulled away. "*Muu-ther!* Do you have to know everything going on in my head? You're such a snoop sometimes!"

Yep, the old Randa was still lingering behind the sweetheart. I gave her a long look. "It's quite all right if you tell me something is personal. I'm willing to accept a reasonable request for privacy. But I am your mother and you *will* show me respect. You know the rules. That tone of voice and your snotty attitude are totally unacceptable, Miss."

She stared at me for a moment, then shrugged and hung

her head. "I'm sorry," she mumbled, handing over the pages. "I'm just trying to write something."

I held the notebook in my hand, not looking at it. "Then that's all you needed to say."

She forced a tiny smile. "Thanks, Mom. I'm just writing some poetry. I got inspired tonight and everything seems so out of place . . . it seemed like a good idea."

Poetry? Miranda? My Randa wouldn't write a grocery list unless I forced the issue. I silently handed the notebook back to her without reading a word. "Go to bed now, baby. It's been a long day for all of us. And be sure to remind me about the money for flowers before you leave for school."

As I made my way to the bedroom, everything felt like it was shifting and changing. As the signs in the mountain passes warned, Unstable Footing, Watch Out for Rolling Rocks. I couldn't help but wonder where the next bend in the road would take us.

MONDAY MORNING BROUGHT with it no sign of Samantha, but instead, a flurry of fog and forecasts for increased cloudiness and probable showers. Joe headed out to talk to his lawyer and, after giving Randa fifteen dollars for flowers, I shooed the kids off to school and called Murray, who promised to come over for lunch.

After I brewed my quad-shot espresso mocha, I put in a call to Harlow. We hadn't spent much time together since she'd had her baby. James arrived home from a long job overseas in late August, just in time to greet his new daughter, Eileen Eugenia Rainmark. Harlow had her hands full with reunions and learning to be a mother and figuring out how she was going to handle the shifts her life had taken. Until this summer, she had been focused on physical fitness, charity work, and using her status as an ex-supermodel to further her causes.

Luckily, they had enough money to hire a nanny, so she was getting enough sleep and wasn't run ragged, but it was still a confusing time and I knew she needed to spend most of it in the comfort of her own home. We tried to get together every couple of weeks for coffee or lunch, but those times were short, and I could tell the entire experience had left her drained. Happy, but dazed and weary.

She picked up on the second ring and I smiled at her voice—Harl was a natural-born bottle of fizzy water, a sparkling drink on a hot day. "Hey babe, how's life treating you?"

"Em! I'm so glad you called," she said, and I could tell she meant it. We chatted for a few moments about Eileen and my kids and Joe and James. I finally sighed and got to the point of my call.

"Listen Harl, I have an ulterior motive, though I did want to talk to you."

She laughed. "What do you need me to find out?" Harl had proved the most marvelous research hound, able to ferret out information that nobody else could seem to dig up. I filled her in on all the happenings and she drew a sharp breath.

"Freaky!" Her usual response to me and my exploits. "So you need to find out who this Brigit O'Reilly was, and how she was connected to the Brunswicks? I can probably dig up something, but it may be a day or so. Can you wait that long?"

I snorted. "Well, she doesn't seem to be going anywhere. I just wish those damned corpse candles would leave us alone." We gossiped a few more minutes and then I hung up when the baby cried in the background. Even with the nanny, Harlow insisted on taking over as much of the rocking and feeding as she could. She wasn't producing enough breast milk, probably due to the years of anorexia she'd undergone while still a model, so after a long discussion with the doctor and several unsuccessful attempts to spur on lactation, they'd switched to a formula to supplement what she could offer.

A quick call to the shop confirmed that everything was fine. Cinnamon said business was picking up and that the annual holiday gift buying had commenced. Satisfied, I set to making thick roast beef sandwiches for lunch. I'd barely finished when Murray's truck pulled up outside. A light drizzle had started and she shook off her coat before tromping in the kitchen door.

"Man, I'm beat," she said, looking exhausted. "This past week has been a nightmare. But there's one piece of good news. We found out who sent that scummy E-mail to Chief Bonner."

"Who?" I poured her a hot cup of lemon tea and pointed toward the food. "Eat. You look tired."

She slid into a chair and, with a long sigh, picked up one of the sandwiches, chewing thoughtfully before she answered. "Did I ever mention a guy by the name of Rusty Jones?"

I thought back, then shook my head. "I don't think so."

She raised her eyebrows. "Seems good old Rusty, who's a clerk in the office, has developed a major crush on me and I never knew it. He certainly isn't my type—very prim . . . owlish glasses, pocket pen protector. He also happens to be horrendously nitpicky and an annoying asshole."

"And Rusty sent the note?" My mouth watered and I bit into my sandwich, hungrier than I'd been in a while.

"Yeah, he got mad because I never paid any attention to him. Well, no more than I pay to the other employees that I don't know very well. I'm always polite and I always say good morning and so forth, but I guess that just didn't cut it with him. So he's been trying to sabotage me."

Jeez, leave it to some nutcase to cause trouble. "How'd you find out it was him?"

"The Chief dropped into my office to ask a question and found Rusty there, on my computer, trying to hack in. He was trying to break my new password while I was in the bathroom. Bonner fired his ass right there and I came back to a very messy scene with Rusty screaming at Tad."

"Not too bright, screaming at the chief of police."

"Well, Rusty isn't the brightest bulb in the socket. When he saw me, he went ballistic." She shuddered. "He seemed so nice but it's like I always say—don't trust anybody at face value. You never know what's going to be behind that smile." She finished off her sandwich and started in on the fruit salad she'd brought for dessert.

A thought struck me. One I didn't want to think, but that I felt obligated to mention. "Do you think he might be dangerous?"

Mur looked at me closely. "Why? Do you?"

I closed my eyes. There was a precarious undercurrent flowing through the situation, I could see it—like rapids on a stream that was supposed to be smooth. "Yeah, you need a good smudging and you need to ward your place in case he opts for revenge."

She grimaced. "You know, I thought I felt him latching on to me. I already called White Deer and she'll be here tonight. She's blended a new banishing incense that should help get him off my back. Rusty isn't allowed back in the building, and the front desk is keeping watch for him. Of course, now that it's all come out, Bonner's being really nice to me and he even apologized for his cracks about Jimmy."

The fact that her boss had backed off on the relationship issue was just gravy on the potatoes, but what made me even more relieved was the knowledge that White Deer was headed our way. Murray's aunt lived on the Quinault reservation. White Deer was a medicine woman, one of the most eclectic and practical people I knew. Her elders weren't always happy with the way she mixed traditions, but she kept telling them, "Times are changing. We either change with them, or we die out." She kept alive the best of her ancestors' training and mixed it with what she'd learned from other traditions.

"Does Rusty know where you live?"

She shrugged. "Probably. He was in charge of all the files. No doubt he's been through my records with a fine-tooth comb. Makes me feel violated, but there's not much I can do about it right now. I'll be careful, Em, I promise. I won't write him off. He's . . . peculiar." She paused, then shook her head. "So finish your salad and let's go see this room of yours."

I pushed back my plate. "I'm not that hungry. Let's head over there now. It's daytime. Maybe those damned Will o' the Wisps won't bother us." I led her out onto the back porch where we bundled up and grabbed flashlights before heading over to the basement room.

As we passed through what once was the gate and picked our way through the debris that still littered the ground, Mur glanced around nervously.

"I don't like it. Something's hanging around and it doesn't feel very friendly."

"Several somethings," I said. "The lights and Brigit and who knows what else." We started down the stairwell. As we approached the mulch, I inhaled deeply. Stepping back into it seemed to invite trouble, like walking into a wave that was riding high on the shores, but I needed to know what we were dealing with. My foot sank up to my ankle and I tried to follow the trail we'd left the day before, but the path seemed to have filled in.

Murray coughed. "There are a lot of fungus spores down here. You don't have an allergy to those too, do you? Last time you played in the forest, we had to haul you out on a stretcher."

"That's because I crawled through a patch of stinging nettle," I said, turning back to stick my tongue out at her. Actually, I was grateful for the diversion. I found it hard to quit thinking about the lot and my ghostly visitors. It was as if they were hiding there, in the back of my mind.

We propped open the door to the bedroom and light streamed in. In the pale autumn sun, the artwork stood out, vivid and brilliant. Even after all this time, even after the inevitable weathering that had made its way through cracks in the walls, the work was still stunning.

Mur took it all in, shaking her head. "This is something else, all right." She closed her eyes. "Can you feel it? There's someone here. What's that?" She pointed toward the door and I turned just in time to see Samantha rush past. We rushed out into the basement. Samantha was sitting on the steps. My heart leapt as I broke into a wide smile.

"Sammy! Baby? Kitty? Kitty?"

She paused, waiting for us, but as we drew near she gave me a fleeting look and I realized that it wasn't Samantha. Her paws weren't white in the right places. Then I noticed that I could see through the cat.

"Kitty?" I slowed. "Mur, that's not Samantha. That's a ghost!"

She looked at the calico, cautious not to make any sudden moves. "You're right. But they look so much alike. I can see how you'd mix them up if you didn't have a clear glimpse."

The ghost cat was sitting on the bottom step. She stared at us, then mewed so loud we both jumped. I had the distinct feeling that she wanted us to come over to her and so began walking toward the little spirit. Orange and black and white, the calico eyed me with gleaming topaz eyes—again, different from my own Sammy's green. As I reached her side and leaned down, I heard the echo of a purr and then she vanished before I could say a word.

Murray was almost by my side. I took a deep breath and shook my head. "Well, that was interesting," I started to say but stopped when a strange look crossed her face. "What is it? What's wrong?"

She pointed to the steps. "Em, what's that brownish stuff?"

I took a closer look where she was pointing. Sure enough, reddish brown stains splattered the stairs. We hadn't seen them before—perhaps foliage had been covering them, or maybe we'd just been too busy watching the Will o' the Wisps to notice them, but now they were plainly visible.

"I don't know . . . it almost looks like . . ." I didn't want to say it, but Murray finished my thought for me.

"Blood. Em, I'll bet you ten to one that's dried blood." She pulled out a knife from her pocket and flipped open the blade.

"Do you have anything I could scrape some of this into?"

I felt through my pockets and came up with an old grocery list. She folded it into a small envelope and scraped quite a few shavings of the material off the steps. "I think I'll have this analyzed."

A thought occurred to me. "I bet you're going to find it's human blood. And I'll bet it belonged to Brigit O'Reilly."

"Why?"

"The cat was the one she was holding in the photograph. I've been chasing a ghost, thinking it was Samantha. I'll bet you anything, the kitty is trying to tell us something."

Mur folded her blade and shoved it back in her pocket. "You could be right, Em. You know," she glanced around, taking in the basement and foundation. "Whatever happened here wasn't good. I won't even venture a guess at this point, but . . . whatever it was caused a whole lot of hurt."

As we climbed out of the basement, I thought to myself that we'd better find out soon, because I didn't want these critters hanging out in my backyard any longer than it took to send them on their way.

Seven

⸸

From Brigit's Journal:

> One thing I'll say about my home and my village: Blood binds. If I was hurting, my parents gave me solace. If I was hungry, they fed me. Even if they didn't agree with all of my choices, not once did my father ever turn on me and browbeat me with shame. My mother would never have stood for such a thing. How can parents act like that? How can they treat their children as pawns in a war of social niceties?
>
> Oh, I suppose it happened at home, too, but we were never rich, and so never saw such a thing among our friends. Some days, I think I should just pack and leave without a word. Go home, make what life I can for myself there. And then I think . . . what's left for me? William is gone, as are my Ma and Da . . . but still . . . the village was so lovely, and I miss it so much.

BY THE TIME Joe got home from the lawyer's office, I'd packed a load of clothes into the washer, picked up enough of the clutter from the living room so I could vacuum, baked two batches of frozen chocolate chip cookies, and scrubbed the counters and all the other small appliances. I was sitting at the table, my second triple-shot mocha close at hand, reading through Brigit's diary when Joe popped through the kitchen door. He didn't look happy.

"What's wrong?" I asked, setting aside the journal.

He leaned over to plant a kiss on my cheek, then slipped into the opposite chair and sighed. "What's wrong? I no longer have any claim to the lot next door, that's what's wrong. This sucks. I can't believe that her lawyer made such a stupid mistake."

"What are you talking about?" I leaned my elbows on the table.

"Okay, here's the deal. Apparently Irena Finch misunderstood which parcel I was talking about. I gather she owns several houses and lots around town. Her lawyer said that she can't proceed with the sale since she and her brother jointly own the lot next door."

"And he has a problem with selling the land?"

"Apparently so. He lives in Europe, so I can't just run over to talk to him about it, either."

Great. Joint ownership could cause massive headaches when the two parties didn't agree. I'd forced Roy to buy me out of the house that we'd owned together since I didn't want to keep it and he didn't want to sell.

"And she has to have his permission?"

"Yeah." Joe sighed. "Their parents left a stipulation that neither can sell the land without permission from the other. And for some reason, Brent Brunswick won't agree." He leaned back and picked up a cookie, toying with it as he stared at the table. "So that effectively screws me over. After all the work I did clearing it. Irena wasn't too happy to hear about that part, either. I guess she doesn't like the idea of the foundation being open. Maybe she's afraid somebody will fall in and sue her."

"Maybe. Or it could be something else she's worried about," I said, thinking about the reddish stains Murray and I'd found. Animal blood? Possibly, but something in my gut told me otherwise. "Well, I've got some more news to add to yours." I told him about the ghost cat and our suspicions.

"*Blood* stains? Human?"

"Murray doesn't know yet. She's having them analyzed. I'm telling you, something happened over there, and whatever it is, it's been hidden for almost fifty years."

Joe reached for the journal. "What's this? You're reading it? Anything interesting?"

I shrugged. "She goes around and around, never saying anything directly, but from what I can gather, there was something wrong that—if the Brunswicks found out—they'd be terribly upset over. She missed her home, and wanted to go back, but her parents were dead . . . and someone she refers to as her 'sweet William.' And her cat was named Mab—I know that much."

"Your ghost cat?"

I nodded. "Yes. Mab was a faerie queen, which ties in with the Will o' the Wisps."

"Did Brigit ever make it back to Ireland?"

I shrugged. "I don't know. I've glanced through a few entries but haven't read the entire diary yet."

Joe sighed. "My idea to dig up the brambles started all this, didn't it?"

I thought about it for a moment, then shook my head. "Not started. No, whatever's going on was set in motion long before we came along. But I think our activity sparked the catalyst that awakened the corpse candles from their dormant state. Or maybe the ghosts and the Will o' the Wisps were always there—just hidden away in the basement beneath the vines, never peeking out into the light. Whatever the case, there's no going back. Whether or not you own the land, we have to do something to stop the energy before it spills over into my yard."

"What have you got in mind? An exorcism?"

"No, not yet." Maeve's cautions were still fresh in my mind. "I don't know enough about what went on in order to do that. I could make matters worse. And with this new development—the blood stains, if that's what they are—then we may have other factors to consider."

Joe took my hand, squeezing it tightly. "Do you think somebody was murdered there?" he asked.

I'd had quite enough of murder, whether it was in the past or the present. But I couldn't escape the feeling that a violent death had been involved. I shrugged. "I don't know, but I haven't got any desire to tune in and find out. Suppose we wait and see what Murray has to say? Meanwhile, how's your arm?"

He rolled up his sleeve. The bruise was brilliant purple and yellow, and the lacerations were beginning to heal. "It'll be okay."

The buzzer in the pantry sounded and I pulled the clothes out of the dryer. We sat at the table, folding clothes in silence, then I brought out one of the leftover sandwiches that I'd saved from lunch. "Eat, you need it."

"You know, I think I'll pay a visit to Irena's lawyer this afternoon. My lawyer doesn't want me to; he said that it's best to avoid pressuring them, but I can't just sit here." He grabbed the sandwich, downed a glass of milk, gave me a quick peck on the cheek, and took off out the front door.

As I watched him pull out of the driveway, I realized how easy it was having him here. At first, I'd been afraid of losing my privacy, of losing myself in the relationship. But Joe fit into my life in a way that I thought no one ever would. He meshed without intruding. He worked with us rather than trying to take over. Slowly, my resistance had faded and now it was hard to imagine life without him.

Brushing away thoughts of murder and ghosts and dangerous faeries, I retreated upstairs to put away the clothes. Then, grabbing my keys, I headed for the animal shelter. Almost eleven months ago, I'd walked into the building and come face-to-face with Sammy and her babies. They stared out of the cage at me, so hopeful, and I knew I couldn't leave without them. Even though I knew she was alive, I didn't know where she was—and one thing Nanna always taught me: Always do the practical, before you trust the magical.

I wandered through the line of meowing cats, my heart aching. One calico, in particular, caught my eye. A Persian, her scrunched-in face was so sweet that I almost broke down and took her home. She reached from between the bars of her cage and lightly pawed at my hand. I glanced at the volunteer who was cleaning out cages.

"They're all so wonderful. I hate working here, but somebody has to do it." She poured litter into a pan and set it back in with a little black shorthair who tried to engage her in a game of bat-bat.

I nodded, unable to say a word. A thorough check of every cage provided no sign of Samantha and, heavy-hearted, I headed home, stopping to pick up a couple of movies that the kids had wanted to see. I knew they'd have a hard time with the news that Sammy wasn't back yet, and the least I could do was distract them the best I could.

*   *   *

BY THE TIME that Joe got home again, Miranda and Kip had persuaded me that, since we were watching movies, we should also order pizza. Since Joe had joined the household, we'd been eating a lot more home-cooked meals but for tonight, I gave in and called the Pizza Shack. I'd just hung up the phone when Joe walked through the door.

"Pizza okay?" I asked.

He nodded. "What toppings?"

"Pepperoni and extra cheese on one, Canadian bacon and pineapple on the other. How'd the meeting go?"

"Not too great," he said. "He couldn't tell me any more than my lawyer. They're drafting out a check to return my down payment and earnest money. I won't lose anything on the deal except the time spent. In fact, I gather Irena instructed her lawyer to give me an extra thousand dollars for work done on the lot, but they're serious about us keeping off the place. Her lawyer said they're bringing in an excavator to fill the foundation and bury it for good next week."

"That's odd, very odd." Something wasn't tracking right, but I couldn't place it. I shook it off and plugged a movie into the DVD player, hoping that the kids would be able to relax. Both had been visibly depressed when I told them that I hadn't found Sammy at the animal shelter.

By the time nine o'clock came around, everybody in the house was ready for bed. Joe and I had just snuggled down to some seriously good foreplay when a yell echoed from the hall. I leapt out of bed, grabbed on my robe, and raced out to find Kip standing outside his door, staring into his room.

"What on earth's wrong?" I checked to make sure he was okay, but he seemed unhurt.

"I thought I saw Sammy in my room, but she vanished! Is Sammy dead? Was that her spirit?"

I sighed as Joe, dressed in pajamas and a robe, joined us. Leading Kip back to his bed, I sat next to him. He rubbed his eyes as Randa peeked in to see what the fuss was about.

"I'm glad you're here," I said. "Okay, kiddos, I wanted to wait, but I guess I'd better tell you now." They settled down to listen. "Two ghosts have moved in next door. A woman and her cat." I turned to Kip. "Randa saw the woman's ghost, by her bed. Anyway, the ghost cat looks a lot like our Sammy."

"But it's not her?" Kip asked. I could hear the fear in his voice.

"No, baby. It's not Sammy, that much I can tell you."

"How can we tell whether what we see is the ghost or really Samantha?" Randa asked.

"Good question. From a distance, it's hard to tell the difference. But up close you'll notice that her paws are different and her eyes are topaz, not green." I snapped my fingers. "I've got a picture downstairs. The woman's name was Brigit, and the cat was hers." Of course, they had to see so we all trooped down to the kitchen where I showed them Brigit's photograph.

Miranda held it for awhile, looking softly at the photo. "That's the lady who was by my bed. Can I look at her journal?"

I silently handed the diary to Randa.

Kip stared at the photograph. "That's the cat I saw. The lady was pretty."

"I bet she was in love, wasn't she?" Randa said, flipping through the pages. "She missed somebody, right?"

I jerked my head up. "We think so. How did you know that?"

She shrugged, twirling the end of her hair around her finger. "I dunno . . . just a feeling. May I read the journal?"

I hadn't seen anything remotely objectionable in my perusal. "I suppose, but don't lose it or take it out of the house," I said. Carrying the half-century-old volume, she started for the stairs, mumbling under her breath. "What did you say?" I asked.

Without turning around, she said, "I just said that I thought she looks like a damsel in distress. You know, like in the old days with knights and ladies-in-waiting, when everything was still romantic."

And then, my precocious, logical daughter raced upstairs to bed, leaving me speechless. I took a deep breath, wondering what had come over her. She was usually so focused on her astronomy that I found her new dreaminess disconcerting at best.

Kip took another look at the photograph, then handed it back. "Is the lady ghost dangerous?"

I shook my head. "I don't think so, honey. I don't even know if she's what we usually think of as a ghost. We might be seeing an image of something that happened in the past, like a filmstrip from an old movie."

He thought for a moment, then bounded off to bed. I turned to Joe and gave him a wistful look. Ghosts and poetry and murals. Randa was right. This was the stuff romance was made of, even when it got a little spooky. He seemed to sense my mood because he held out his hand and led me to the bedroom, where our passion overrode our weariness and we finished our lovemaking in a frenzied burst of energy.

* * *

JOE WANDERED IN while I finished toasting the waffles. He set the table as the kids dragged themselves downstairs. We gathered around, nobody saying very much. After a moment, I remembered to ask Randa about her visit to Gunner.

She shrugged. "He's pretty depressed. His folks are still in intensive care and the doctors say that even if they make it through, they'll take a long time to heal. They both are going to need a lot of plastic surgery. I bought a big bouquet of chrysanthemums and roses with the money you gave me. Gunner sends his thanks."

Poor kid. He was probably scared as hell. "Would you like to invite him over for dinner? It might do him some good to get out for a bit."

She brightened. "Yeah, in a day or so. Thanks, Mom." She wiped her mouth neatly on her napkin and then pushed her chair back. "I need to get to class early. I've got a science experiment I want to check on."

Grateful to hear the enthusiasm in her voice, I waved her off. Maybe she wasn't entering that mopey, angst-ridden phase all girls seem to go through when they discovered boys. At least, I hoped not.

"Okay, but come home right after school. I'm making an early dinner."

She grabbed her pack and ran out the door. Kip followed more slowly, turning back to plead, "Could you call me at school if Sammy comes home?"

He looked so forlorn that I swept him into my arms and gave him a tight hug. "Sure thing, kiddo. Now off to school, and please try not to worry."

Joe polished off the last of his waffles. "I should go down and check on things at the station. What are you planning for the day?"

I shrugged. "I guess I'll head out to the shop for a bit."

Truth was, I was getting bored of being at home 24/7. The stress from coping with the spirits and Samantha's disappearance didn't make playing house very appealing.

Joe vanished with a kiss and a wave. I gathered my purse and keys and headed out the door. By the time I reached the Chintz 'n China, Cinnamon was just opening shop. She seemed surprised, but happy, to see me.

"Emerald! What are you doing here? You're still on vacation."

I grinned. "Maybe not. Plans are falling apart. I thought I'd drop down and take a gander at how things are going."

Going, they were. Business was brisk and I was impressed by how smoothly Cinnamon and Lana were running the shop. Of course, there were things they couldn't tend to but overall, they were doing a good job. I headed for my office to spend an hour or so catching up on paperwork. Twenty minutes in, my cell phone rang. It was Harlow.

"I've got the information you wanted about the Brunswicks. Do you want me to run it on over?" She sounded excited and I could sense that she'd found something that wasn't quite so run-of-the-mill.

"Can you bring it down to the shop? That's where I'm at right now."

"Do you mind if I bring Eileen?"

"Mind? Why should I mind? Bring my goddess-daughter down here so I can spoil her."

Harlow had recently discovered New Age philosophy. I had the feeling it was her way of compensating for all the psychic work that Murray and I did together, but wasn't about to say so. It made her happy, and so far, there was no harm in it. She'd joined a local women's empowerment group, and therefore, I had a goddess-daughter instead of a goddaughter. Made no difference to me, as long as I got to see her.

We made plans to meet at lunchtime and I went back to my inventory and invoices. The Abbotshire China Company was offering several seasonal teapots and I wanted to order a few Christmas-themed ones. I knew they'd sell; the craftsmanship was high quality. I also needed to restock water biscuits, lemon curd, marmalade, and chocolates that we ordered from a London-based supplier. After that I should call Beatrice MacAlvy, a local candy maker, and place an order for Christmas mints and handmade candy canes.

I sighed as I stared at the ever-growing to-do list and added a note to restock all the regular teas and jellies and cookies, and to pay the insurance. It was almost noon by the time I finished making phone calls and had worked my way through the pile of invoices and accounts. I sat back, satisfied. After lunch with Harlow, I'd take off for home, but right now, the work felt good.

Cinnamon was busy with Farrah Warnoff, one of our regulars, who was trying to decide between a plain pumpkin teapot or a jack-o'-lantern teapot.

"Who's it for?" I asked, stepping in.

She gave me a helpless smile. "My niece. Mandy turns thirteen next week, and I have no idea which she'd prefer."

I thought about Miranda, who had always been a little older than her years. "Pumpkin," I said. "That way, she can use it year-round."

Farrah grinned. "What would we do without you?" She selected a handful of teas—maple, cranberry, and a new cinnamon-pear flavor that had just arrived, and Cinnamon packaged her order and gift wrapped it for her.

My work done, I headed into the alcove that nestled

our tearoom and staked out the staff's table. Larry had delivered two types of soup—chicken noodle and pumpkin—along with sandwiches befitting the season. I dished up a big bowl of chicken soup and thumbed through the sandwiches until I found a pastrami on rye. I'd had just settled in when Harlow strode through the door, all five-foot-ten of her.

Her hair gleamed in golden cornrows that hung down to her shoulders, and her flawless lips broadened into a huge smile. She carried a Louis Vuitton handbag in one hand, a diaper bag slung over her shoulder, and was pushing a snazzy stroller. Little Eileen, just two months old and bundled up like a butterball, snoozed away in the seat. Harl had already lost every ounce of pregnancy fat, but I had the feeling she would never return to her pre-pregnancy gauntness. Her curves were in all the right places, and while before she had been a beauty, now she was stunning.

She parked the stroller next to me and hurried over to the counter, where she asked Lana to bring her a bowl of pumpkin soup and a turkey on whole wheat. By the time she returned, I was engrossed in a staring match with the sleeping Eileen. A real cutie, all right. Harl had given her Randa's middle name, an honor and a gift, considering that Randa had helped her deliver the baby on my kitchen floor.

Harl plunked herself down in the chair and began to nibble on her sandwich. "I'm beat. We've been shopping for the past two hours. Eileen is such a good girl—she didn't fuss at all. But I think this motherhood stuff is taking more out of me than I want to admit. I need a nap and I still have to work out today. And my feet are swollen—that ticks me off." She held out one foot and I saw that the narrow Prada shoe was playing tight squeeze today. Like most tall, thin women, Harlow had long narrow feet and could pull off the designer look without a hitch.

I grinned. "Lily helping any?" Lily was Harlow's baby nurse. It would have been nice to have a baby nurse when my two were young, but those days were long ago and far away, thank heaven.

"Oh, yeah. I'm just worn out."

"I remember that bone-weary tiredness," I said. "You never forget it."

Harl shook her head. "How did you do it, Em? You raised two children without any real input from Roy, no nurse, no time to yourself. I don't know if I could have managed it. You're amazing."

A warm glow rushed through me. Harlow was so perfect in so many ways that it felt good for a change to hear her admit that she admired me.

"So, what did you find out about the Brunswicks?" I poked at her shopping bags. "And then tell me what you bought." Harl's shopping trips were notorious for their length and scope. She seldom ever left a store without a handful of bags and boxes.

She pulled out a notebook and flipped it open. "Did I tell you that I'm going back to work next month? Professor Abrams wants me back as soon as possible. He said I can telecommute without a problem. And I'm signing up for a class in antiquities come winter quarter. Next fall, I'll ease into half-time."

So she was going through with her plan to go back to school. I had to hand it to her—she was a trooper. Though I had my B.A., the thought of returning to school at this time in my life would have overwhelmed me. Harlow was thirty-five, only a couple of years younger than I, and here she was, just stepping into motherhood and planning a return to college to get her degree.

She pushed the notebook in front of me. "It wasn't hard to find out the basics about the Brunswicks, but I also dug up a few skeletons that were hidden." With a satisfied smile, she sat back and ate her soup while I glanced over the material.

"Normal rich family?"

She gave me a lopsided grin. "Eh, normal is as normal does. In many ways yes, but there are a couple things you should be aware of. Everything seems fine with the mother, father, and daughter, but the son had some serious problems. The family told everybody that he went overseas, but he actually had a breakdown and was committed to Fairhaven Psychiatric Hospital. The kicker is, he's still there. Almost fifty years after he was first locked up."

I jerked my head up. "The son? Brent Brunswick? Irena's brother?"

Harlow checked over her notes. "That's the one. They were twins. Irena married a banker named Thomas Finch and they're still married. The parents moved back east and both died there some time later, the father from a heart attack, the mother from booze."

Hmm . . . something was wrong. Irena had specifically said her brother lived overseas, and that he had refused to sell the property. She was obviously lying about the former, but what about the latter? Had Brent even heard of the deal? Or was he just a convenient excuse to keep hold of the lot? And if so, why?

"Does it mention why Brent's there? And when did they commit him?" I finished my sandwich and picked up my cup of soup, slurping it down much to Harlow's dismay.

She grimaced. "Try a spoon, babe. Anyway, let me see . . ." She flipped through the pages. "Here it is. Brent was committed when he was twenty years old. A few days later, his parents told everyone in town that he'd run off overseas. Given his family name and their place in society, nobody ever questioned the matter. A month or so after that the house burned down, Irena got married, and Mr. and Mrs. Brunswick moved back to the east coast."

A warning bell rang in my head. Something was off. "Is there any mention of a cousin or anybody named Brigit O'Reilly?"

Harl snorted. "Not likely. The Brunswicks are old money. They can trace their family origins back to Henry the Lion, a powerful German prince back in the 1100s. I doubt if they'd even admit to cousins from Ireland—from what I gather, Edward and Lauren Brunswick were hoity-toity types. Edward especially. Irena took after him. Lauren was a lot nicer, I gather. So nice, she turned to drink in order to keep her mouth shut around her husband, according to Patricia Jones, who knew the two after they moved. I made a few calls."

So where did Brigit fit in? Was she an exchange student? A friend? A maid? Her clothes suggested genteel poverty; her journal, youthful angst.

"Okay, thanks. Can I keep all this?" I gathered up the papers.

"Sure, as long as you let me know when you find out what happened." Harl then launched into her morning's shopping, pulling out all of the baby clothes she'd bought, including Eileen's miniature leather jacket. I stifled my amusement and let her prattle on. After awhile, the baby woke up and I held her, breathing in the smell of baby shampoo, burp-up, and Ivory soap, then transferred her to Harlow and led them back into my office where she changed the baby and fed her. By one, they were ready to head out.

As she kissed my cheek and waved, pushing the

stroller toward the door, I couldn't help but feel a little wistful. Whether it was because I missed the days when Harl and I could hang for hours together, or whether it was because I missed the days when my own children were babies, I didn't know. And maybe, I thought, it was better that way.

BY THE TIME I got home, Joe was gone. He'd left a note. Robert Kindle, from the station, called in sick and they needed a substitute. Since Joe had been on vacation and all the other men had worked long shifts lately, it was only right that he take up the slack. He warned me he might not be back for a day or two, depending on how busy they were, and asked me to call him down at the station.

I put in a quick call to reassure him that everything was fine. I also filled him in on the fact that Irena had lied to him about her brother and spelled out exactly what I'd learned. Joe was furious, but right then he was called out—a small brush fire had got out of hand—and I stood holding a silent receiver. I puttered through the house, thinking I should start dinner. The kids would be home soon.

We had a quiet evening of macaroni and cheese and broccoli, and then Randa retreated to her room and Kip headed upstairs to play. I read for a bit, glanced over the info that Harl had found for me, and decided to make an early night of it. After making sure the kids were asleep, I crawled under the covers. The bed felt so big without Joe. We spent every night we could together now, and it was hard for me to sleep without his strong arm curled around my waist, but fall asleep, I eventually did.

At some point, I awoke with the feeling I was being

watched. I sat up and saw the ghost cat on the bottom of
my bed.

"Well, hello," I said softly, trying to avoid startling her.

She looked at me and mouthed a "meow" and I had the
strangest impulse to follow as she hopped off and headed for
the door. I hurried into a sweat suit and chased after her. In
the darkened night, every sense seemed heightened, every
nuance of perception clarified.

She silently padded down the stairs and through the
front door as if it didn't exist. Without a second thought I
followed, into the rainy night, flashlight in hand as the cat
led me under the cloud-covered sky. The wind was whip-
ping around my shoulders, stirring up a granddaddy of a
storm.

The calico led me next door, through the maze of roots
and branches, into the darkened lot. I wondered where the
corpse candles were, but was grateful for their absence. I
was getting tired of my unwelcome neighbors.

We stopped near the back of the lot where the ancient
yew rose out of what had been a huge patch of brambles,
but was now reduced to roots and scrub. Its branches were
gnarled and bent as if the weight of a thousand years
rested on them. The massive trunk was woven of many
smaller trunks that twined together to form the whole,
calved off the main root. Mother and children bound together forever. I could almost see faces etched within the
burled bark, filled with pain and anguish, with hope and
trepidation, and the entire area felt prickly, as if there was
deep earth mana flowing here.

I stood there for a moment, then turned, uncertain what
to do next. My flashlight beam caught a puddle that had
formed at the base of the tree from the rain. As I glanced
into it, the reflection of a woman stared at me from the
water. Brigit, her eyes closed in endless slumber. My

breath caught in my throat and—without thinking about what I was doing—I dropped to my knees and began clawing at the thickly layered mulch around the trunk.

After a few minutes, I uncovered a depression leading under the trunk—a hollow at the base of the yew that was deep and wide. As I pulled away another clump of old branches and leaves, I began to wonder what the hell I was doing. A spider ran over my hand and I stifled a scream. Enough! Time to go home. As I started to stand, I happened to glance at the excavated cavity beneath the tree again, and my flashlight caught something in the beam. I paused, unwilling to believe my eyes. But there it was—stuffed into the hole beneath the yew, reaching out from what looked like a swath of tattered material still covered by compost.

A skeletal hand. Bones. Gleaming ivory bones.

At that moment, I knew that I'd found Brigit. She'd rested beneath the yew in a long night's slumber of almost fifty years. Unclaimed and missed by no one, she had remained hidden from the world until we awakened her by opening the door to her secret world.

Eight

❖

From Brigit's Journal:

The Missus is crying today, so she'll be wanting her martinis, and I never can seem to fix them right. I'll have to have Angela teach me how to make them properly. I don't think Maggie knows how.

I think Mr. Edward slapped the Missus. He went into a fury when B. came home from the university. He gets terribly mad when his family won't follow his orders. I still say there's no call to go and take your anger out on a woman. I wouldn't ever stand for it, myself.

And Miss Irena is all aflutter over her young man and what B.'s homecoming will do to their wedding plans. She and her father are two of a kind, mean as spit. Sometimes I thank my lucky stars I'm not from fine folk. Poverty isn't the worst curse that can plague a family. Madness and anger are far more dangerous than a little bit of hunger.

*　　*　　*

I SCRAMBLED BACK and slipped in the mud, falling on my butt. I grunted, then pushed myself onto my knees, staring at the skeletal hand that glistened in the beam of my flashlight.

A trickle of rain started again, plopping down around me in fat droplets. As I gingerly peeked back in the cavity, I saw a simple gold band on one of the fingers of the hand—the right hand. The roots of the yew had entwined around the bones, like a mother holding a child. Could this really be Brigit's remains? My gut told me yes, my mind waxed uncertain.

I slowly pushed myself to my feet, exhaustion weighing heavily on my shoulders. A glance at the sky told me that the rain was about to turn into a downpour. I'd better call Murray before it got any worse. Bones buried in old trees usually meant that whoever put them there hadn't wanted them found.

After four rings, Mur's voice grumbled over the line. "Hello?"

"Hey, it's Emerald. I need you to get dressed, get a couple of your men, and come over here."

A pause. Then, "Em, it's three in the morning. What the hell's going on?" Even as she said it, I could hear her moving around and I knew she was grabbing her clothes.

"I found Brigit . . . or at least, I think it used to be Brigit. Buried in a hole beneath the yew tree next door."

Another brief pause, then Mur exploded. "You what? Oh good God, you found a body?"

"Yeah," I said, not wanting to acknowledge the fact that I seemed to be destined to discover death in an all-too-congenial manner. "Well, a skeleton."

"And you say she's buried by the yew tree?"

"Not so much by the tree, as *in* the tree. I found her in a hole beneath the roots. So, you coming over?"

"Of course I am. I'll get hold of Deacon and we'll be there in twenty minutes. Meanwhile, you get back over there and make sure nobody goes near that skeleton. I doubt if anybody will even notice, but you never know."

I debated calling Joe at the station, but there was nothing he could do except fret, so I nixed that idea. It wasn't like I had just stumbled over a fresh corpse with a murderer on the loose. I slipped upstairs and quietly woke Randa.

"Huh? Whaa—?" She blinked against the light filtering in from the hall.

"Honey, I have to go next door for awhile and wait for Murray. I just wanted you to know in case you or Kip need me for a bit. I'll be right over there, though, and if you yell out your window, I should be able to hear you."

I smoothed her hair back and she nodded sleepily, then turned over and promptly fell right back to snoring. I scribbled a note, reiterating what I'd told her, and left it plastered to the bathroom door in the hall. That way both Kip and Randa would know where to find me if they woke up before I returned.

After gathering several flashlights and—just because I just felt better with a weapon—a handy little switchblade Jimbo had given me on the sly, I headed next door. The tree remained undisturbed, as did its ghastly contents, though the rain was starting to blow in. I scrounged around and found a piece of tarp that we'd used to protect the tools and covered the hole with it to prevent any storm damage to the skeleton.

Ten minutes later, Murray jumped out of her truck and hurried across the lot. "Deacon will be here in a few. Let me see what you've got."

I knelt down and pulled back the tarp. "Mur, those are Brigit's remains. I know it."

She gazed at the skeletal hand for a moment, then took a deep breath. "Well, you're right about one thing. It's a skeleton. Okay, let me put in a call to the station. We're going to have to cordon off the area. We'll do our best to find out whoever she—or he—was, and if this was a murder. God knows, I doubt if she crawled in there and died by herself. We'll need to preserve all the evidence that we can. Where's Joe? Is he around? I'd like his permission to search the property, just for formality's sake."

Oops. Of course there had to be fallout over him losing ownership of the lot. The universe wouldn't have it any other way.

"There may be a problem with that."

"Why? He working tonight? I can have Deacon drop over there—"

No, that's not the problem." I cleared my throat. "See . . . uh . . . Joe is no longer the legal owner of the property. Irena revoked the sale." I quickly filled her in on all that had happened.

"Shit, that means I'm going to need a search warrant. Even if Irena gave us permission, she could rescind it at a later date if she got huffy later on. With a warrant, there's not much she can do."

She sighed. "Okay, when Deacon arrives, I'll send him over to the station and have him ask Judge Chambers for a warrant. The judge has always looked kindly on me and I think he'll be willing to help. Then I'll send someone to notify Irena. However, Judge Chambers—and my boss— are going to want to know how you came across the skeleton, and I don't think that saying 'A ghost cat led me to it' will do." She gave me a long look. "Anyway you could reword things? Without asking you to lie, of course."

I glanced up in the tree above us, where the corpse candles swarmed. "How about this: I saw what I thought was my missing cat. I tried to catch her, she ran next door, right up to the yew tree. I fell on my butt and disturbed some of the leaves." I pointed to a small space under the roots that bordered the cavity. "And that's when I found the skeleton."

She snorted. "Actually, that's plausible enough to work. And since Sammy's still missing, it makes sense." She glanced up at the treetop where the bare branches were starkly silhouetted against the cloud-covered sky. She sucked in a deep breath. "Autumn is the loneliest time of the year, don't you think? The night always feels so ancient, and the days so barren."

As I turned my face upward, a few drops splashed on my cheeks. Yes, the rain was about to start again. "This year seems particularly harsh."

Mur nodded and pulled out her cell phone. She flipped through the stored numbers, then pressed the dial button, moving off to one side. I could hear her explaining to someone why she needed a search warrant and asking if one could be issued right away. Apparently whoever was on the other end was short and to the point, because within five minutes she'd hung up and turned back around.

"Judge Chambers said no problem. He told me to send Deacon over when he gets here, and we'll have the search warrant in just under an hour."

"There's Deacon now." I pointed to the Honda Accord that pulled up in the driveway. Deacon hurried over to us with a worried look. I'd developed a distinct fondness for the officer; he was a good cop, and it didn't hurt that he was handsome—his eyes and skin as brown as warm chocolate. He was pulling the Yul Brenner "do." Bald looked good on him.

He gave me a quick smile, then turned to Murray. "What have you got, Detective?" He always gave Mur her due, and I knew she was planning to recruit him onto her team as soon as she could do so.

"Take a peek in that hole under the tree," she said and he knelt down and flashed his light in the cavity.

"What the hell—?" The look on his face told me that Deacon Wilson had caught a glimpse of the skeleton. "Now I see why you called me out of a warm bed. Whoever that is has been there awhile." He glanced up, nodding at me. "Emerald, good to see you. How's Joe?"

"On duty right now," I said. "Good to see you too."

Murray cleared her throat. "Okay, here's the deal. Deacon, you need to run over to the courthouse. Judge Chambers will meet you there with a search warrant for this property. When you have it in hand, bring it back to me. After that, I'm sending you over to let Irena Finch, the owner of the lot, know what's going on. Under no circumstances is she to be notified before we have the warrant. I want to get excavation underway before she shows up, complaining."

"Anticipating trouble?" he said.

She shook her head. "I hope not. But this will eliminate any problems down the road. I'm headed over to Emerald's to grab a cup of coffee and call the M.E." He saluted her, waved at me, and took off.

Murray and I replaced the tarp and she surrounded the area with crime tape. After that, we returned to my house, where I stuck the kettle on. "What's your poison? Apple spice? Mint?"

"How about caffeine? I have the feeling I'm going to need it by the time Deacon gets back with that warrant."

Caffeine. Now that was a good idea! I pulled out the grinder and beans and went to town. "Triple espressos on the way," I said.

"I'm going to call Jimmy. He's at my house and I don't want him to worry." She pulled out her phone.

I grinned. "You guys have been spending a lot of time together. Any hope for an engagement?"

With a snort, she said, "Right. Em, you should know by now that when—if—we get married, it's going to rock the status quo at my job. It's hard enough dealing with—hold on." Jimbo must have come on the line, because she said, "Hey, it's me. I'm at Em's and it looks like I'll be here until morning . . . yeah, there's something weird going on next door. I'll tell you all about it when I get back. Okay . . . Well, if you have to take off before I get home, would you make sure that Sid and Nancy are firmly locked in their cages? Thanks, babe. Love you too." Sid and Nancy were her boas—one a congenial red tail boa, the other a nasty-tempered nocturnal green tree boa.

As she hung up, I had to ask. "What about his cats and chickens and goats?" I knew that he brought Roo, his three-legged dog, with him when he stayed at Murray's, but I wondered how his other animals were faring.

She grinned. "Snidely and Whiplash are living at my place right now—they've adjusted to life in my house and as long as we make sure the snake cages are securely locked, the cats are safe. Jimmy spends a lot of the day out on his land and he takes care of the goats and chickens while he's there."

I set the espresso maker to brewing and fixed us piping hot triple mochas with a slathering of Redi-whip. As we settled in at the table, Kip came padding into the kitchen, rubbing his eyes.

"What's goin' on? Is something wrong? Is it morning yet?"

I pulled him to me and gave him a hug. "It's real early,

kiddo. You still have a couple hours to sleep. What are you doing up?"

"I heard you guys and wanted a glass of water, so thought I'd come downstairs to check." He yawned and I grimaced. He'd obviously been into the candy stash, his tongue was a brilliant blue. Thank God his teeth were still white, but we'd have to have a little talk about not eating after brushing his teeth. That would keep, however.

I poured him a glass of water and said, "Murray and I need to talk. Listen, in a little while, I'm going to go next door with her. Both Randa and your alarms are set, so you guys will wake up in time for school. You'll remember where I am, right?" My hands on his shoulders, I guided him back to the stairs.

He leaned against me briefly, then trudged back up the stairs without complaining. I listened as his door opened and closed. He'd be back to sleep in no time. When I returned to the kitchen, Murray had her hand in the cookie jar. She grinned at me, sheepishly wiping peanut butter crumbs away from her mouth.

"I'm sorry, I was hungry—"

"Sorry? What have you got to be sorry about? You're family and you know it." I slipped back into my seat and finished my mocha. "Mur, I have something to show you. Brigit's picture and journal." I reached across the table and pulled them toward me. "She was in love with somebody, and from what I've read, she had a hard life and more than a few secrets, though it doesn't say what they were. But it sounds like something she was ashamed of and afraid for people to find out. It also looks like she missed her mother and father, and the man she'd been in love with. Appraently, they were all dead."

Mur shook her head. "This is all very strange, Em. If we can prove that the remains are hers—and I'm not promising anything because it's harder to identify old bones—then what the hell happened? Why was she stuffed in a tree, for God's sake?"

"Murder?" I said, thinking for a moment, although I didn't like the direction my thoughts were going. "Irena stopped the sale on the lot. She said her brother, who supposedly owns joint custody of the family land, refused to sell. She also told Joe that her brother lives in Europe. Harlow found out that Brent does *not* live overseas. In fact, Brent isn't even really living in this world—he's been in an asylum outside of Bellingham since he was twenty. Which means, chances are he wasn't consulted about the land sale. Which means . . ."

"Irena didn't want to sell the land for some reason," Murray finished.

"Right. We were ordered to stop work on the lot. But now, thanks to Brigit's ghost cat, I find a skeleton stuffed into a yew tree. I think the question of the day is: Does Irena already know the skeleton is there? If so, is that why she doesn't want to sell the land?" Everything fit together in a very weird way.

Murray looked at me closely. "And if Irena does know about the skeleton, that begs the question: Did she help put it there? Is she responsible, or partially responsible, for this person's death?"

Troubling questions all. A knock on the door interrupted our thoughts and I opened it to find Deacon, search warrant in hand. He slapped it on the table. "We're good to go. Judge says since the property has no house, isn't being used, and hasn't been used for years, this is all we need. Want me to go inform Irena?"

Murray gave him a wide smile. "You're a mind reader, Deacon. Okay, I'm calling for the M.E. and a few more of the boys. Come back afterward. And tell her that if she wants to scream, she can scream at me."

As Deacon took off, Murray phoned Nerissa Johansen, Chiqetaw's new medical examiner. Nerissa had been hired to replace Bob Stryker, who had been found guilty of any number of infractions. Once they surfaced and Chief Bonner had gotten wind of what was going on, Stryker was out on his ass and had moved out of town.

After talking to Nerissa, Murray put in a call to Greg Douglas and Sandy Whitmeyer, two of the other officers who had her back, then glanced at me.

"I'm headed over. You stay here. There won't be much to see. We need to mark off the area, which will take a little while, and then we have to wait for first light so we can have a good view of what's out there. The last thing we want is to lose valuable evidence because we can't see it. I want to know just who this was, and why he or she was buried inside a tree trunk."

As much as I wanted to go with her, I knew she was right. At this point, there wouldn't be anything to see and I'd only hamper efforts. "I hope the Will o' the Wisps stay away," I said.

"I think with the activity out there, and without you there to act as a blue-light special over on the astral aisle, they'll keep quiet. After all, they didn't show up when you found the skeleton."

"I know, and frankly, I can't help but wonder where they are. Maybe with me finding the skeleton, their job is done? Or maybe not. I don't know and I'm almost scared to find out."

"Well, get a couple hours more sleep, and I'll talk to you in a bit."

As she headed out, I closed the door behind her. What was it like to carry a gun and badge, to constantly be on the lookout for crooks and con artists, murderers and rapists and every bad guy in the world that might be passing through town? Mur was a good cop and I felt safer with her around, but it wasn't the life for me. And for my children's sake, I was supremely glad of that.

BY 6:00 A.M., I had dozed on the sofa for thirty minutes, and read the entire contents of Brigit's diary. I was a lot more depressed than I'd been—the girl's life had sounded so unhappy, though I couldn't figure out exactly what had been wrong. I got the impression, however, that Brigit had been a servant of some sort in the Brunswick household.

The lot swarmed with activity. Kip and Miranda woke early, clamoring to know what was going on, but I told them I couldn't say a word until Murray gave me the go-ahead, and they quieted down. As they ate their breakfast, the phone rang. It was Joe, wanting to know what was happening. He'd gotten wind of the activity via the police scanners. I filled him in on what had gone down and reassured him that I was fine, when Mur knocked at the back door and slipped into the kitchen.

"I thought you might like to come watch," she said as I replaced the receiver. "It's light enough to start excavating the site now. We're going to be putting in some time there today. We have to cut some of the roots so we don't disturb the skeleton when we remove it from the cavity." She helped herself to a Danish and a slice of bacon.

"What did Irena say? Is she giving you a hard time?" I brewed a couple of shots of espresso for her and poured them into a pint-sized carton of chocolate milk since she didn't have time to sit down with a proper demitasse cup.

She laughed when I handed it to her, but didn't hesitate to chug it right down.

"Thanks, I needed that. I'm exhausted." She wiped her mouth and sighed. "Actually, Irena's not being a pain like I expected."

I scarfed down the last of my biscuit with egg and cheese and bacon, sent my protesting son and daughter off to school after enjoining them to keep quiet about matters until Murray gave us the thumbs up. Then, grabbing on my jacket, I slipped my keys in the pocket and headed out the door with her.

"Jeez, it's cold this morning," she said.

As we headed across my yard, I jammed my hands in my pockets. The temperature had plummeted in the past hour or two and I could swear I smelled snow on the horizon, but it was far too early for that.

"So Irena's okay with this?"

"Well, she's not giving us any trouble. I was rather surprised. Deacon says she appeared properly shocked when he told her that we'd found a skeleton on the property and insisted that yes, of course we need to investigate. She 'can't for the life of me figure out where it came from.'"

I could see my breath. Winter was going to be nice and cold, which was fine with me since it was my favorite season. I was hoping for a white Christmas and—if it was anything like the year before—expected to see one.

"Think she's telling the truth?"

Murray shook her head. "Nope. She knows something about the body, I'll bet my next promotion on it. Deacon says she paused a second too long before launching into her "oh my" routine. Long enough to tell him that she wasn't all that surprised by his news. She conveniently has a day trip to Bellingham planned and regretfully declined our offer to let her watch."

"That's weird. If somebody found a skeleton on my property, I'd want to be there to find out what the hell was going on. What about the foundation? She was going to fill it in."

Murrary shook her head. "Ain't gonna happen. I thought about that and called the judge. He added a restraining order to prevent her from doing so." She shivered as a blast of wind caught us from the north. The rain had stopped, but the clouds were hanging heavy overhead. "I swear, we're due for an ice storm or snow. The temperature's hovering about thirty-five right now. It's cold for this time of year—way too cold."

I stepped back to let her go first as we crossed onto the lot. "Thirty-three. I checked the thermometer on our way out."

Sandy, Greg, and Nerissa were near the tree, along with several techs assisting the M.E. Sandy was taking photographs while Greg prepared evidence bags. Nerissa looked bent out of shape, and I heard her yell at one of the techs that the equipment hadn't been stored properly, and if it happened again, he'd be out of a job. Watching her, I had none of the squeamish feelings I'd had when I met Stryker. Ms. Johansen seemed more than capable.

As Murray joined them, they cautiously began scooping all the mulch they could find around the area into large bags.

I wandered over to the basement and peered down the stairs. No sign of the Will o' the Wisps yet. With luck, they'd stay out of the way until everyone was gone. The tree looked bare and naked after the area had been cleared of debris.

Nerissa probed the cavity with a flashlight and then withdrew, shaking her head. "Detective, you might want to take a look. Then we'll start photographing and remove the body . . . skeleton."

Murray knelt down and then called me over to her side. "Emerald, look at this." I peeked over her shoulder. There, wrapped in what looked like a sheet of some sort and cradled by the roots of the yew, rested the skeleton. Against its chest, snuggled in ivory arms, rested yet a smaller skeleton. Even I knew that the second set of bones were those of a cat.

"Oh my God," I whispered. "That is so bizarre." Murray said nothing, but nodded. She stood up and wiped the mud off her hands with a towel that Deacon offered her.

"Okay, here's the situation," she said. "Somebody put that body in there. We're looking at the possibility of this taking place fifty years ago. Maybe more, maybe less. I don't know yet. I want this entire lot canvassed. Whatever you find, bag it." She turned to me. "Those things you took out of the room when you thought you owned the land? That's fine, but we're going to need them as possible evidence. If you could bring them over, I'd appreciate it."

She was fully in command. When she slipped into her cop mode, she intimidated even me, but I didn't mind. This was who Murray *was*, down to the core. A cop. And a good one at that. I gave her a quick nod.

"Of course. I'll go get them now."

There was no real reason for me to stand around and watch, so I headed back to the house, wanting to see what else they found, but knowing that I'd hear about it later. I no sooner stepped through the door when the phone rang. I grabbed it up and was greeted by a voice that I neither needed nor wanted to hear.

"Emerald? It's me, Roy."

Great. My scumbag of an ex. Roy was like spoiled

meat—rotten through and through and likely to be dangerous to your health if you got too close.

"What do you want? Have you figured some new way to destroy our kids' image of you? Or are you just calling to make me miserable?" I'd ceased any veneer of being civil when the kids weren't in earshot. Roy ran roughshod over me whenever I offered an olive branch. I was done with playing nice-nice.

I was especially furious that, after months of ignoring Kip and Randa, he'd finally ruined the one visit they'd had in a year. He agreed to meet them in August when he drove up to Bellingham for a business trip, but had spent the entire time ragging on Kip for not being more athletic and calling Randa stupid for her interest in astronomy. And then he sealed the deal when he started bragging about the new half-brother they were supposed to have, and how good it would be to have a child in the house again.

He let out a loud sigh. "I'm always the bad guy, aren't I? You never take any responsibility for your problems that led to the end of our marriage."

I'd heard this all before. "Get real, Roy. What do you want?"

"I'm headed out of the country for a month. I'll have my secretary pick out Christmas gifts for the kids and send them over just in case I decide to stay away longer."

I sighed. "Let me offer you some advice for a change." He was always telling me what he thought about my lifestyle, my choices, and it was never very pleasant. Time to turn the tables.

He muttered something under his breath but said, "What is it now?"

"If you don't want to lose our kids—and I mean lose their hearts, lose their love entirely, get your act together and start being a father to them instead of a jerk. Trust me,

I'm not thrilled about offering you this advice because I want you as far out of our lives as possible. If I had it my way, we'd never see you again. I just hope you treat Tyra and your new child better than you ever treated the kids and me, because if you don't, someday you're going to wake up alone. People don't hang around when they're not appreciated."

After a pause, he startled the hell out of me by saying, "Yeah, so I seem to have found out."

I stared at the phone. "Say what?"

Another long pause. Then, "Tyra left me a week ago. She lost the baby and she blames me. She filed divorce papers yesterday."

My heart leapt, but I managed to restrain myself from singing the "I told you so" song when a cold thought swept through me. "Roy, how did she lose the baby?" My ex had roughed me up a couple of times during our marriage—ending in a black eye.

"She fell," he mumbled, then quickly added, "I've got a plane to catch. Tell the kids . . . I love them."

The line went dead. I slowly replaced the receiver, wondering what the real story was. But I wasn't curious enough to call him back, and no way was I going to hunt down Tyra to ask her side of things. As sorry as I felt for her right now, she was still the woman who'd been screwing my husband behind my back.

I shook off the call, scooped up Brigit's journal and photograph, and availed myself of the copy function on my printer, duplicating all fifty-three pages in the notebook, the handwritten copy of *The Lady of Shalott*, and the picture. As I gazed into the eyes of the woman long vanished, I knew without a doubt that we'd found her final resting place.

Now if we could just find out what her secrets were.

Nine

From Brigit's Journal:

    B.'s having a bad day again and there's nothing I can do. Why can't Mr. Edward leave him alone? Why can't the Missus stand up and say something? It's as if they're ashamed of him—ashamed of his problems, but Mother Mary, I'm certain that they're really the cause of his troubles. Who could withstand such browbeating?

    I need to talk to someone about my feelings, but there's no one I can trust. Even my friends slip and tell secrets. And I don't dare let this secret get out . . . not now—especially not now. I havent' told him yet, but I have to soon. I'm going to church on my next day off, and confess. Maybe the priest will be able to help me decide what I should do. I've no one else to turn to but God. Pray for me, diary, that He doesn't turn his back on me.

*   *   *

BY THE TIME I returned, the crew had excavated the skeleton. Both bones and the sheet they were loosely wrapped in rested on a tarp to prevent contamination from mud or other debris. While an examination would be necessary to determine the sex, I was pretty sure it was a woman. The skeleton was dressed in a tattered skirt and blouse. Whoever she was, she'd been twisted and contorted to fit into the tree, with the cat cuddled in her arms. They had slept there together, slowly melting back into the earth until I'd found them.

Rather than chance losing evidence to rain or wind, Nerissa ordered that the tarp, bones, sheet and all, be lifted into a body bag. The sound of the zipper closing was fraught with stark finality. Brigit's long night of obscurity was over; now she would be exposed to harsh lights and probing instruments that would ferret out her secrets. In a way, I almost wished I hadn't found her and that she'd been left to her slumber. What good could we do at this point? Of course, logic argued, if she'd been murdered—and why else would her body be stuffed into a tree—perhaps we could put to rest unfinished business, and a troubled spirit.

As the techs loaded the body bag into the ambulance, Murray motioned to Greg. "We've got a long day ahead of us. Take Sandy and go pick up some coffee and food. I want a quad venti mocha frappuccino. Get a quad venti mocha for Emerald, too." She pulled out her wallet. "Add raspberry to hers, no whipped cream, and make it iced."

Greg jotted down her instructions. "What do you want to eat?"

She shrugged and handed them thirty bucks. "I'm fine with a couple of sausage-egg muffins and some hash browns. Make that three muffins—it's been a long night and my stomach's rumbling. You guys get whatever you want. While you're at it, check in with the chief and tell him what's going down. Make sure he knows I'll be tied up here for awhile so if anything urgent happens, he can reach me by radio. And get hold of Deacon. Tell him I said thanks for the help last night. I'll talk to him later myself, but I want to keep him in the loop."

Greg and Sandy headed out in a cruiser. As they turned off Hyacinth onto Wilson Street, I handed Murray the photo and diary.

"The Brunswicks were seriously dysfunctional, if you believe some of the entries. The father was cruel, and Irena was no saint. Harlow wasn't kidding when she told me the mother died of booze. A lot of entries mentioning Lauren Brunswick's drinking."

"Anything saying that Brigit had enemies who wanted to kill her?"

I shook my head. "No, but she seems to have been terribly unhappy. A lot of hints about guarded secrets and innuendos in there, but nothing I could figure out on a concrete level. Today, her doctor would have her on Zoloft."

Regardless of exactly who it had been, the remains had once belonged to a living, breathing woman who had laughed and cried and loved. And upon her death, someone had seen fit to hide her away, to stuff her under a tree out of view. The fact that she was holding the skeleton of a cat—most likely the one in the picture—didn't help my mood any.

"What could have happened?" I said. "And what about her cat? Did they die at the same time?"

Murray shrugged, her lips a grim line. "I don't know, Em. We'll have a better picture of what went on once Nerissa examines the remains. Sometimes this job sucks." She paused, glancing around at the rain-sodden ground.

"You know what gets me the most? The damned cat. The fact that she's holding a cat makes me want to cry."

I hung my head and whispered, "Me, too." In fact, the skeleton of the cat was a harsh reminder that Samantha was still missing. A sense of helplessness washed over me. This woman, whoever she was, and her cat were beyond help. And even though I was positive Samantha was alive, I couldn't get the idea out of my mind that she was trapped somewhere alone, thinking we'd forsaken her.

"You're running a guilt-trip, aren't you?" Mur gave me a speculative look. We'd been friends so long she could sense my moods the minute they shifted.

I nodded. "The cat's skeleton . . . the ghost cat . . . I miss Sammy. I know she's alive somewhere out there, but that doesn't mean she's safe. And until she's back, all the intuition or hunches in the world won't comfort me as much as seeing her face staring into mine in the morning when I wake up. I have to put on a strong front for the kids, but her disappearance is tearing me up." Kip and Miranda loved Sammy dearly, but she'd taken to me, while her kittens had bonded with the kids. Samantha was *my* cat.

Mur slipped an arm around my shoulder. "I know, Em, I know. Hang in there. Tell you what, White Deer should be here by this afternoon. Maybe she can think of something to help."

The knot between my shoulders loosened a little. If anybody could help, it would be White Deer. "Thanks, Mur. You know I appreciate it."

"I know," she said. She glanced back at the yew. "Regarding this case, though, a thought crossed my mind that perhaps this might have been the end result of some form of ritual burial? I remember reading that some cultures bury their dead in trees."

There was a thought. It wasn't like the body had been cut to pieces or maimed, as far as we could tell, and whoever buried her had kept her with the cat. That spoke of some compassion, didn't it?

"It's an idea, I guess. But around here?"

"Bear in mind that if this is Brigit, then whatever happened took place at least fifty years ago. It was easier to cover your tracks back then. There were a lot of immigrants around who came from overseas after World War II. Many of them brought their customs with them. Not to mention that you yourself said Chiqetaw is a magnet for psychic phenomenon. Maybe it also attracts those with unusual beliefs. After all, you're here, aren't you?" She grinned.

"If you're trying to cheer me up, keep trying," I said, but smiled despite myself. Murray had a way of making me laugh, even when I didn't feel like it.

"Detective?" The M.E. strode over. Ms. Johansen certainly had an air of authority about her, I thought. She was no-nonsense, but I had the feeling she'd be on the square far more than Bob Stryker had ever been.

"Yes? What is it?" Mur turned around.

"We're ready to take the body to the morgue. I've got an autopsy scheduled for this morning, but things have been pretty dead lately." Her straight face didn't belie a single twitch of the lip, but her eyes smiled. "I should be able to start in on the examination this afternoon."

Murray nodded. "Good. Let me know what you find. I'll make sure we hunt down any evidence here and get it right into the labs."

"Just pray this isn't the body of one of the tribal folk around here," Nerissa muttered under her breath. She seemed to recognize her mistake the minute she said it but there wasn't time for a graceful retreat.

Murray gave her a cool look. "And why are you worried about that?"

Nerissa cleared her throat. "I just thought . . . well, neither one of us wants another case like the Kennewick Man."

The Kennewick controversy surrounded the nine-thousand-year-old remains of a man found in the Columbia River near Kennewick, Washington. Even though examination showed the remains to be of Caucasian origin, the question remained: How did the Kennewick Man show up in what was supposed to have been purely native territory at that time? Who was he and where was he from? Natives wanted to rebury him out of respect—they said the bones belonged to them. Archaeologists wanted to study him. The controversy was still being battled out in court.

Murray snorted. "Don't worry about it, Nerissa. I sincerely doubt if these bones are over fifty or sixty years old. And if they're native, they'll be reburied."

Trying to salvage the conversation, the M.E. said, "I just meant, we don't want an archaeological nightmare on our hands. You're probably right, though. We'll know more later today." She climbed in her car and took the lead, the ambulance following.

Murray watched her go, shaking her head. "I think she worked on the Kennewick case. That's her one stumbling block, as far as I can see. Science takes precedence over everything with her. But I guess it's a good attitude for her line of work—just so long as she doesn't have to interact with the families of the deceased. She's not very tactful."

"She seems competent, though. You couldn't say that about Stryker."

"You've got me there," Mur said. "Not to change the subject, but I've got a favor to ask of you."

"What is it?" I glanced at her warily. Anytime anybody had a favor they wanted to ask me, it usually involved me getting hurt or having some run-in with an astral beastie.

"I was wondering if there's a chance I can cajole you into tuning in to see if you can pick up anything about the skeleton? I know you're nervous about the thought—"

"Nervous? Try terrified." I thought about the retreating ambulance and sighed. The bones resting in the back made everything real. We weren't just dealing with spirits and otherworldly creatures now. I wiped my mouth, gauging what I could do without putting myself in jeopardy. "And it's not just the Will o' the Wisps that worry me."

"What, then?"

I looked at the yew for a moment before answering, the aura both fascinating and frightening me. No longer just a tree in a neighboring lot, it had transformed into a graveyard, a silent witness to a death long forgotten.

"Do you know anything about the lore of yew trees?" I finally said.

Murray shook her head. "Not much, they don't play a big part in the traditions in which I was brought up."

"Well, I know a little of their history. In Irish myth and legend, yews were considered some of the longest-lived beings on the face of this planet, and they represent rebirth and reincarnation. Their spirits can be wild, unpredictable."

"Is that why the Will o' the Wisps congregate around it?"

"I think they're here for two reasons. One, because of Brigit. She was Irish and probably had some sort of connection to the *Sidhe*. But the yew is also connected to the Otherworld—supposedly to be one of the five sacred woods brought over. It seems natural that the corpse candles would be attracted to it, much like a moth to a flame. Yews are often found in graveyards."

Murray contemplated what I had said, then nodded. "I can see why you'd be leery of touching it on a psychic level."

"Not only did the Celts hold the tree sacred, but the Norse, too." I stared up into the wild branches that wove together against the sky. Without meaning to, I tuned in— just a little—and the nimbus surrounding the tree flared to life. "I can believe that Yggdrassil was a yew. The World Tree."

And in fact, the tree radiated like a torch, warming my skin as it penetrated the chill that clouded the early morning air. It became obvious that its roots ran deep into the ley lines that formed the psychic grid of Chiqetaw. A sentinel, a guardian of the area. I broke away, disconnecting before it noticed me.

I shook my head. "I can't. I'm sorry, Mur."

"Not a problem," she said. "It would be nice, though, to know what it's seen over the years. I imagine not much that happens around here escapes its notice."

I nodded. "Yeah, it's sentient, all right. I've been thinking. I believe that when Joe and I started clearing the brambles and found the basement, we awakened the spirits of Brigit and her cat."

Murray sighed. "Probably. I think it's time to go have a talk with Brent Brunswick. Do you want to come along?"

"Brent? But he's in an institution." Even as I said it, I realized that the thought of visiting him made me nervous. I wasn't sure why—maybe I was picking up on something I really didn't want to know, or shouldn't know.

She shrugged. "Irena obviously isn't prepared to come clean with us. Maybe we can find out something useful from Brent."

I considered the idea. We had no idea whether Brent

was coherent yet dysfunctional, or whether he was totally out of touch. A lot of people were locked away when they shouldn't be, slipping through the cracks of the system. We couldn't count him out of the picture until we'd actually met with him. Even if he wasn't able to provide any information on the mysterious skeleton, maybe, just maybe, he might shed some light on why Irena wouldn't sell the lot to Joe, and maybe I could get him to agree to the sale.

"I'm game. I should give Joe a call first, to let him know what we've found out. He was . . . shall we say . . . less than shocked when I told him I'd found the skeleton." I snickered. "Joe seems to have accepted that I have a knack for stumbling over dead bodies. Now if *I* could just learn to live with it, I'd be a happy camper."

"I wish I could have been a fly on the wall for that conversation," Mur said with a grin. "Give me a couple more hours. Here come Greg and Sandy with the food. We'll get started hunting for evidence, and once I know they're up to speed on what to look for, I can slip away. We'll take my truck. No sense in both of us driving."

"Sounds good." I waved at her as the guys climbed out of their car, loaded down with breakfast. Sandy handed me the mocha and I saluted Murray with it, then headed back to the house, my stomach rumbling like a freight train. The Danish I'd eaten for breakfast was a distant memory, as were the eggs and bacon I'd managed to snag. I decided it was time for lunch, even if it was only midmorning, and was in the middle of fixing a sandwich when the phone rang.

"So what's the buzz?" Joe's low-slung voice echoed over the line, making me melt. "Any more bodies in the tree?"

I stared at my roast beef sandwich, gauging whether it

was thin enough to allow me to talk and eat at the same time. Nope, too thick. I wistfully set it on the counter and told him what we'd discovered.

"We're going over to Fairhaven Psychiatric Hospital to meet Brent. Maybe I can find out what the deal is with Irena and the land. Murray thinks maybe Irena knew the skeleton was there and didn't want to sell for that reason."

Joe cleared his throat. "Did you ever think that maybe Brent's in that hospital for a reason? Maybe he's dangerous and his family knew he did something he shouldn't have?"

I had to admit, the thought hadn't occurred to me. I wondered if Murray had been mulling it over. "I suppose you have a point. I doubt if the possibility's escaped Murray's notice. She thinks by the book." I wiped up a trail of mustard dripping off my sandwich and licked my finger. Yum.

"Are you eating while you're talking to me?" Joe laughed. "I bet you're sitting there, staring at a big old mug of mocha or something, just dying to get me off the phone so you can chug it down. Well, am I right?"

The ice in my mocha was melting, and the sandwich was tempting me to cave in and admit that he was right, but I had my pride. "No."

"Right, and I'm not sitting here wishing I was right there next to you so I could rip off your clothes and drag you up to the bedroom, either. But we both know that's a lie." The lonely note in his voice caught my breath short. My appetite disappeared and I dropped into a chair.

"I wish you were here. I like having you around."

He seldom stayed at his apartment anymore, using it more like a pit stop between my house and the station. I suddenly felt bad for him—he must feel so ungrounded with no real home base. Earlier in the year, he'd mentioned that he was going to ask me to marry him on my birthday, but we hadn't talked about it since then. I wondered if he remembered, but didn't want to ask. No sense setting myself up for heartache if he'd changed his mind.

"Do you have to work tonight?"

"Yeah," he said, sounding depressed. "But I can get away for dinner. Want me to come by? I can eat at the station if you have plans with the kids."

"The only plans we have are to continue looking for Sammy. I'm scared, Joe. What if she doesn't come home?"

He let out a sigh. "I don't know, love. I don't know. We'll weather it through, whatever happens. I'll be over there around six. That good?"

"That's wonderful." I suddenly wanted him with me now, his arms wrapped around me, holding me close. "I'll make fettucine Alfredo."

With a smack of the lips, he blew me a kiss through the phone, and signed off. I hung up, feeling unaccountably lonely. As I was staring at the phone, it occurred to me that maybe Margaret Files, Joe's aunt, might know something about the Brunswicks. She had lived here during the same time they did.

I dialed her number but got her answering machine. After leaving a message I finished my second breakfast, then headed upstairs to change for our trip. What did one wear to a mental institution?

I decided to err on the side of conservative. After a quick shower, I slipped into a brown suede skirt, a hunter green cowl-necked sweater, and zipped up my knee-high brown leather boots. I hooked a gold chain around my neck and slipped matching hoops in my ears, then quickly brushed my hair back and deftly wove it into a French braid, fastening it with a gold barrette. I'd just finished dressing when the doorbell rang.

Murray's voice echoed from the hall. "Em? Are you ready to go?"

I dashed down the steps, and stopped short. Apparently Murray had decided to change too. She wore a deep burgundy pants suit with black leather pumps, and was carrying a shoulder-bag briefcase. Her hair was pulled back in a chignon. I was used to seeing her in both jeans, and her everyday suits for work, but she looked so classy and chic that I caught my breath.

"Where did you get that? I love it!" I circled her, examining the suit. This wasn't her usual business suit. No, indeed. "This is an Anne Klein!"

She blushed. "I asked Harlow to go shopping with me last month. Once I accepted the promotion, I needed a few really nice outfits for times when I have to appear as a consummate professional. After all, I am the head of detectives now."

"That you are," I said with a smile.

"I may not know fashion, but I knew the look I needed. So Harlow helped me find a few things that I can wear into meetings or to address the press, when necessary. I told Bonner that I'm not about to let the department stay sloppy—Coughlan may have let the men slack off on both attitude and fitness for the job, but that's going to change under me."

I scribbled out a note for the kids, should they arrive home early, and grabbed my cell phone and purse. Too bad Horvald had taken off on his mini-vacation—I'd gotten used to having him around. He was as wonderful about looking after the kids as Ida. With both of them gone until Halloween, the neighborhood felt empty.

Arming the security system, I turned back to Murray. "Still having trouble with the guys at work?"

She shrugged as we climbed into her truck. "Well, it's

not like it's a huge department. They can either shape up or find another job. Bonner agrees with me on this, at least, especially after Rusty's stunt. The place has gotten slack. Half the guys there couldn't pass their physical entrance exam if they had to right now. So I told them to hit the gym, cut down on the carbs, and tone up that muscle."

I snorted. "Do you really think they'll listen?"

She nodded. "I know they will—they don't like being beaten by a woman when it comes to arm wrestling. I made them a deal. If they can't beat me in the best two of three, and if they can't pass the number of push-ups I can do, then they have to shape up. I've got three detectives under me. All of them lost the bet. Their egos are bruised and they all want a rematch."

"Now that you know none of them are the ones trying to get you fired, do you think things will get easier?" I was hoping that her discovery of her not-so-secret admirer was going to shift the mood.

She eased onto the main highway and we headed toward Bellingham. "Honestly? I don't know, Em. But I think Rusty was stirring up some of the trouble. Right now, it's a wait-and-see situation."

We headed north on Highway 9 for ten miles or so, then veered west toward Bellingham. The Fairhaven Psychiatric Hospital was located a mile or so east of the city. Residents had, many years ago, feared the type of people who would be housed there and insisted on the state removing it from near the boundaries.

As we rounded a curve, a large sign proclaimed that Fairhaven was just ahead, to the right. Murray flipped on her blinker and veered onto the wide, spacious road. Lined with maple and horse chestnut trees, the drive was lovely. The long meadows of grass were covered with brightly colored autumn leaves, and the trees looked

sparse against the overcast sky, but there was still a genteel feel to the place. I had a feeling this institute was
more of a private haven for those from well-to-do families
who had decided their loved ones weren't well enough to
withstand society. It certainly didn't resemble a state-run
facility, that much was for sure.

We'd barely driven one hundred yards along the park-
way before a wrought iron gate barred our way. Booths sat
next to it on either side, manned by security guards wearing olive uniforms. I had a feeling they were packing guns
beneath those jackets.

I glanced at Murray. "This isn't a day spa, tell you that
much."

She nodded, rolling down her window. The guard remained behind his bulletproof glass and motioned for her
to speak into the intercom.

"I'm Detective Anna Murray with the Chiqetaw Police
Force. I've come on official business. I spoke to Dr.
Ziegler this morning and he said you'd have me on the
list." She flashed her badge.

The guard checked over a list and nodded. "And your
guest?"

"Emerald O'Brien," she said. "She's connected with
the case in question."

The guard made a quick phone call, then stepped out of
his booth and handed Murray two passes—one for each of
us—and a sticker for the truck. He admonished us to wear
our passes at all times while inside. Along with the passes,
he gave us a brochure about Fairhaven, then returned to
his booth and the wide gates swung open.

Murray slipped her pass around her neck—they were
on long ribbons—and I did the same. She slapped the
sticker on the dashboard so it was visible through the win-

dow shield, face up, and then slowly eased the truck through the gates.

In the distance, I could see a clock tower rising from a building shrouded by the trees and a wave of melancholy swept over me. Even from here, I could feel the years hanging heavy over the institute and, in the pit of my stomach, I had the feeling that most of the residents weren't even aware of the time that passed in the outside world as they waited inside for something to change in their lives.

Ten

❦

From Brigit's Journal:

Sometimes my room gets so cold at night that it feels as though my hands are going to freeze. I talked to the Missus about it; she said she'll see what she can do. The family had a shouting match over breakfast, with Miss Irena screaming at her brother, and their father yelling at both of them. As usual, the Missus slipped out for a drink.

I found her in the laundry room with a bottle of sherry. She let me help her up to her room for a nap. Sometimes she can be so sweet—it gives me hope that maybe things will work out. If only she wasn't so afraid. Mr. Edward has a temper, though I've seldom seen him strike her.

I checked on the price of passage to Ireland. I have almost enough saved up to pay for it, should circumstance make it necessary. I told Maggie I might be leaving. She doesn't know why and thinks I should stick it out. If she only knew the truth . . .

*   *   *

A JUNCTURE BETWEEN never-never land and the twilight zone, Fairhaven Psychiatric Hospital seemed poised on the crux of a vortex of energies, partially created from—I suspected—the neuroses and instabilities of those making their home there. It was as if a large dragon coiled overhead, brooding as it spied on the complex. Whether poised to pounce or to protect, I wasn't sure.

Murray glanced over at me. "Can you feel it?" she asked. "As if something stopped time here."

When I thought about it, I saw she was right. People came to the institution to mark time—whether to rest and recuperate from some devastating breakdown, or just to wait it out. To wait for death, wait for life, wait in limbo. I nodded, shivering.

"Yeah, I can feel it. Creepy and yet, incredibly sad."

We followed the road toward the main building. Fairhaven was comprised of four buildings. The main structure housed the administrative offices, dining hall, classrooms, the infirmary, and several meeting halls. Two of the other buildings were the dormitories, segregated by sex. And the fourth was, according to the brochure the guard had given us, restricted to authorized personnel. Apparently, violent cases were treated and housed there.

A circular drive in front of the buildings spun off several smaller roads—one to a parking lot for visitors, a second to a staff parking lot, and a third to an undisclosed location. Murray parked in the nearest open space for visitors. There weren't many people here today, I noticed as I climbed out of her truck and smoothed my skirt.

I took a deep breath and looked around. The lawns were perfectly manicured—a state my own would never see. A few people crossed from one building to another under the covered walkways, but most looked like staff. Only once on our way to administration did we see someone that I assumed to be a patient, led by a rather hassled-looking nurse wearing a pale blue pantsuit.

As we entered the main building, a hush descended, and I felt like a child entering a library, although there were no Quiet Please signs hanging in the hallway. A locked door prevented us from going any farther, and a cubicle to the left housed a guard behind a bulletproof pane of glass.

"The nature of your business, please?"

"Police business," Murray said, and held up her badge as she leaned close enough for him to scan the pass she wore around her neck with a handheld scanner.

"I'm with her," I said and moved forward to allow him access to my pass. He flickered the gun-shaped object over the bar code on my pass and nodded.

"If you have weapons, you'll have to check them here. No weapons allowed in the main facility. And I need to glance through your handbags, please."

Murray reluctantly surrendered her gun, getting a receipt for it. I had nothing to declare, but when the guard peeked in my purse, he pursed his lips.

"How about this?" he said, pointing to the little switchblade that Jimbo had given me.

I blushed. "Oops, sorry. I forgot I had it with me."

Unsmiling, he wrote out a receipt and handed it to me. After a second, he glanced at Murray and then motioned me close. He whispered, "Ma'am, I hope you know that switchblades are illegal to carry in Washington State. I'm not a police officer like your friend there—she would know better than I—but next time, I'd leave this little beauty at home."

I noticed Murray was trying hard to avoid listening, but a faint grin played across her lips as she studiously pretended not to hear our exchange. I thanked him for the advice. He punched a button and the heavy double doors clicked. Mur pushed them open and I followed her inside.

As we passed into the facility, Murray murmured to me, "Remind me to have a talk with Jimmy about what kind of gifts he's handing out to our friends. The guard's right—you shouldn't be carrying that around in your purse."

I cleared my throat. "What about a pocketknife?"

"No problem as long as it doesn't open automatically. If the blade doesn't exceed about three to three-and-one-half inches, you should be—" She stopped abruptly. "My God, it's ugly in here."

The walls were pale blue, the furniture cream and brown, and everything was covered in a wash of antiseptic sterility, worse than most hospitals and clinics. Cinder blocks formed the walls, big rectangular stones, and the floor had been polished until the linoleum shone, a mottled blue and peach pattern. The place was totally devoid of character or personality.

The receptionist's desk sat in the middle of a four-way juncture. An older woman in a white pantsuit sat behind the desk. She was stout, with her salt-and-pepper hair pulled back in a bun, and she wore rectangular wire-framed glasses that were about a decade out of date. She beamed as though we were exactly the people she'd been waiting to see. For the first time since we'd entered the grounds of the institution, I felt like there was a human being attached to it.

"I'm Nurse Martin. May I help you?" she asked. Her tone immediately put me at ease; she sounded sincere instead of just mouthing a rote response, the perfect choice to meet and greet family members.

Murray must have sensed the same thing I did because her demeanor softened and she gave the woman a gentle smile. "Thank you. Is Dr. Ziegler here? He assured me it would be all right to drop in. We need to talk to him. I'm Detective Anna Murray and this is Emerald O'Brien."

When Mur pulled out her badge most people flinched or looked a little intimidated. Not this woman. She eyed it carefully, gave a respectful nod, and picked up the phone. After paging the doctor, she pointed to a row of uncomfortable-looking chairs.

"If you'll wait over there, Dr. Ziegler will be here in a few moments. I'm sorry the chairs aren't softer, but if you girls would like some coffee or tea, I'd be happy to get you a cup."

We declined graciously, and took our seats. Nurse Martin went back to her work, fluttering over the desk. We had been waiting about five minutes when a man of around sixty strode into the waiting room. The doctor was swathed in a white coat with a stethoscope around his neck, so tall that he towered over Mur by a good six inches.

She held out her hand. "You said we could come by and talk to Brent Brunswick?"

"You caught him on a good day. He's actually having one of his lucid moments. If you'll follow me." We swung in behind him and headed down the hall. "I had him brought to the main facility. He usually spends most of his time in his room except for meals," Ziegler continued. "I need you to understand that Mr. Brunswick has been with us for fifty years. He's going on seventy-one, and while he's capable of functioning on his own to the degree that he can dress himself and feed himself, he doesn't speak often. When he does, he doesn't always make sense." He stepped along so briskly and was so tall that I had trouble keeping up.

"What exactly is wrong with him?" Mur asked.

"Schizophrenia. The condition developed when Brent was twenty years old. His records indicate that he was always a moody boy, but one day something snapped and he made the break from reality. He lived for years in a fugue, and then slowly began pulling out of it for short periods of time. Back when he was first diagnosed, we didn't have the treatments we do today. At this point, the illness has a firm hold on him; stronger than anything we can offer to treat him with."

"There's no hope he'll ever get better?" I asked.

The doctor glanced back at me. "Ms. O'Brien, Brent is seventy years old. Even when young, he was a hypochondriac, with an overactive imagination that seemed to take on a life of its own. I gather he claimed to hear voices when he was in his early teens, but his family overlooked it because it never seemed particularly dangerous."

"Does he have a family history of schizophrenia?" I asked. The condition was often passed down through heredity.

"Apparently, he had a grandfather with the disoder. I take it this is germane to your case?"

Murray nodded. "As I said, we've made a discovery in the lot where the house that he grew up in stood—a skeleton. Perhaps from the time when he was around nineteen or twenty. We need to question Mr. Brunswick. We're not labeling the find a homicide yet, but that could change, depending on the results of our investigation."

Dr. Ziegler gave her a long look. "Do you think Brent may have had a hand in this? Something like that could easily cause that final break in his psyche."

Murray shrugged. "Right now, we just want to find out if he can tell us anything about the skeleton."

"I see," he said, stopping to glance through the thick file he carried. "I can tell you this: It's a matter of public

record that Mr. Brunswick's grandmother committed sui-
cide when she was around thirty-five. The story was in the
papers, even though the family tried to have it covered up.
She probably suffered from some sort of mental disorder,
though there's no way to prove it. And one of his uncles
ended up being treated for alcoholism after he was ar-
rested for raping a young woman."

He thumbed through the file. "Again, our records indicate that the family tried to hush it up, but Mrs. Brunswick
said that the authorities wouldn't let it go and the story apparently hit the papers and was the catalyst that forced Mr.
Brunswick and his wife to move away from Seattle to
Chiqetaw."

"So Brent's probably going to be here for rest of his
life?" Murray asked.

"Brent Brunswick has spent five decades in this facility, first in the old building, then this one when it was
built. I sincerely doubt that he'll ever walk the streets on
his own again. He's . . ." He paused, looking around as if
trying to find the right words.

"Waiting to die," I said, staring at the doctor. If he
wouldn't say it, I would. Murray sucked in a breath but
the doctor nodded very slowly.

"Actually, yes. I do honestly believe he's looking forward to the end. During his lucid moments, he often asks
how long he has left."

Dr. Ziegler stopped in front of a door and unclipped the
ring of keys from his belt. He pressed the intercom button
beside the door. "Ziegler here. I'm bringing in two guests
to see Brent." He tapped in a code on the security panel,
then when a click sounded, he unlocked the door and we
followed him in.

The walls were the same icy blue as the rest of the

complex, but the room felt close and heavy, as if swathed in cotton.

Two attendants stood by another door that led out the other side. In the center, a Formica-clad table held a single cup of coffee. Four plastic chairs surrounded the table and, in one of those chairs, sat an older gentleman. He was wearing a business suit thirty years out of date, and a blue plastic bracelet encircled his wrist—a hospital bracelet impervious to tearing. He looked up at us and a flicker in his eyes told me he was aware of our presence.

Murray took a step forward. As I stared at Brent Brunswick, my stomach knotted. The doctor was right— he wasn't all there, even though he looked perfectly normal. It was obvious in his feel, in his aura, in his eyes. I gave Murray a nudge and she nodded ever so slightly as we sat down at the table across from him.

"Brent, I want you to meet two ladies who've come to talk to you," Dr. Ziegler said. "This is Detective Anna Murray, and her friend, Emerald O'Brien."

Brent ignored Murray but he turned to me and, with what felt like a spark of recognition, whispered, "You know her."

"Who?" I asked.

"*Her*, you know her," Brent said, leaning forward.

Taken aback, I swallowed. Dr. Ziegler sighed and joined us at the table. "Sometimes he talks about a mysterious woman, but I haven't the faintest idea of who she's supposed to be. He's never mentioned a name, and his sister's never given us any clue as to who she might be. A dream, perhaps."

Murray leaned forward. "Brent . . . Mr. Brunswick? I'd like to ask you a few questions, if I could."

Again, he ignored her, this time directly focusing on me. "You want something, don't you?"

His gaze fastened on mine, and the age slid away from his shoulders. For a moment, it was almost as if I could see him when he was still young and tall and handsome. His face was that of a poet's, with a delicate bone structure, despite his wide shoulders, and a spark flickered in his eyes, swimming in the depths, dancing, waiting—orange in an ocean of blue, almost drowning. The spark of a life unlived, of an active and brilliant mind caught in the trap of mental illness.

And then, the flare faded and once again, I found myself staring into the age-worn face of a man who had lived far too many years in the fog. Weathered like the mountains, Brent had fought all of his storms on the inside. I stared at him, gauging what I could get away with asking.

Murray slid a piece of paper my way and I glanced at it. She'd written, "He seems to respond to you, go ahead and ask about the lot."

I sucked in a deep breath and said, "Brent, do you remember the house where you grew up?"

He did not blink, did not move, did not flinch, but I knew I'd caught his attention. After a moment he whispered. "Yes. Hyacinth Street. I lived on Hyacinth Street."

I nodded. "That's right. Do you remember who lived there with you?"

Again, an interminable pause. Then, "Mother . . . Father. My sister." A wounded expression spread over his face. I felt like I was watching someone on a cliff, teetering on to the edge.

I let out a long breath. "Do you remember someone named Brigit?"

He shifted and looked away. After a moment, he whispered, "I want my paints."

I glanced at the doctor. "Paints?"

Ziegler smiled. "Mr. Brunswick is quite the painter. He loves to paint castles and trees and cats."

"What kind of cats?" I asked.

"Calicos, mostly." The doctor looked over at Brent, who was staring off into space. "He's at his happiest when he's got a brush in hand."

Murray cleared her throat. "Can we see some of his paintings?"

"I'd like to oblige you," the doctor said, "but as soon as he finishes them, he tears them up. We figure it's a harmless diversion, and it keeps him content, and that's the best we can hope for."

Brent drifted back out of his fugue. He blinked and pointed at me. "You want to ask me something about the house and the land, don't you?"

I was willing to wager Brent had more than a smattering of psychic awareness. It might have driven him over the edge, considering the atmosphere he'd grown up in. Or maybe something more sinister had been at play. I thought about Dr. Ziegler's comment to Murray. Could Brent have killed Brigit and then lost grasp of reality?

I glanced at the doctor, who nodded. "Brent, my boyfriend and I want to buy the lot where your house stood. We need your permission, along with Irena's." I wasn't sure what to expect, but I might as well give it a try.

"I don't care," he said, sounding surprisingly clear. He shrugged and, for the first time, glanced up at the doctor. "I should sign something?"

Dr. Ziegler stepped forward. "Brent, do you understand what she's saying?"

"She wants to buy the land. I said I don't care."

The doctor looked at me. "You can have him sign

something, but I don't know if it would hold up in court, should his sister object."

I sighed, wondering vaguely if I might be taking advantage of Brent, but I couldn't let Joe down. He wanted the land, and Brent would never use it again. I pulled out the form I'd typed up in advance and put it down on the table.

"Do you understand what it says?" the doctor asked Brent, reading it to him.

Brent nodded and held out his hand for a pen. He signed, and I folded the paper and put it back in my purse. Whether it would help or not, I didn't know, but it was worth the chance.

After I had tucked the paper away, I decided to try one last time. "Brent," I said softly, leaning forward to stare in the eyes of a young man trapped in a body which had gone on blithely through the years without him.

"Brent, do you remember who Brigit was?"

This time, he began to shake. His eyes grew wide and he stumbled to his feet, breathing rapidly. "Brigit! Oh Brigit, God forgive me, I'm sorry. Brigit, please forgive me—don't hate me, please don't hate me. I'm so sorry, so sorry!"

The attendants leapt to his side, taking gentle hold of his arms. Dr. Ziegler stepped forward. "Brent, calm down or we'll have to sedate you."

Appalled, I watched as the older man shrank away, twisting against their grips. He was clearly terrified, but the attendants held fast rather than trying to calm him down.

"Brigit! Please—don't hate me! Don't hate me!" And then the doctor injected something into Brent's arm and he went slack in their arms. As they led him away, Ziegler turned back to us.

"That's the most lucid I've seen him in months," he said.

"Was that little display necessary?" Murray said, and I could tell she was as revolted by their strong-armed tactics as I was.

Dr. Ziegler sighed. "Ladies, have you forgotten that you're in an institution for seriously dysfunctional people? Brent could have hurt himself if we'd let him go. What else are we supposed to do? Soft words and a gentle hand don't always do the trick."

Without another word, Murray and I rose to our feet and left. As we reached the parking lot, I looked back at the building. I couldn't get the image of the frightened old man fighting against the attendants out of my mind. I leaned against the side of Murray's truck, swallowing the lump that was rising in my throat as I wondered if I was going to vomit.

"Em, Em? Are you okay?" Murray draped an arm around my shoulder.

"I just . . . that is not a good place for me to be."

"Take a deep breath, come on, that's right—and another. Good." Her voice soothed my frazzled nerves and after a moment, I shook my head to clear my thoughts.

"What do you think?" I asked. "Brent was begging for Brigit's forgiveness. Do you think he killed her?"

Murray frowned. "Em, I know it seems like a good lead, but remember—Brent is over the edge. He's lived in his own little world for half a century, and who knows what he's dreamed up in there? For all we know, he's confusing Brigit with a childhood pet or something. I wasn't sure what I expected to get when I came here, but it's obvious he's not playing with a full deck."

I sighed. What she said made a lot of sense. How could we trust him? And yet, he painted castles and trees and calico cats, and he knew Brigit's name, and he desperately wanted her forgiveness. For a crime committed? Or simply because he was a confused old man?

"So where do we go from here?"

Murray hopped in the truck and started her up. "I think I'll check on Brigit O'Reilly. See if I can find a record of her leaving the city."

I climbed in and fastened my seat belt. "Good idea. I've got to make dinner—Joe's coming for an hour or so. I hope they don't make him work the next couple nights. I want him home for my birthday."

She gave me a quiet smile. "Home? So Joe is home when he's at your house?"

I couldn't help but grin at her. "Yeah, I guess he is." We headed back to Chiqetaw in better spirits, but my thoughts kept drifting back to Brent. Just what had he done, that he needed forgiveness?

AS I WHIPPED together a quick meatloaf, the phone rang. It was Margaret, Joe's aunt. "Hey Maggie," I said. "Want to join us for dinner tonight?"

Her cheerful voice rang out over the line. "No, my dear, I can't make dinner, but perhaps I'll drop by this evening if you don't mind."

"I'd like that."

Margaret Files was a delightfully spry and surprisingly sharp old gal. She was also Joe's only family in town; his brother lived back east, his father had long disappeared, and his mother lived in California with her latest boyfriend.

I finished dinner just in time to hear the kids slam through the door. They rushed in, asking about Samantha, and I had to tell them that no—she wasn't home yet. De-

jected, they trudged upstairs to wash up for dinner. Kip
looked so forlorn that my heart felt like it was cracking in
pieces. So many sorrows, so much pain in the world.
Randa set the table while Kip went out back to call for
Sammy with a can of cat food. In the midst of all our bus-
tle, Joe popped in and I wrapped my arms around him.

"Mmm, I need this," I said. "It's been a long day,
Files." I filled him in on what we'd found out and showed
him the paper. "I don't know if this will help, but now
Irena can't use the excuse of not being able to get her
brother to agree."

"I suppose," he said, setting the paper on the desk and
pulling me into a long, leisurely kiss, his tongue probing
my mouth, questioning. "I wish I could stay the night," he
whispered. "I want to make love to you, to kiss your neck,
your breasts, your thighs. I want to wrap you in my arms
and slide inside you."

I caught my breath, flushing as desire grew like a flame
from a lightning strike. Just then, Randa called from the
kitchen and I gently disengaged myself.

"Duty calls," I said, wistfully.

He slapped me on the butt. "Then make me some dinner, woman. We'll find the time to satisfy our other
hunger later."

I sliced the meatloaf and arranged it on the platter
while Randa finished heating a jar of gravy in the mi-
crowave. Baked potatoes and diced beets finished the
meal, along with the promise of a chocolate cream pie that
I'd bought on the way home.

We ate in silence, Kip staring at the door every few
minutes. I was worried. If we didn't find Sammy soon, I
had the feeling I'd have more than one breakdown on my
hands. While Joe served the pie, I made a pot of mint tea
and carefully placed the chintz pot on the table, along with

the honey. Randa poured while I fed the cats. I didn't have the heart to ask Kip to attend to the task. He was taking Sammy's absence hard, as was I, but he didn't have the resources or experience to cope with it. Randa also seemed withdrawn.

I took her hand when she offered me a cup of tea. "Randa, honey, is anything wrong?"

She bit her lip, then hung her head. "I got a B today."

"B? In what?"

Blushing, she said, "Math."

Math? My genius girl had gotten a B in mathematics, one of her best subjects? I frowned. "Well, honey, that's a good grade, but I'm kind of surprised. You usually manage an A. Did something happen that you want to talk about?"

With a quick shake of the head, she dove into her pie. "No," she said, mumbling through a mouthful of whipped cream and chocolate custard. "I screwed up, okay?"

I dropped the subject, not wanting to embarrass her in front of her brother and Joe. It wasn't the end of the world, by any means, but a radical departure from the usual, and it raised warning flags in my head. I filed it away for later and turned to Joe.

"Your aunt is coming to visit tonight. Will you be able to stay?"

He shook his head and wiped his mouth on his napkin. "I wish I could, but I've got to get back to the station. And I may have to work tomorrow night, but I'll definitely have your birthday off, so chin up, sweetie." He shook the crumbs off his shirt and leaned down to give me a kiss. "Gotta run. Say hi and love to Aunt Margaret for me."

"I will," I said, watching as he slipped into his jacket and headed out the backdoor after a quick good-bye to Kip and Randa. Somehow, my birthday seemed to be dropping further and further into a fugue of its own. I wondered if I should bother celebrating at all. With Sammy missing, and a possible murder next door that may have been committed by a man who had lost his grip on reality . . . with ghosts and Will o' the Wisps hanging about, and the spirit of a woman who seemed caught forever in a freeze-frame of time. . . . Perhaps I should stick to honoring my ancestors the way Nanna had taught me and forget about a celebration.

Outside the wind kicked up a fuss and a tree limb went crashing into the backyard, narrowly missing the shed. Oh yeah, this was shaping up to be a Halloween I wouldn't forget.

Eleven

⁘

From Brigit's Journal:

I went to book passage home. I stood in the rain for an hour before the agency opened, and then, when I was almost ready to hand over my money, I couldn't do it. Not yet. Not while there's still a chance. Hope is such a bitter, cruel dream. I looked out of my tower and fell in love. But if I approach the castle . . . will I find there's a place waiting for me within?

Some secrets can be kept only so long before they become public knowledge. I can't wait any longer for him to make a decision. My cousin is right. I'm a dreamer, a silly girl whose head is filled with old sonnets and poems. Tomorrow, I'll book my trip, and I'll go home to Mary Kathryn and make a new life. There's nothing else for me to do.

WHILE I WAS waiting for Joe's aunt, Randa handed me her notebook. "Would you read this, Mom? We have to write a poem for English class and I tried, but . . ." She shrugged. My daughter was more fixated on the stars than on verbs, for all of her new obsession with writing poetry. An obsession which I fully believed to be Gunner's influence.

I took the notebook. "How's Gunner, by the way?" I asked casually. "You haven't mentioned him in a day or so."

"He'll be back in school next week, the teacher says. His parents are still critical, and he's staying with his aunt until they know what's going to happen. He's pretty shell-shocked."

"I would think so," I murmured. I opened the notebook to the page she indicated and began to read.

> *Once upon a golden morn,*
> *A lady fair of face was born.*
> *In a tower she did stay,*
> *Telling fortunes all the day.*
> *Until a knight came riding by,*
> *And a tear fell from her eye.*
> *Her heart it broke in two that day,*
> *She loved him dear from far away.*
> *But in her tower she did stay,*
> *Until she faded quite away.*

I glanced up at Randa. As far as I knew she'd never read Tennyson, but then again, perhaps I'd read him to her as a baby—I'd read everything and anything to my kids when they were little that I figured wouldn't terrify them. I wondered if anything in Brigit's journal had influenced her.

"Honey, have you ever heard of a poem called *The Lady of Shalott*?"

She scrunched her face up, thinking. "Nope, don't think so."

"How about a poet named Tennyson?"

Again the concentrated frown and a shake of the head. "Why?"

I sighed. Too many parallels, too many connections for comfort. I felt like we were swimming in a vast pool of oddities that just kept pouring in, and I knew they were all related but couldn't see the stone for the ripples.

"Nothing," I said. "It's very good, sweetie. What made you think of it?"

She shifted from one foot to another. "I've been having weird dreams about a woman locked in a tower who is dying of a broken heart. Do you think it has anything to do with the skeleton in the tree? That's kind of like a tower and it was a lady who died there, right?"

Bingo. She'd put her finger on it, but I didn't want to scare her. If I could put a logical spin on it, she might accept it for what it was, at face value, without worrying too much.

"Hey, it probably does but not for the reasons you might be thinking. Look at the facts—your friend Gunner's parents are seriously burned in a fire. Not only do we have an infestation of nasty faeries next door, but we also find a skeleton hidden in a tree over there. Toss in with that the fact that Sammy's missing, and that at school, you're in a much harder class than last year . . . honey, that adds up to a lot of stress. I'm not surprised you're having nightmares and writing poetry like this. Your mind just puts everything in a jar, shakes it all up, and out come the dreams."

She chewed on this for a bit then nodded. "Yeah, that makes sense. Okay, I'm going to check the sky to see if it's clear enough to stargaze for awhile. Maybe while I'm up there, I'll see Sammy."

"Bundle up before you go out on the roof," I called as

she headed for the stairs. She tossed me a quick wave as I glanced around the living room. The place was cluttered, but not dirty, and I began tidying up, trying to distract myself. I was actually glad that I'd be back in the shop come Monday—I was sick of shadows and half-veiled glimpses of the Otherworld.

Usually, the supernatural came in with a bang and I was able to resolve the issue without too much stumbling around, but this time was different. As I'd told Randa, with skeletons and a haunted lot next door, and the Will o' the Wisps, and odd dreams, and questions about a possible murder from the past, no wonder I felt disoriented.

Actually, though, when I thought about it, it made perfect sense that Brigit was wandering the earth again. Not only had we disturbed her resting place, but the energies of the season were beginning to turn. Halloween night lifted the veil between the worlds for a brief time, and spirits walked the earth, looking to communicate with those they had left behind. Especially those souls who had died unexpected or violent deaths. Most people went through their days never realizing how many ghosts brushed by them, sharing their space. The traffic increased at this time of year, and those who were psychic, who could "sense" things, often felt discombobulated.

As I plumped the sofa pillows and straightened magazines, Kip came trudging down the stairs. He settled himself on the floor, crossed his legs and stared at me, his eyes full of hurt. I knew what he was thinking and I sat down beside him, taking his hands.

"We'll find her, kiddo. She's out there, I can sense it. I just can't seem to pinpoint where she is. But Samantha is alive." I stared into his eyes, willing him to believe me.

He swallowed. "I know you're right, but I still . . ." A

brief pause and I suddenly understood what the problem was.

"You're scared I'm wrong, but you don't want to make me mad or hurt my feelings by saying so?" The flicker in his eyes told me I had nailed it. "It's okay, kiddo, you can go ahead and say it. It's okay."

With a sniffle, he wiped his nose. "I thought you might get upset 'cause it sounds like I don't believe you."

I slipped my arm around his shoulders and squeezed. "You know, I always want you to be able to tell me what you're thinking. I know it's hard to believe she's still alive when we don't know where she is, and I know how scared you are. I'm scared, too. But, kiddo, we have to keep our hopes up. I really do believe she's out there, you know. I don't know why she can't make it home right now, but there's something blocking her way."

He leaned his head against my arm. "Okay, but I wish whatever it was would go away and leave her alone."

"Me, too, hon. Me, too." The phone rang and, with a quick kiss on his head, I jumped up to answer it. Surprise of surprises, it was White Deer.

"Boy am I glad to hear your voice," I said. "Has Murray told you what's been going on?"

"Yes, she did. Interesting," White Deer said, and I could tell she was being her usual reticent self.

"I hate to ask this, but is there any way you could help with Samantha? We're worried sick about her." I could hear the edge of exhaustion in my voice and realized that I was starting to run on fumes. The past few days had been a blur of energy and chaos, and all the mayhem was draining my reserves.

She was silent for a moment, then said, "What about if I come over later tonight? We'll talk then."

"Thank you—thank you. I've been so frazzled lately,"

I said. "There's just been so much going on here. What with ghosts and faerie lights and now this skeleton business, I feel like I'm being slammed around in a tidal wave of energy."

"I can be there around eleven. If that's not too late for you, I'll drop over then. Meanwhile, you look around and see if you can find any fur you might have from Samantha—stray hairs in a brush."

"Will do," I said, not even asking why. I trusted White Deer implicitly. "Eleven's fine, I'm not sleeping that well anyway."

"Okay. I'll see you then. And Emerald," she paused. "Samantha will come home, but I sense there's a long bridge that she has to navigate first. I think . . ." She paused and I could feel her tuning into something that I couldn't quite touch. "I don't know how to explain this but there was some sort of crossover. I'm not sure of what I mean by that, but it's as if something came through and exchanged places with her. Whatever that is, it has to return to the spirit world before Sammy can come home."

I hung up, thinking about what White Deer had said. Something had taken Samantha's place in this world, something from the spirit world. Brigit's ghost cat—that had to be what she was sensing! Somehow, the cats had managed to trade places, but the ghost cat had retained its ghostly status in our world, while Samantha was still alive and trapped in the spirit world. We had to forge a link that would allow them to each return to their respective homes. But would it work?

I glanced at the clock—half an hour until Margaret arrived. Long enough for a little research. Taking the stairs two at a time, I raced to my room and pulled out Nanna's trunk. My grandmother had taught me, from the time I was little, how to work the charms and spells she learned from her grandmother. When she died she'd left me her special trunk. Hand-carved from ironwood, it was filled with her charms and the core of her folk wisdom.

In the bottom of the trunk, within a secret compartment, rested the five-hundred-year-old *seax* dagger that had become my own. I seldom used it but every month under the full moon, I gently polished the blade, then smudged it with white sage, an herb whose smoke purified and sanctified everything that it touched. The dagger had served me well during the few times I'd had call to bring it out, even to the point of getting rid of astral nasties on occasion.

However, the real treasure in the trunk—the one I'd taken care to preserve and would one day pass down to one of my children—was Nanna's journal. The leather-bound pages were filled with handwritten charms, some in her native German, some in English. A compendium of knowledge she'd learned from her grandmother.

I could make out some of the German words, and was planning to take a class in German so I could read her entries and notes as well. In fact, I thought, I should do that this winter. I jotted a reminder to myself on the notepad sitting on my nightstand.

Sifting through the pages, I looked for anything that might be useful in our situation. I had just hit a page with a charm on it designed to call lost loves home when I felt a presence near me. I glanced up and there was Nanna, sitting on the bed.

"Nanna!" I dropped the book and turned to her, overjoyed. My grandmother had become a regular visitor since she died. In fact I saw more of her now than I had in the years right before her death when my ex, Roy, refused to visit my family. She offered comfort, and now and then helped me out of a mess that I couldn't handle on my own.

Now, she sat there bold as life, holding Samantha in her ghostly arms.

I reached out for Sammy, but my hands passed through the vision and my heart quivered. Could I be wrong? Was Sammy dead? But then the cat looked at me and I heard, rather than felt, her mournful meow. That was no spirit, but the wail of one very lost kitten who wanted to come home.

Nanna pointed toward the journal. I glanced at it. "Are you telling me the answer to bringing Sammy home is in the book?"

She tapped the page with the love charm on it.

"I'm supposed to cast this? That will bring her home?" I thought about it. Samantha was a lost little love. It made sense. Nanna nodded and smiled, then blew me a kiss and faded out of sight, taking Samantha with her. I watched her disappear, and only then did I realize I was crying.

I picked up the journal and headed downstairs as the doorbell rang. It was Aunt Margaret. Margaret Files was a spry woman in her early seventies who had been a county clerk before she'd retired. She liked romance novels, played a mean game of pinochle—and I do mean *mean*—and was staunchly in Joe's corner on his choice of girl-friends. Not once had she mentioned our age difference, and not once had she expressed anything but support for our relationship.

I invited her in. "Would you like tea? I think we have some leftover cake in the fridge."

Margaret dropped her purse on the coffee table and slipped out of her jacket, draping it over the back of the rocking chair. "Tea would be lovely, dear, but I'll skip the cake, if you don't mind. I overdid it at dinner tonight."

"Where did you go?" I asked, heading for the kitchen.

"To the FED," she said, following me. The FED was

short for Forest's End Diner, one of the more upscale bistros in Chiqetaw. "Lanny took me there and we had a wonderful dinner—steak and lobster."

I grinned at her as I put the kettle on to boil. "You guys are getting awfully chummy, aren't you?" She'd been seeing Lanford Willis, a retired physician, for the past couple of months. Joe and I suspected that they were more than friends.

Margaret blinked, then gave me a cagey smile. "Well, my dear, you know as well as I do that age has nothing to do with desire."

With a laugh, I arranged cups and saucers on a tray and picked out my prettiest pumpkin teapot and filled it with Spicy Autumn tea bags. "Oh, I know. I've just noticed you two have been seeing quite a bit of each other." I sat down at the table across from her while we waited for the water to heat. "You like him, don't you?"

She giggled. "Yes, I like him. And he seems to fancy me. We get along. It's comforting to have a companion at this age."

I reached over and took her hand, squeezing it. "I think it's comforting at any age to have a companion. So, are you two planning on getting engaged?" I might as well have asked her if she was going to start smoking crack for the look she gave me.

"Engaged? No, and don't you go spreading rumors like that to Joe. I've never been married and I don't plan on it now. Years ago, when I was just graduating from high school, I told my father that if he expected me to be a wife and mother, he could just kick me out of the family right then." She snorted. "I never had the desire to have children of my own, but I have loved playing Auntie to my nephews and nieces. I seem to do a fine job of it."

I poured the steaming water into the teapot. "So you don't ever want to get married?"

She laughed again. "My dear, I've lived seventy-three years in peace and comfort without a man around the house cluttering up things and telling me not to buy the spicy sausage or the German chocolate cake. I do things the way I want to do them and have no intention of breaking the habit now. Why, I couldn't do half the things I like to do if somebody else lived with me. But I do enjoy going out to dinner and to the theater." Her cheeks flushed and she gave me a naughty smile. "And a little hanky-panky is always good for the soul." With a satisfied sigh, she leaned back in her chair. "Perhaps I will take some of that cake."

I peeked in the cupboard for the cake tray. There was just enough chocolate cake left over for two so I divided it onto dessert plates and handed her one, keeping the other for myself. As I settled back in my seat, she poured the tea and we ate in silence, munching away and sipping at the fragrant and spicy blend. After a moment, I sighed and pushed back my plate.

"Margaret, you were here in Chiqetaw fifty years back, weren't you?"

She blinked. "Actually, yes. I moved here when I was nineteen. I was hired to work as the county clerk right after graduating from Bellingham High, and against my parents' wishes, moved to Chiqetaw, rented my first apartment, and settled into the working girl's life."

"That must have been unusual for the time," I said.

"Oh, it was scandalous. But my father was busy with his own life and finally accepted my choice after one nasty argument. My mother died the year before I left, you know, and he didn't want to lose me too. Shortly after I moved, Father remarried to a very nice woman and started a new family. I have two half-brothers. The oldest, Dexter, is Joe's father. He came along a year after I moved to Chiqetaw, and he's twenty years younger than me. Well, he played the good son, stayed in Bellingham and got married, until something snapped."

I knew Joe's father wasn't around, but I had never pried. "What happened? Why did Dexter leave town?"

"Dex wasn't good at handling responsibility. He's a compulsive gambler and Terri, Joe's mother, kicked him out when he lost their life savings. He took off for Vegas and Joe and Nathan grew up without their daddy. They saw him on holidays but seldom more than that. Terri tried, but she always resented raising the boys alone. She drank a little too much, brought home too many strange men. When both boys were both in college, she moved to California and opened a little wine shop. I think Joe talks to Dex a couple times a year, but he's never forgiven his father for putting his addiction ahead of his family."

So that's what had happened, and that's why Joe sternly refused to even think about visiting a casino. I filed away the information and returned to the subject at hand. "Well, the reason I wanted to know if you lived in Chiqetaw at that time is this: Do you remember a house on the lot next to mine? The lot Joe's trying to buy?"

Margaret leaned forward, propping her elbows on the table and resting her chin on her hands. After a moment, she snapped her fingers. "Yes, I remember that house. In fact, I knew someone who lived there."

"Irena Brunswick, perhaps?"

"No," she said, shaking her head. "I didn't rub elbows with Irena—she was high society and I was a working girl. No, my friend was Brigit O'Reilly, the Brunswick's maid."

I sucked in a deep breath. So my thoughts that Brigit

might have been a servant were right on track. She hadn't been a distant relative. No wonder her bedroom had been in the basement. "What was she like? Where is she now?"

Margaret looked at me closely. "You have a reason for wanting to know this, don't you?"

I nodded. "I'd rather not tell you why yet, but yes—it's important."

She inhaled slowly and let it out in a thin stream. "Brigit O'Reilly. I haven't thought about her in years. She was a lovely girl. Close to my own age, you know, although I can't remember just how old she was when we met. She was tall, at least five-ten, and willow-thin, like a reed. I remember being so envious of her hair, it coiled down her back, long and curling and thick, a deep russet red. But I think the thing I remember most about her was just how fragile she was."

"Fragile?"

"Emotionally. Like a flower. If you even breathed on her, you thought she might blow away in the wind. She seemed to have so much sorrow in her young life—her parents were dead and she'd lost a fiancé at a young age. She never talked much about her personal feelings, though."

That would fit with the poems she wrote. "What was she like?"

Margaret closed her eyes and I knew she was reaching back in memory. "Brigit was the sunshine of a spring morning. She always had a kind word for everyone, no matter how awful they were to her. Back then, folks around here didn't treat servants with much civility, you know. And she was incredibly passionate. If she believed in a cause, she'd fight tooth and nail for it. She came over from Ireland, hoping to earn enough to go to school and become a teacher, but something happened and she ended up hiring on as a housekeeper. In the time I knew her, she withdrew and grew despondent."

"What happened? Did she stay in Chiqetaw?" I held my breath, but Margaret could shed no light on the situation.

She shrugged. "I think she went back to Ireland. She told me that she was leaving town. 'Maggie,' she said, 'I'm going home. I mean it this time.' She always called me Maggie."

Maggie . . . Margaret must be the Maggie mentioned in Brigit's journal. "Go on, please," I said, feeling like the young woman's spirit was suddenly taking on a life and substance I had only been able to imagine before.

"By the way she talked, I assumed she meant it. I think she had a cousin over there, though from the hard times that had befallen her family, I couldn't understand why she'd want to go back. But people miss their homes, unhappy memories and all. The last time I saw her, she kept saying that things would never work out and that she didn't know what she was going to do. I wasn't sure what she was talking about. She was a tightlipped thing."

"Thanks," I said, mulling over this information. If Brigit *had* left for Ireland, how would we find out? "One last question. Did she have a cat?"

Margaret laughed. "How funny you should ask! Oh my dear, her cat was almost the spitting image of your Samantha. I remember she named the little thing Mab, after the legendary faerie queen. Brigit loved reading poetry and mythology. Speaking of cats, did you find your wayward girl yet?"

I shook my head, thinking about Brigit and her faerie sprite of a cat. Another part of the puzzle clicked into place. "Thank you," I said. "I appreciate the information."

After a moment, a thought struck me. "Did she leave before or after Brent was put away?"

"Brent? Oh, Brent Brunswick. You mean before he went overseas? That was big news back then, I'll tell you that. I think, if I remember right, Brigit left about a month or so before he took off."

Another interesting tidbit. I tucked it all away for later and segued onto another subject, sipping tea until nine o'clock, at which point Margaret kissed me on the cheek and left for home.

WHITE DEER LOOKED a little thinner since two months ago when I'd seen her at Murray's annual family fish fry over on the reservation, but her eyes were still that same deep brown that held me spellbound, and she had a look of peace about her that felt both ominous and restful to me. I gave her a big hug. She returned the embrace with a warm smile.

"Emerald, it's good to see you again. Anna told me all about your problems. Sounds as though you've stumbled onto a real mystery."

I offered her a chair. She sat on the sofa.

"The problem is, we're not at all sure what's going on. Whether the skeleton is someone who was killed or who died naturally. I think I know who it is, but can't be sure until tests are run."

"Well, I can put that question to rest—the one about how she died." White Deer unzipped her boots and set them aside, crossing her legs on the sofa. "Anna asked me to tell you that they've determined that the skeleton is a woman who was probably in her early twenties and she didn't die of natural causes. The skull was fractured

across the front of the forehead. The cat's skeleton, however, doesn't look like it suffered any trauma at all."

So the woman had been murdered, but the cat had died
naturally? "How odd. Are they treating this as a homicide?"

White Deer pulled out a notebook. "Anna jotted down
a few things for me to tell you and said for you to call her
tomorrow." She consulted the page of notes. "For all intents and purposes, yes, they think this was a homicide,
and they're placing the death at some fifty years ago,
based on the style of the dress and the condition of the
bones. The dress matches the size of those found in the
basement room, and so they're checking into Brigit
O'Reilly's history to see if there's a record of her leaving
town."

"I'll have to call Murray and tell her what Margaret
told me about that subject. Might give her a heads-up on
the time period in which to check." I sighed, then
launched into what had happened with Nanna's spirit that
afternoon. "So she seems to think this love spell will bring
Samantha home to me." I retrieved Nanna's journal and
flipped it open to the page, then handed it to White Deer.

She read and re-read it. "Oh, this is a simple one. We
can easily pull this together. Let's see, what do we need?"

I glanced through the spell. "Amber, some crystals,
rose petals, and honey. A picture of Samantha or something that belonged to her. I've got a picture on the desk
over there—we were using it for the fliers that we posted
around the neighborhood. And I think that using the fur
you wanted me to find from Sammy would be a good idea
too—a bond to call her home."

White Deer laughed. "I knew that I brought these along
for a reason!" She opened her backpack and withdrew a
small bundle, wrapped in soft felt. As she pulled open the

flaps of material, I gasped. Six beautiful carved-and-polished quartz spikes rested within, each a good five to six inches long.

"Oh man, those are gorgeous. I have an amber necklace—that should work for the amber. I'll go get it." I ran upstairs to fetch the necklace out of my jewelry box, then handed it to White Deer when I returned and headed for the pantry where I kept my stash of herbs. Rose petals, peppermint, and a brown bear bottle filled with honey. On the way out of the pantry, I snagged the cat brush. There had to be Sammy fur in there—the kids hadn't cleaned it for a couple of weeks by the amount of fuzz poking through the bristles.

White Deer was holding the necklace up to the light when I returned. "Nice—very nice. Beautiful inclusions." She tilted it under the lamp to look at the bee that had been encased within the thick mass of hardened resin. The oval cabochon was honey colored and rich, almost as big as an egg.

I set everything on the table. "Okay, what do we do next?" At that moment, Kip and Randa appeared at the bottom of the stairs.

"What are you two doing up?" I asked. "It's past your bedtimes, both of you."

"I heard voices down here," Kip said. "I knew it was White Deer!" He ran over and threw his arms around her. "Heya!"

"Kip woke me up," Randa said, close on his heels. She gave White Deer a peck on the cheek. "I wish you lived in Chiqetaw. We never get to see you enough."

As much as they loved Mur, they loved her aunt even more. White Deer had a way with kids. She listened to them, really listened, and made them feel that what they had to say was important. As their mother, I'd never be able to pull that one off—they wouldn't let me get away with it.

She kissed them both and motioned them to the ends of the coffee table. "Sit, you can help us. That is, if your mother doesn't object."

I glanced at her and saw that she really wanted them to join in.

"Okay," I said. "But as soon as we're done, it's off to bed again. No whining about it, either."

"What are we doin'? Magic?" Kip's eyes lit up. He loved working Nanna's charms with me, but I had to be cautious about what I allowed him to do. Kip had the predilection for going off half-cocked; more than once he'd gotten himself in deep trouble. I finally had to accept that he wasn't ready for the responsibility yet. Until he was older, I had decided to just try to help him understand his psychic abilities, so he wouldn't grow up afraid of them.

"We're putting out a call for Samantha. Your mother is positive she's alive and so am I. So we're trying to guide her home through magic," she said, arranging the crystals in a hexagonal pattern over the picture of Samantha. "We'll send out a psychic S.O.S. signal and hope that she's able to follow it."

She draped the amber necklace around the picture and crystals and scattered the rose petals and peppermint over the top. Then she opened her pouch of herbs and withdrew something I immediately recognized as catnip. Within moments, Nigel, Noël, and Nebula came racing into the room, meowing.

"I think the catnip will work better than honey, considering we're trying to lead a cat home rather than a person. Don't you?" White Deer said. I nodded. She laughed as one of the kittens scrambled up in her lap and batted at the pouch. "You want to help, too, don't you? You must be missing your mama something fierce." White Deer sprinkled the catnip around the coffee table's legs and the kittens went wild, squirming on the floor, playing and wrestling.

"What do we do?" Randa said. Usually she was reticent about magic, but this was Sammy we were talking about. Randa would walk through hell and high water to get her back. She'd already proven that by going down into the foundation of the old Brunswick house.

White Deer gave me a glowing smile. "I sense she's trapped somewhere—not in a house or garage, but somewhere between the worlds. Something crossed over and took her place, bouncing Samantha into the spirit world even though she's still alive."

"I was thinking about that," I said. "Brigit had a cat named Mab. Joe's aunt said that Mab and Samantha look so much alike that it's hard to tell them apart, which would account for the sightings the kids and I've had. Somehow the two exchanged places."

"Is Mab the spirit of the skeleton cat?" Randa cocked her head, looking at the picture of Sammy.

"I think so," I said. "But I can't prove it."

"So if we can get Mab to go back where she belongs, Sammy will come back to us?" Kip asked.

White Deer nodded. "That's the theory. I can't promise it will work, but I think that it's worth a try."

I glanced at her, grateful that she'd added a caveat. Magic and charms were powerful forces, but there were no guarantees in life—with anything, be it mundane or mystical. I cleared my throat and White Deer gave me a look that told me she knew exactly what I was thinking.

"Trust me," she said with a slow smile, and I had the feeling she was talking more to me than to the kids. "Are we ready then? Let's join hands and focus on Samantha. I want you to follow my lead. When I start calling her, you join in by chanting her name, softly, over and over."

And then, in a hypnotic and resonant voice, White Deer began chanting, and we joined in. We were calling Samantha home.

Twelve

❖

From Brigit's Journal:

Sometimes, I think that image means everything to this family. Substance, real heart, matters very little. I bought my ticket today. Tonight, I break the news. I still have hope I won't have to use it, but as my hope fades, so does my fear. It's time I stopped being afraid. There's no choice but to move forward. I'm not sure I care what happens now. I'm lying, of course, but sometimes, we have to convince ourselves we really believe we're doing the right thing. Sometimes, it's the only way we make it through difficult times.

WHITE DEER AND I headed next door after I made sure the kids knew where I'd be and were tucked back into bed. The rain pelted down, sparking in the illumination of the streetlights as it hit the sidewalk. I huddled in my coat, wondering if things would ever get back to normal.

White Deer picked up on my mood. "Emerald, this will

pass. It always does, and you always come out stronger than before."

"I know," I said, "but this time, something feels different. The spirits here are old and rooted deep. And even if Joe manages to buy this lot, what are we going to do? Unless we can put Brigit to rest, she'll haunt us for the rest of our lives. Not to mention the Will o' the Wisps. They're like a nest of hornets. I'm really worried, White Deer. About the kids, about Samantha. Even about whether or not I'll be able to keep my home. Those things are dangerous!"

White Deer laughed, a throaty, dusky laugh. Her long hair was more salt than pepper and hung down her back in a single, thick braid. She reminded me of a lynx, secretive and observant and mysteriously lovely.

"Good God, Emerald, when are you going to accept that you're a magnet for this sort of thing? It's not going to stop, you know. No matter where you go, you're bound to attract the fringe elements of the world. So you might as well dive in and test the waters. The more you resist, the harder the lessons get."

I frowned at her, a little irritated by her flippancy. "What about the kids? What about the ghosts playing loose in my house? What about my cat who has apparently transported over to a different . . . whatever you want to call it. Dimension? Reality? Walked through the veils?"

White Deer reached out and caught my arm, yanking me toward her. "Stop whining! Life isn't safe. You have to learn that the hard way. It's up to you to make it as secure as you can without getting paranoid."

She paused, then shook her head. "Your children are smart, and most important, they listen to you. So yes, you have ghosts running amok in your yard that scare the hell out of you. You've met a legendary beast face-to-face. But you've handled it all, haven't you? And Samantha . . ." With a sigh, she held up her hands. "Samantha got caught in the hands of fate. She's alive, though. You know it, and I know it. We've had this discussion before. When are you going to start trusting your intuition? When are you going to start believing in what your gut is telling you?"

I froze, trying to force a protest out, trying to counter what she was saying, but she was right. I was too afraid of being wrong to trust that I was right. I was afraid of hurting my children by following my instincts. And most of all, I was mourning the lack of normalcy that everyone else seemed to have.

"All my life I'd lived with one foot in the mortal realm and one foot in the spiritual realm," I said. "Most of the time I love it, but I'll never be able to go through life without always knowing there's more out there than meets the eye. Without always being able to sense things other people can't. Without always being pegged as crazy, or besieged for help by everybody who thinks I can solve their problems. Sometimes the Sight isn't a gift. Sometimes it's a curse."

White Deer stared me down. "Do you really believe you're the only one in the world with problems? Get a grip. Most people in this world are focused on just surviving until tomorrow. And look at you! You've found love, you have wonderful children, you own a comfortable house, and your business is going great. You honestly think that half the population on this planet wouldn't jump to change places with you, ghosts and all?"

I hung my head, letting the rain pound down around my shoulders. My hair was stringy and wet, and I was numb from the cold, but that didn't seem to matter. "That doesn't invalidate my feelings or my fear."

She backed off, smiling quietly. "No, Emerald, it doesn't. But you need to put things in perspective. You're starting to scare yourself and that won't help. You have the ability to handle whatever it is that's happening here. You just don't know how yet."

I inhaled deeply, then let my breath out in a thin stream. She was right, as much as I hated to admit it. Once again, I'd let fear get the best of me. "Nanna used to say that there's always a solution. Sometimes you just have to redefine the problem."

"Your Nanna was a wise woman. I wish I could have met her."

"Stick around long enough and you might." I gave her a wry grin.

White Deer held my gaze fast. "Emerald, I love you almost as much as I love Anna, and sometimes you seem just as much my niece as she is. Ever since you became friends all those years ago, I've felt a kinship with you. You are her sister, you know. Not by blood, but by spirit. And therefore, you're my kin."

I suddenly felt ashamed of my outburst. Here I was, getting advice and comfort from the strongest woman I'd ever met, and I'd been fighting her every step of the way.

"I love you too, White Deer, and so do my kids. And you're right, I know you are. I'm just frustrated." We turned in at the driveway and I stared at the empty lot that spread out in front of us. Faint glimpses of the corpse candles flickered in and out, like lightbulbs ready to fail. They were at it again.

She wouldn't let me off the hook. "Why? What's bothering you?"

"So many things." I sighed. "Joe not being able to buy the lot the way he'd planned, and then all this crap going down—more ghosts and more unhappy souls. Who the hell put that girl in the tree? I mean, who would do something like that? And damn it—what about Joe? Will he get tired of all the woo-woo stuff and goblins that take up residence in my life? Hell, I'm going to be thirty-seven years old the day after tomorrow and I'm in love with a man ten years younger than me. Is he still going to love me when I'm approaching fifty?"

"So is that what's at the bottom of your fear?" White Deer asked.

I clapped my hand over my mouth. What had I just said? Could I really be that worried about the difference in age between Joe and me? I thought I was fine with it. Nobody else seemed to think it was a big deal, but suddenly I could sense the creeping tendrils of doubt. The worry that maybe, in a year, or five, or ten, he'd find someone else. Somebody not always prattling on about the psychic world or . . . did I dare even think it? Somebody . . . younger?

White Deer chuckled, her eyes merry. When I flashed a hurt look at her, she said, "Please don't be mad! I can't help but laugh. I'm just surprised to hear those words come out of your mouth. Are we all still sixteen under the surface, still so insecure and frightened?"

I plunked myself down on a rock that was jutting out of the ground near the fence leading to my yard, not caring that I was getting wet from the rain that puddled around me. "Maybe we are. I never thought of myself as insecure—at least not lately. I didn't even realize that I was worried about losing Joe. Maybe it's just my past. The breakup with Roy still haunts me. How could he do something like that to me? To Randa and Kip? Do we really ever know the people we fall in love with? Or, maybe I really do sense there's something to worry about, and I just don't want to face it. What do you think?"

"You mean, do I think you're having a premonition about you and Joe breaking up?"

I nodded, afraid to speak.

White Deer pulled her hood farther over her eyes. The rain dripped off, forming thin streams that drizzled to the ground. "Emerald, do you want my honest opinion?"

Good question. She didn't lie, and she seldom gave advice. When she offered to voice her opinion, it would be the real McCoy. I inhaled and watched my breath go drifting off into the night, a thin stream of white mist that dissipated in the darkness. "Okay, let's hear it."

She patted my arm. "Joe's a good match for you. He'll remain true, as long as you don't play games with him. He's honorable, and he's madly in love with you. Don't be so quick to think the paranormal irritates him. He's more interested than you realize."

I glanced over at her. "Ya think?"

"I think," she said and I knew that was the end of the discussion. She'd said what she had to say and that was all I was going to get. It was enough.

"Okay then," I said, hoisting my butt off the rock. "I'll stop borrowing trouble. Do you want to see the lot?"

White Deer followed me, her hands jammed into the pockets of her white fleece jacket. We entered the lot. Even though the Will o' the Wisps were mere flickers, I could feel energy oozing around the lot, old fears and worries and tragedy. Almost as if the land were a black hole, sucking up joy and laughter.

White Deer seemed to have the same thought. She took a step closer to me and said, "This land needs cleansing. It's stagnant, like a pond that's covered with bracken. If you don't clear it out, you'll be courting trouble."

I showed her around, cautiously navigating the bricks

and tendrils and pieces of wood that littered the lot. "I thought you said not to worry?"

"Don't worry about Samantha or Joe—those issues will take care of themselves. This, on the other hand . . . isn't conducive to good health." I could see the emotions wage war on her face. "I still believe you can handle this, but the energy is a lot darker than I thought. Not evil, but old and tenacious. The very plants are rooted deep in misery."

I led her over to the yew. "Here's where I found the skeleton."

As she knelt by the base of the tree a gust swept through, forcing the rain sideways, stinging bullets against our skin. I winced, turning my back to the wind.

White Deer placed her hands on the roots and moaned softly. "Emerald, the spirit who was buried in this tree is still walking the world. She can't break free, she's entwined in this realm just like the roots were entwined around the skeleton." She abruptly pulled her hands away as a loud "pop" echoed through the air. "Damned tree shocked me!"

"Let me see." I flashed the light on her hands.

She winced. Her palms were singed, covered with a strange sooty substance. I lifted one to my nose and sniffed. The faint scent of ozone—yeah, she'd been zapped all right.

"I think that we'd better leave the tree alone," I said, a rush of adrenaline racing through my veins. This afternoon it became apparent to me that it's alive and sentient, and I'm not quite sure just how much it can react."

White Deer laughed. "Oh, it's not going to go marching across the lot, trust me on that one." She sobered. "But you're right, there are powerful forces here. I think that we'd better cleanse the lot as soon as possible."

"We?" I looked at her hopefully. "Does that mean you're offering to help me?" I could use all the help I could get, considering just how deeply the hauntings were embedded in the ground. They had anchored themselves, growing right along with the brambles and the roots of the tree, coiling out from both Brigit's bedroom and the shelter of the yew to encompass the whole lot.

White Deer sighed. "I think it's going to take more than just you or Anna to set this place to rest. Let's think about the situation for awhile. It would help if we can find out more about Brigit."

As we hurried out of the lot, I wasn't so sure that even with White Deer's help we'd be able to exorcise the energies here. They were stronger than we were. I just hoped we didn't end up making things worse.

AFTER A LONG talk with Joe on the phone, where he broke the news to me that he'd be away for one more night, I fell into an exhausted sleep. My dreams were a kaleidoscope of images—a red-haired woman crying, Samantha and Mab running side by side through a stark and barren landscape, Will o' the Wisps darting around the exterior of my house, seeking a way in. When the alarm went off, I felt like I'd been run over by a truck. I dragged myself out of bed, grumbling.

After making breakfast for the kids, I chased them off to school and brewed my mocha, chugging it. I needed my fix as fast as possible. Just as I drained the mug, the phone rang. Murray was on the line.

"White Deer told me about your talk last night. She's studying up on some possible ways to cleanse the lot."

"That's good," I said, squinting at my mug. The caffeine was barely touching the edges of my fog, eating away at the weariness that ran through my body. One hell of a way to be facing my birthday, all right—worn out and freaked because I'd found out I was living next door to spook-central. "So, have you found out anymore about the skeleton or Brigit?"

"Yeah," she said. "I found out that Brigit never left the States, and nobody knows where she went. She could have disappeared anywhere, but I'm leaning toward the thought that she stayed right here in Chiqetaw. Especially with what Nerissa discovered."

I perked up. "What? Did she find some way to identify the skeleton?"

Murray let out a low sigh. "I think we can be certain that we've found Brigit. I managed to track down Mary Kathryn O'Reilly, a cousin of hers who still lives in the village of Glengarriff."

"The Mary Kathryn in the journal?"

"One and the same. It seems that Brigit never returned to Ireland. They lost touch with her back in 1955. Brigit had faithfully written a letter to her cousin every two weeks since she moved to the States. Then, one day, they just stopped coming. In her last letter, she'd mentioned she was thinking about returning home, that she had one last thing to do and—if it didn't turn out as she hoped— she'd be booking passage on a boat. She added that she had a surprise to tell Mary—though not altogether a happy one. And then—silence. No more letters, no post-cards. Nothing."

I took a deep breath and let it out slowly. "Joe's aunt knew her, Mur. Brigit told Margaret that she was thinking of leaving town, and Margaret just assumed she'd left when she disappeared." I gave her a quick rundown on what Margaret had told me. "So, if she never left, never went home . . . then . . ."

"She died right here in Chiqetaw. There's more. In talking with Mary Kathryn, I asked if Brigit had any identifying characteristics that might show up on the skeleton or in her possessions. Mary remembered two—one physical and one a keepsake. It seems that Brigit was born with six toes on her left foot. The skeleton has six toes on the left foot. And Brigit owned her mother's wedding ring. According to her cousin, Brigit never took it off. She wore it on her right ring finger. The description matches the ring that was on the skeleton's finger."

I stared at the table, my muscles twitching. That cinched it. We'd found the mysterious Brigit. Poor girl, unmourned and forgotten for all these years. Except, perhaps, for the murderer. Had Brent been responsible for her death? Was there any way to find out?

"And you say her death was no accident?"

"She had a skull fracture on the front right temple. Though we can't be sure what caused the break, it seems to fit with a heavy blow from a blunt object." Murray sighed. "I hate this shit. It's hard enough to solve a murder that's recent, let alone one that took place fifty years ago. Whoever stuffed that girl's body in the tree didn't want her to be found. They just hid her out of sight like a bag of old rags. Bastards."

"So, what's our next step?"

"We interview Irena. Want to come? You can talk to her about Brent and the lot while we're there."

"Will that be okay?" I asked, knowing that Murray had already pushed the envelope by letting me tag along to see Brent.

"Yeah, don't sweat it. I can always think of something to tell Bonner if he bitches, but with this case being so old, he's not really paying much attention. Cold cases like this seldom ever find resolution. Luckily, the crime rate in town the past few weeks has been pretty sparse, so I've got some leeway."

We agreed that she'd swing by to pick me up around noon. I glanced at the clock. 9:00 A.M. Time enough to run a few errands before she got here. I pushed back my chair, grabbed my keys, and headed out the door.

A QUICK STOP at the shop reminded me just how much I missed being back at work. Monday was looking better and better, and I could hardly wait for things to get back to normal. I made sure Cinnamon and Lana had everything under control and then headed out to the animal shelter. Never ignore the practical, even when hoping the magical would work. The charm could bring Sammy home in a number of ways—the neighbors might spot her, or animal control might find her, or maybe she'd saunter home on her own.

Once again, my heart fell as I made my way back to the cats' room, where at least fifteen felines of varying ages waited behind bars, their expressions mixtures of desperation and hope, of fear and weariness. How I wanted to take them all home. But even if I had the space, by tomorrow, the cages would be full again. I hurriedly glanced through, but Samantha wasn't anywhere in sight. I forced myself out of the building as fast as I could, unable to handle the loneliness that emanated from the very building itself.

A quick stop at the grocery store took my mind off the shelter. Until I stocked up on cat food, that is. After depositing our brood's favorites in the cart, I stared at the shelves for a moment, then hoisted two twenty-pound bags of dry food on top of everything else. Before I headed home, I dropped in at the shelter and donated the food. Maybe I could only feed a few mouths, but at least I would know that the cats were getting a good meal.

Once I got home, I slipped out of my jeans and into a calf-length brown rayon skirt and a burgundy turtleneck sweater, then zipped up my tan suede boots. If things went right, maybe I could persuade Irena to sell Joe the lot now that she couldn't use Brent as an excuse anymore.

I finished putting away the last of the groceries when the doorbell rang. Mur was dressed, once again, in a fancier-than-usual suit, but she looked no-nonsense. She strode in, gave me an approving glance.

"Ready?" She glanced at her watch.

I nodded and gathered my purse and keys. As I slipped into her truck, I looked at her. "Do you think Irena had something to do with Brigit's death?"

Mur grimaced. "I have no idea. Whatever happened, it was a long time ago. Irena seems awfully cagey, but maybe she's just worried about word getting out that Brent's been stuck in an institution all these years. She's a schmoozer, runs in high society right up there with and above Harlow. Some of those folks take a dim view of oddball relatives. I think that was especially true back in the fifties when she first got married. On the other hand, maybe Brent did it and she knows and has been trying to protect him all these years."

Both thoughts made sense to me. And if she knew he'd killed Brigit, it might account for her trying to keep things undercover. Maybe she was protecting him but felt guilty about it. If people heard about him, they might ask why he was there and bring up unpleasant questions. We passed through the west side of Chiqetaw, where the lawyers and doctors congregated their practices, into one of the garden suburbs. Chiqetaw might be small, but it had its neighborhood districts. Or cliques, should I say.

Irena's house was buttressed up against the Chiqetaw Links Country Club & Golf Course. Harlow had been offered a membership, but she turned it down with a quick and icy "no." The club was known for its subtle racism and Harl refused to take part in any such discrimination. She'd made her displeasure known around town, but only a few of the members tried to strike back. Her philanthropy and substantial wealth buffeted her from criticism.

We slipped out of the truck and headed up the walk. Apparently Irena had her housekeeper waiting for us because she opened the door before we had the chance to ring the bell. Murray introduced us, and the maid led us into a long foyer, then off to the right into a formal living room. As she withdrew, closing the double doors behind her, I glanced around nervously. The furniture looked like it cost more than my entire house.

"Jeez, just don't spill anything," I said.

Mur grinned at me with a wry smile. "I don't drink on the job, luckily." She rubbed her foot on the white carpet. "Who in the hell buys white carpeting? It has to be a status symbol, especially in areas like this where we get so much rain. Rain equals mud, you know."

I was about to agree when the door opened and a woman who looked to be in her mid-sixties stepped through. Irena. She and Brent bore a resemblance to one another, but it was obvious that Irena had been under the knife a few times; since they were twins, therefore, she had to be seventy-one, the same as Brent. She had that taut, overstretched look that some stars get when they've had a little too much plastic surgery.

"Detective Murray, it's nice to meet you." She held out her hand, smiling, although her expression said she was anything but happy to see us. Murray introduced me. Irena peered at me for a moment, then said, "Oh yes, the fireman's girlfriend. You own the tea shop. You have a quaint and charming store, my dear."

I forced myself to bite my tongue. I'd dealt with her type before. Dazzlingly polite and aloof, she'd already negated any worth I might have, categorizing me as "Joe's girlfriend" which meant I wasn't worth bothering with.

Murray indicated the black leather sofa. "Shall we sit down? I have some questions I need to ask you."

Irena took a seat in the wingback, while Murray and I gingerly sat on the overstuffed leather couch. I felt dwarfed—the thing had been made for giants.

"I can't imagine how I can help you, but ask away." She fidgeted in her seat and I noticed her hands were in constant motion, twisting her handkerchief. My guess was that Irena wasn't the best poker player in town.

Murray sighed. "Why don't we start with your brother? All these years, you've told people he's been living overseas and yet, all this time he's been at the Fairhaven Psychiatric Hospital. Would you tell me why you've kept up this charade, and why Brent was committed?"

Irena winced. "Committed is such a harsh word, Detective. Brent was a danger to himself. Even as a child, he wasn't very stable, he was always so emotional and passionate about life. He was an artist, you know, but our father was only proud of him when Brent made the football team. Father thought it might snap Brent out of what he considered his 'sissy ways', but all it did was point out how different he was from the other boys. He spent a year at Yale, failed miserably, and had to come home."

Mur regarded her quietly. "How old was he, and what happened when he returned?" She was jotting notes as quickly as Irena gave them to her.

"Brent was nineteen when he came back. He stayed home for a year, trying to regroup. Father insisted he give it another shot—he'd pulled some strings, gotten Brent back into school on conditional acceptance. Before he was supposed to leave, something just snapped. He collapsed into his own little world. The doctor recommended shock treatment. That was routine back then, and so our parents signed the papers and committed him to Fairhaven."

Up until then, she'd been telling the truth. I could hear it in her voice, see it in her aura. But she'd glossed over something with the last—left something unsaid. Not a lie, really, but an omission.

Murray's gaze flickered toward Irena and I knew she'd picked up on the shift, too. She nodded, though her expression remained passive. "I see. Can you tell me why your parents, and later on *you*, lied about his whereabouts?"

Irena shrugged, a bitter expression crossing her face. "Detective, you weren't even alive at that time. You have no idea of how easily any hint of mental illness could ostracize a family. My parents were high on the social ladder, not only here, but in Seattle and on the east coast. They were only thinking of me. It was better to have people think that Brent ran off to Europe, if I were to have any hope for a normal life. They told me never to talk about his problem, so I did as they asked. And the lie became habit, and then—in its own way—the truth. Brent really is in a foreign country, but one that exists within the confines of his own mind. Why, even my husband doesn't know that Brent is living at Fairhaven. After all these years, I've never told him."

"Do you ever go see him?" I asked.

Irena gazed at me quietly. "Once a month. I tell my husband I'm going to have lunch in Bellingham, and I go sit with Brent for the afternoon. He never seems to care, but I do it anyway."

I liked her a little better, and forced a smile to my lips, which she gently returned.

Murray let her breath out in a slow stream. "All right. What can you tell me about Brigit O'Reilly? She was your maid, was she not?"

Irena nodded. "Yes, lovely girl, around my own age. She was quite competent, and we were sorry to lose her but she wanted to go back home to Ireland. I think she missed her family."

There—again the omission. I nudged Murray ever so slightly.

Murray's eyes flickered and I knew that once again, she'd caught the shift in energy. "When did she leave?"

"Oh, I don't know. I was in and out of the house that summer getting ready for my wedding. I really don't remember," Irena said. She paused for a moment, as if thinking, then shrugged. "I'm afraid I can't help you."

Murray sat her notebook and pen down on the coffee table. "Mrs. Finch, what would you say if I told you that Brigit never left Chiqetaw? That the skeleton we discovered on your lot is hers? We've confirmed it, for all intents and purposes."

Irena gasped, delicately fluttering a hand to her throat. "Oh my! You can't be serious?" She gave Murray a wide-eyed correct-me-if-you-dare look. Murray returned it with her own icy stare.

"I don't joke about death. Brigit's remains were found stuffed in a hole beneath the yew tree on the back of your lot. We found her diary, her suitcases, and her clothing hidden away in a basement room. We think she may have been murdered, and we want some straight answers. I might remind you that there's no statute of limitations regarding murder."

I was suddenly glad that I wasn't on the receiving end

of Murray's interrogation. Irena sniffed; I could feel her waver. Then she let out a loud sigh.

"I'd help you if I could," she said, "but I simply don't know what happened. As I explained, I was heavily involved with wedding plans and at that age, wasn't thinking too clearly about anyone or anything else."

Murray flipped her notebook shut. "I see. Thank you for your cooperation."

I piped up. "Mrs. Finch, on a different subject, may I ask why you don't want to sell the lot to Joe? I've spoken with your brother and he's given his permission." I held up the paper he'd signed and she paled as she looked at the signature.

"Yes, I'm also curious to hear your answer," Mur said. "Why didn't you want to sell the land, Mrs. Finch? Could it be that you knew the skeleton was there all along?"

I watched Irena wage war with herself. Finally she motioned for me to wait while she picked up the phone, hitting number five on speed dial. After a moment, she said, "Williams? This is Irena. Put through the sale of the lot that fireman wanted. Files. Yes, I said put it through. We have permission from my brother. Yes, from my brother. In writing."

She replaced the receiver on the cradle. "You made your point. I'll need a copy of that note for my lawyer. He'll confirm it with the doctor. You can mail it to him—George Williams. He's in the book."

Turning to Murray, she added, "I had no ulterior motives in keeping the land away from Mr. Files. I simply didn't think my brother was capable of giving the permission needed, but apparently it seems that you and Ms. O'Brien . . . she flashed me a searching look, "have taken care of that little problem."

We stood to go. Murray said, "Mrs. Finch, one last

question, if you would. Do you know why your brother might feel like he'd done something terrible to Brigit? While we were at the hospital, he broke down and began begging for her forgiveness."

Irena froze. I could see her throat muscles contract as she breathed. Slowly inhale, slow exhale. After a moment she shook her head. "I can't think of anything. They barely ever spoke. I'm surprised he even remembers her name." She blinked and the reserved matriarch was back. "You have to understand something about my brother's condition. Schizophrenia often includes both paranoia and delusions. Whatever he's concocted in his mind about Brigit exists only within his own tormented imagination." She gestured to the door. "And now, if you'll both excuse me, I have a meeting to attend."

Murray nodded. "Thank you for your time."

"I trust you'll be as discreet as possible about my brother's information? I'd rather not have it come out now that he's been locked away all those years."

I couldn't read the look on her face, but it wasn't a good one. We took our leave and headed out for the truck, mulling over what Irena had told us. No concrete answers, and so much unsaid. I wondered if we'd ever find out the truth of the matter. That is, if anybody knew, after all these years.

Thirteen

❖

From Brigit's Journal:

> I was thinking of stories this morning—I'm going to have to remember a lot of the family stories quite soon.
>
> When I was little, my mother told me that our family had been blessed by the Sidhe. My great-grandfather, Jonathon, was hiking down to the water one morning to go fishing, when he saw a little girl sitting on the side of the road. He stopped to ask if she needed help. She said she was hungry, and he gave her the bit of bread he had in his pocket, even though it meant he'd have no lunch. He offered to take her back to his home so his wife could give her a proper meal, even though it meant going out of his way.
>
> The little girl stood up and transformed into a tiny little man, no bigger than Great-grandfather's knee. He said that since Jonathon was so helpful, without begrudging the help, he'd bless the family. We might have times that were hard, but no one would ever stay lost— no matter what happened. We might run away, or be

swept out to sea, but somehow, we'd always end up
home again. The faeries would watch over us.

SINCE JOE WAS coming for dinner, I decided we'd order Chinese takeout. I could hardly wait to spring the news that Irena had agreed to sell the lot after all, though I was still a little worried she might try to back out of the deal again. I glanced at the clock. Five-fifteen. The kids wouldn't be home till near six and Joe had said he'd arrive around six-thirty.

On a hunch, I pulled out the pages I'd copied from Brigit's journal and began reading through them again, to see if I could find anything I'd missed. And then—there it was. A story about her great-grandfather and the faeries.

I read through it, silently thinking about the Will o' the Wisps. We'd barely seen them since the night I discovered the skeleton. Could their purpose have been to lead us to her? Perhaps they were the faeries that were watching over Brigit's family. Now that we'd found her body, they could fade back to wherever it was they'd come from. I had a sudden urge to put flowers out for Brigit, to assure the powers that be that we were thinking about her. No doubt her bones would be returned home to her cousin, so Brigit would be going home, in a manner of speaking. I wanted her spirit to rest, as well.

Perhaps the only way to do that was to cleanse the lot. And perhaps that was the final key in bringing Sammy back home and returning Mab to her ghostly owner. Brigit had loved her cat; they rested together even in death. And maybe that's why she was still walking the world, even after we'd discovered her final resting spot. She was looking for her cat.

I'd just started listing ingredients that went into the

strongest exorcism ritual I was familiar with when a brief knock announced that Joe was home. He popped his head around the corner, wearing one of the biggest smiles I'd seen in awhile.

"I'm early. That okay?"

"Okay? Of course!" I dropped my pen and raced over to give him a big hug, breathing his scent into my lungs. He smelled like cinnamon and spice and cloves, and my desire flared as he gathered me in his arms and glanced at the clock.

"Do we have time before the kids come home?"

It was six o'clock. The kids got out of their after-school activities at six-fifteen and it would take another twenty minutes for them to arrive home.

"C'mon!" I grabbed his hand and dragged him upstairs. Quickies had their time and place, and right now twenty minutes in bed with Joe was one luxury I wasn't about to take a pass on.

We tumbled out of our clothes, laughing. I reveled in the feel of his hands on my skin, on my breasts, on my thighs as he traced circles with his fingertips, drawing vines and tendrils. He leaned over and slid his tongue against my own and I welcomed his presence in my home, my bedroom, my body. Joe reached for protection and then rose above me, bearing down with the mastery of his ancestors—robust and full of vigor. As my legs entwined around his waist, I forgot all about ghosts and spirits and long-forgotten bones in a sweep of love that brushed them into the dark corners of my mind.

BY THE TIME the kids came trooping through the door, we were dressed and back in the kitchen. My heart ached at the look on their faces when I broke the news that

Sammy hadn't come home yet. Tears in their eyes, they headed into the living room to play with the kittens. I ordered the takeout, then Joe and I talked over coffee while we waited for it to arrive.

He leaned back in his chair. "You met with Irena today, didn't you?"

I blinked. "Did she call you?"

"Her lawyer did," he said, breaking into a wide grin. "The lot's mine. He's working up the final papers now. We can get back to work on it, though I have to tell you, that damned place scares me out of my wits. What the hell are we going to do about it?"

I went over everything that had happened with Brent and Irena and White Deer. "I've come to the conclusion that Brigit must be searching for Mab. The Will o' the Wisps were there to lead us to her body, thanks to the pact the faeries made with her great-grandfather," I said. "I'm thinking that if we clear the lot, Sammy and Mab will be able to exchange places and Brigit and Mab will be free to rest or go off and do whatever it is that spirits do."

"Maybe so," he said, musing. "Broken hearts and ghost cats and skeletons in trees . . . the stuff legends are made of. I wonder who killed her."

"If you ask me, I think it was probably Brent. According to Irena, he was always unstable and, unless I miss my guess, for some reason he snapped and killed her, then tried to cover it up. When Irena heard that a skeleton was found on the lot, she must have put two and two together."

"Maybe." He toyed with his coffee mug. "Meanwhile, though, I want to talk about something else. Specifically, your birthday."

I blinked. We'd barely discussed my birthday since we'd found the basement and the hauntings had started.

"Yeah, tomorrow night. I'll be thirty-seven. Joe," I said, hesitating.

"What?"

Taking a deep breath, I took the plunge. "Do you think . . . in ten years, do you think our age difference will bother you? I'll be closing in on fifty by then. Well, forty-seven, and you'll still be in your prime."

He stared at me, puzzled, then a look of understanding spread across his face. "Good God, woman! Has that *really* been worrying you?"

I nodded, blushing.

He laughed. "Emerald, I'm in love with you. Not your age. You're beautiful and vibrant and everything I want in a woman. Whether you're thirty-seven or sixty-seven, I'll still love you." With a soft look, he reached across the table and took my hands in his. I hung my head, embarrassed to have questioned him in the first place.

"Yes, you're ten years older than I am, but does that matter? I'm not going anywhere. I'm not looking for anyone else. I've never been a player, and I don't respect the sort of man who toys with a woman's affections. Like Andrew."

I blinked. Joe had a thinly disguised disgust for the man I'd been dating before he came into the picture. I didn't blame him. Hell, it had been a bitter pill for me to swallow when Andrew dumped me. When he came crawling back a few months later, I'd been secretly overjoyed to be able to tell him thanks, but no thanks, not interested. We'd tried being friends, but that hadn't worked out. He'd called a few times since then, once getting Joe on the line—which hadn't been a pretty sight. Every time he'd sounded whinier and needier.

I looked up into Joe's face. He held my gaze for a moment, questioning, and then I broke down and laughed.

"Oh Joe, you're so good to me, and I've been an idiot about this. Thank you for understanding, for not treating me like I'm crazy."

"I never said you weren't crazy," he said sternly, but then snorted. "But, I'd never call you an idiot. Now, where's dinner?"

The doorbell rang and I heard the kids come racing downstairs. "Mom, Mom! Takeout's here!" Kip sounded overjoyed. Dinner could make or break his mood.

As Joe went to pay the delivery man, Randa sidled up. "Mom, I invited Gunner over. He's supposed to be here in a few minutes. Is that okay?"

I gave her a long look. "Well, I wish you'd asked earlier, but yes, it's fine. I ordered plenty of food. Go wash up."

Kip was setting the table when the doorbell rang. I answered and there stood Gunner Lindemeyer. A tall boy, he was already my height. Skinny, blond, the picture of a young Scandinavian lad. But I could tell that he'd been crying recently, and could only imagine how lost and confused the boy must have felt as he tried to find a way to cope with the enormity of his situation. I wanted to wrap my arms around his shoulders, to let him cry. He needed a mother's touch, and his own mother was fighting for her life.

"Come in." I escorted him into the kitchen just as Miranda bounced back from washing up. Her gaze fell on Gunner and she almost tripped. Blushing, she stammered out a greeting. Oh yeah, she had it bad.

We gathered around the table and I took a long look at the boy. He'd survive, I thought. He might be hurting now, but he had a strong spirit. If his parents made it through, he'd help them recover. He was just that kind of kid.

As we dove into the fried rice and pot stickers and sweet-and-sour pork and almond chicken, Gunner didn't say much but the expression on his face told me just how much he missed all of this—family and chatter and bright lights and companionship. I had the sneaking suspicion that he wasn't too happy at his aunt's house.

For once, my darling Kip had the good sense to keep from sticking his foot in his mouth. Not once did he approach the subject of the fire. Randa, on the other hand, morphed into a moon-eyed love child. She hung on every word Gunner said, as infrequent as they were. Her food sat untouched on her plate, until I gently prompted her to eat.

Joe and I glanced at each other. We weren't the only ones in the thralls of love. Bless his heart, Joe launched into telling the kids that he'd be able to buy the lot next door after all and the conversation picked up.

Kip cheered. "Does that mean we can go back over there and look for Sammy?"

I nixed that idea right off. "No, it does not. We've been keeping an eye out for her but there's no way in hell I'm letting you prowl around over there."

Gunner cleared his throat. "Are you and Mr. Files engaged?"

I glanced at Joe and he grinned. "Not really, not yet."

"I'll ask her to marry me when I think she'll say 'yes,'" Joe said.

Kip and Randa stared at us, open-mouthed. I decided to change the subject. "Dessert's in the freezer—Donna Linda's ice cream." The kids had developed a taste for a gourmet ice cream that we could only get at the Shanty Barn.

Thoughts of marriage forgotten, Kip and Randa raided the freezer. Gunner waited politely for a bowl, which Miranda prepared. He glanced around the kitchen and I could tell he was taking in the feel of the house.

"My aunt thinks that you're an evil woman," he said almost offhandedly. "She's nuts, though, so don't be offended."

I stared at him. Where had *that* come from? "What?"

"My aunt. She says that you're in league with the devil because you talk to ghosts and spirits and you don't go to church. I don't like my aunt," he added. "She bitches because I write."

I wasn't sure what to say, especially with his choice of language, but Randa jumped in immediately. "Mom isn't evil! You're aunt's crazy—"

"Randa, hon, that's not a nice thing to say, but I appreciate you defending me." I wasn't sure how to deal with this. I didn't want to belittle Gunner's aunt in his presence, but I wasn't about to let somebody ride roughshod over my reputation. "Gunner, what do *you* think?"

A faint smile appeared on his lips. "I think my aunt and I don't get along very well," he said, accepting his ice cream.

I nodded solemnly. "Yeah, it sounds like you're going to have some problems all right, kiddo. Well, just for your peace of mind, I don't believe in the devil . . . not the way a lot of people do. I do believe evil exists, but it comes in many forms and shapes and behind many facades."

"So does bad luck," Gunner said, staring at his plate.

Randa glanced at him, then at the rest of us, and did something I never expected to see her do—she slid an arm around his waist and rested her head on his shoulder. "It'll be okay—I know it will. And I'm here if you need to talk."

He blushed, but I could tell that she had eased his pain, if just a little.

I quickly looked in Kip's direction—this would be the perfect chance for him to embarrass Miranda, but again, he wisely kept his mouth shut. When I saw he wasn't going to take advantage of the opportunity, I smiled at him and gently nodded. As soon as the kids finished dessert, they decided to head out into the backyard to search for Sammy since the skies had partially cleared. I excused them from kitchen chores and they bolted for the door.

Joe kissed me and headed back for work, and I was alone in the kitchen. The house seemed to breathe with life and, for a brief moment, everything felt calm. I yawned as I cleared the table. Long day, and I wanted a bubble bath and my sweats. I'd just started to stack the plates in the dishwasher when Randa jerked the door open and stumbled in.

"Mom, Kip fell out of a tree—he's hurt."

I was out the door before she could say another word, racing barefoot through the mud. There, near the fence that separated my property from the neighboring lot, Kip lay on the ground beneath the oak. God damn it! Weren't my children safe in our own yard? As I skidded to a halt, falling on my knees beside him, he groaned and looked up at me.

"I saw her, Mom! I thought I saw Sammy. She was in the tree, but then she disappeared!" Samantha . . . Kip must have seen Mab and got the two mixed up. I glanced up at Gunner, who looked confused.

"I didn't see anything," he said.

Randa caught up and knelt beside me. "Should I call the hospital?"

"Where's it hurt, kiddo? Are you okay?"

He shook his head, biting his lip and I could tell he was

in a lot of pain. "M-m-my arm, I think I broke it when I fell."

I grabbed the flashlight that was lying on the ground and trained it on his arm. Sure enough, his right wrist and forearm were twisted in an unnatural position. Shit. I turned to Randa. "Go call Joe. He'll bring a medic unit. Tell him I think Kip's arm is broken."

She scrambled to her feet and raced off while I tried to keep Kip from squirming. "Kiddo, I know it hurts but please, keep calm. Joe will be here right away, and he'll fix you up good and proper."

"Am I gonna have to go to the hospital?"

"Probably," I said. "But I'll be right there with you." I brushed his bangs back. His forehead felt clammy. Shock, probably. I glanced up at Gunner, who was pulling a Bambi-in-the-headlights. Emotional overload, probably. "Gunner? Gunner!"

He slowly shook his head and looked at me. "Huh?"

"If you want to help out, why don't you go see how Randa's doing with that phone call? And ask her to bring me a thick blanket, my shoes, and a coat."

After he disappeared toward the house, I leaned down close to Kip's face. "Kiddo, tell me what happened."

"We were calling for Sammy and then I looked up at the oak tree an' saw her up there. She was meowing. Randa saw her too, but Gunner didn't. Anyway, I started climbing up to get her and I almost had her when . . . when . . ." His lip trembled.

I winced. Not only was my son in pain but the one thing he wanted most in the world had been right within his grasp before she slipped away. It must have broken his heart when he realized she wasn't really there.

"When what, hon?"

"She disappeared—poof—and I tried to grab for her

and fell out of the tree." He shivered and I put my arm around him, taking care not to shift his shoulder. Randa and Gunner came back then, they were carrying my heavy coat, a pair of sneakers, and three blankets.

"Did you get hold of Joe?" I snuggled one blanket under Kip's head, then covered him with the other two.

She nodded. "He should be here in five minutes. He said not to worry."

Yeah, right. Not worry. Good one. "Randa, I think Gunner had better go home for now. I can't drive him, so go call his aunt and have her come pick him up. If she can't, then get a ten-dollar bill out of my purse and call a taxi."

She looked crestfallen and shot one quick glowering look at Kip, but when she saw that I'd noticed her expression, she hung her head. "Okay," she said.

"Ms. O'Brien?" Gunner hung back.

"What is it, Gunner?"

"Thanks for everything. I had fun." After a moment, he added, "Hey, Kip, you get well." He gave a half-wave and followed Randa through the kitchen door.

Joe was good to his word. Within five minutes he and a crew were crowded around Kip while I stood back, watching and biting my nails. They examined him thoroughly, then Joe headed over to me.

"Well, his arm really took a beating. Legs seem fine, he has some bruises and needs to be checked just in case there's any internal damage, but overall, I'd say he escaped relatively unscathed. What the hell happened?"

Keeping my voice low so the other paramedic couldn't overhear us, I filled him in on what had gone down. "We have to do something Joe. White Deer offered to help me cleanse the lot. We'll get started tomorrow."

"But tomorrow's your birthday—"

I cut him off. "And I want to see more birthdays! And I want my kids to see more birthdays. But at this rate, we may not unless we clear up this nightmare that's been set in motion. Listen, do you mind if the kids and the cats and I stay at your apartment tonight after we get done at the hospital?" I wasn't above bumming a safe haven when we needed it.

He nodded. "You don't have to ask, babe. You've got a key."

"All set, Captain!" His partner waved to the stretcher where Kip lay firmly strapped in. "He's good to go."

"I'll see you at the hospital," I said. After giving Kip a kiss and assuring him that I'd be there soon and that everything was going to be A-okay, I stood aside to let the paramedics pull away. As soon as they headed down the street, I raced back to the house where Randa was waving at Gunner as he sped off in the back of a taxi.

"How's Kip?" she said.

"Broken arm, I'm not sure what else. Joe said that he should be okay." I shuffled through my purse to make sure I had everything, then nodded her toward the door. "Randa, did you see Sammy in the tree too?"

She paled. "Yeah, though I thought it was the ghost cat at first. But Kip wanted it to be her so bad . . . I'm sorry." She hung her head. "I told him go ahead and climb up to check it out. Kip's so good at climbing trees that I thought he'd be okay. We didn't have time to come get you. Since we were in the backyard, I thought we'd be safe." As she shrugged into her jacket, she said, "Mom, will Sammy ever come home?"

I smoothed her bangs back from her face. "I really think she will, honey. We're going to stay over at Joe's apartment tonight after we get done at the hospital. Then tomorrow, White Deer is going to help me finish cleans-

ing the lot and maybe that will be just what Sammy needs
to find her way back."

As we hopped into my SUV, my stomach churned.
What if we couldn't clean the lot and it stayed a haven for
sadness? What if Sammy never came home? I pushed
everything out of my mind, unable to cope with any more
stress.

WE REACHED THE E.R. ten minutes after Kip was
trundled in. The nurse glanced at me and smiled.

"Ms. O'Brien, you're here again?" She blushed. "I
mean—"

"I know what you mean," I said and rolled my eyes.
Great. Of all the places where I could be known as a regular, it had to be the hospital. Let's see, how many times
had we been here in the past year? I started counting on
my fingers and then shook it off. Enough of the past. Time
to focus on the present. Hopefully, the rest of the year
would pass without incident.

"Captain Files asked me to tell you he had to return to
the station. He wants you to call him whenever you have
news."

"Thank you. Can I see my son now?"

"He's in the x-ray room. As soon as he's done, we'll
take you back. Meanwhile, I need you to fill out some new
paperwork. We've updated our system since you were in
last."

Fretting, I filled out the forms while Randa plunked
herself down on a sofa and picked up a magazine. Half-
an-hour later, the nurse motioned for me to follow her and
led me down the labyrinth of sterile corridors. We stopped
in front of a set of double doors that looked all too famil-

iar. I took a deep breath as she peeked in, announced my presence, then guided me through.

Kip sat on the table with an oversized hospital gown wrapped around him. He looked cold, and even though he'd put on his stalwart "I'm a big boy" face, I could tell he was tired and worn out. The doctor glanced up as I entered the room.

"You his mother?" he asked.

I nodded. "Emerald O'Brien. How's my son?"

"Kip will be fine once he's mended. His arm's broken, but it's a clean break and the x-rays showed no internal damage. Your boy's a tough customer. Of course, he's going to be in a hard splint for six weeks, and a sling for awhile, but that's not going to be so bad, is it, slugger?" He grinned at Kip and a light shone through the doctor's aura. Curt, but caring.

Kip's "warrior" face disappeared and he perked up. "Yeah, an' I can get all my friends to sign it."

"Whoa, slow down there," the doctor said. "I'm sorry to disappoint you, but the splints we use now aren't like casts used to be. You're going to have to pass on having friends autograph it."

Kip's expression fell. "Aw gee. Can I keep it when they take it off?" He appealed to me. "Mom?"

Oh yeah, my son was already on the mend. "We'll see what we can do," I said dryly, wondering how to preserve a splint so it didn't stink to high heaven or grow moldy. No doubt, I'd find out if it could be done, one way or another.

The med tech took Kip away to be fitted with the splint. While he was gone, I had a little chat with the doctor. I told him exactly what happened: Kip thought he saw our missing cat in the branches of an oak tree in our backyard, climbed up, got startled by something, and fell. Period. End of story.

He nodded. "If your cat's still missing in a week or so, call me. I've got a batch of kittens at home. We adopted a cat and didn't know she was pregnant and now we've got eight little mouths mewing at us."

I headed back to the waiting room where Miranda was impatiently flipping through an old copy of *Discovery Magazine*. She glanced up, her eyes red like she'd been crying.

"Your brother's going to be okay." I settled in next to her and she dropped the magazine back on the table and leaned against my shoulder. "They're putting a splint on his arm, and he'll be in a sling for awhile. It's a clean break, so there shouldn't be any problems."

"I love him, even if he is a pain," she murmured. "I don't want to see anything happen to him."

I kissed the top of her head—no small feat since she was almost as tall as I was—and gently tucked my arm around her. "We can't ever be totally safe, honey, but we do our best. Kids get into scrapes all the time, regardless of whether it's a ghost or a faerie or the neighborhood bully."

"Did I?" She looked at me, her brilliant brown eyes dark and flashing.

I laughed. "You? Are you kidding? When you were three, you fell down the steps at our old house and banged up your nose. Two years later, you tried to climb out on the roof to watch the stars. I had the horrible feeling you were in danger and ran into your bedroom. You were trying to get out the window. I'd left it cracked for fresh air and you were doing your best to open it."

She blushed, but looked pleased. "I don't remember that at all."

"Well, it's true. Of course, you weren't strong enough to manage it but still . . . that's when the safety screens went on. I never told your Dad, though. He would have been furious and would have ended your interest in stargazing." My daughter had been watching the skies since she could toddle.

Randa closed her eyes, drifting off to sleep as we waited for the doctor's return. An hour later I had dozed off myself, but the sound of my name startled me awake. The doctor waited until I'd rubbed my eyes, then sat down next to me.

"You can take him home in a few minutes. No strenuous activity for a few days. Keep him in a sling until we say otherwise. No climbing trees or any other dangerous stunts until it's healed. The nurse will give you a home health-care sheet that explains how to keep the arm clean and how to take care of the splint. Take him to your doctor on Monday, and if there's any noticeable swelling in his fingers or above the top of his cast, bring him back to the E.R. immediately."

"What about pain medication?"

"Children's Tylenol or Motrin. We gave him a mild muscle relaxant so he'll sleep easier tonight, but that's as strong as he needs."

I thanked him, took the handouts, and stuffed them in my purse. We waited for another fifteen minutes until the nurse wheeled Kipling out. He looked tired, but excited. Broken bones and bruises and dangerous encounters with the unknown always seemed to perk him up. I had little doubt that he'd end up an explorer or eco-adventurer.

By the time we were back in the car it was almost eleven o'clock. I drove directly to Joe's place and dropped off the kids, making sure Kip was as comfortable as possible before heading for the door.

"I have to go back home for the cats and clothes. Watch TV, have a snack, and for God's sake, don't go anywhere, don't open the door for anybody, and don't get into anything. And don't take off that sling." I glanced at my watch. "I'll be back in half-an-hour. Randa, watch out for your brother."

She nodded solemnly. She could tell when I'd reached meltdown level and I was dangerously close. I forced myself to drive the speed limit on the way to our house, hoping it was still in one piece.

The lights were blazing, but I remembered that I hadn't bothered to turn them off before leaving for the hospital. I gingerly made my way up the front porch and unlocked the door. As I slid inside, I stopped and listened. Silence. Nothing except a sudden meow as Nigel came rushing down the stairs. He entwined around my legs, happy to see me. I tiptoed into the kitchen, wary but hopeful. With a little luck, everything would be in order. A quick glance around showed me nothing was out of place. So far so good. But what about the backyard?

I peeked out the kitchen window. A faint sparkle of light here and there but at least the Will o' the Wisps were no longer swarming. I couldn't help but wonder what else might be prowling around under the cover of night. At least one spirit kitty that I knew of.

Before retrieving the cat carriers from the back porch I refilled the dish of dry food we had placed just under the porch steps in case Sammy might be around. Something had been eating the food. Probably raccoons, but as long as there was a chance it might be her, I'd keep it full.

As I set the dish on the ground, a flicker of movement caught my attention. There, to my left, shimmering and beautiful and graceful, sat Mab. She sidled up to me, purring loudly. As I let myself tune into her energy, I knew—on a gut level—that she hadn't meant for Kip's accident to happen. The poor cat's aura was rippling with waves of loneliness. She'd probably saw what she thought was a chance to make some sort of contact. Mab looked up at me, a winsome expression in her eyes.

I tentatively reached out, but my hand passed right through the translucent tortoiseshell's side. I sighed. "I'm sorry, little one. I can't pet you. We aren't exactly in the same world."

She gave me a solemn stare but a moth caught her attention and she pranced around, chasing the luminous white insect. She would have caught it, but her paw swept through the wings and the moth flew off, unaware that it had been marked as ghost food.

"Have you seen Samantha?" I asked, kneeling down to get a better look at her. "We miss her. If you can help her get home, I'd appreciate it."

I could swear Mab understood me. She *purped* and blinked, and something in the air shifted. Perhaps it was instinct, or perhaps it was because tomorrow night was almost All Hallows Eve . . . whatever the case, in that instant I knew White Deer had been right. Mab was as lost as my Samantha. She couldn't find her way back to Brigit. The cats had traded places and both were lost in the slipstream of time.

"We'll try to help you, baby. Meanwhile, if you see Sammy, tell her we love her," I said, trying to hold back my tears. Reluctantly, I left her, going inside to pack an overnight bag.

I gathered Nanna's journal, the kids' homework and school clothes, then managed to hunt down Nigel and his sisters. They protested their incarceration, but I ignored their indignant mews and managed to herd them into their carriers, promptly depositing them along with their food, litter box, and the rest of my gear, into the back of the Mountaineer.

After arming the security system I took one last look around and locked the door. Tomorrow we'd finish this. Tomorrow we'd try to put Brigit to rest, and to build a bridge over which Mab and Sammy could cross.

Fourteen

✦

From Brigit's Journal:

The end of secrecy is almost upon us. Today is the day, and Mother Mary, I pray that they welcome the news. If not, there's nothing left for me to do but pick up the ticket I bought, and go home. Thank heaven my parents will never know what happened—how could I face them? At least my cousin loves me. Mary Kathryn will be sorely disappointed in my behavior, but she'll take me in and help me rebuild my life. Oh. I can't help but hope there's no need for that. The Missus might take pity on me . . . on us. She treats me kindly enough, if with a firm hand.

But Mr. Edward, somehow I don't think we'll find much comfort in his words. With no love in his heart even for his children. how can I expect sympathy or kindness for myself? Mary Kathryn is right—I'm a fool and a romantic. When I first came to this country. I had such high hopes. Now they're all but dashed on the rocks.

*   *   *

TECHNICALLY, JOE OWNED a condo, but it was really a unit in a renovated apartment building on the out-skirts of Chiqetaw, near the turnoff that led out to Klick-avail Valley. He had a spacious one-bedroom. Although decorated in utilitarian fashion, it was clean and neat. I had never seen any sign that he reveled in his bachelorhood. No pinups, no beer bottles on the floor or dirty clothes scattered around. The refrigerator even had food in it, food that hadn't gone the way of the mold patrol.

When I returned with the cats and our clothes, Randa helped me carry them up to the apartment. As soon as we were inside, I asked her to set up the litter box while I made up the sofa bed for Kip. Randa and I would share the bedroom. I rummaged through the linen closet and came up with clean sheets and warm blankets, then tucked Kip in for the night, propping pillows on either side to keep him from rolling over onto his broken arm. He was out like a light before I could even kiss him good night.

"Poor little guy," I whispered, staring at his sleeping form.

Randa fed the cats, then leaned against me, watching her brother. "He seems okay."

"He is."

She yawned. "I'm going to bed. Are you staying up?"

"For a little while," I said, and gave her a kiss on the cheek. She headed into the bedroom and I settled down next to Kip, desperate for a few minutes when I didn't have to do anything, or worry about anybody. I leaned my head back and absently petted Nebula, who crawled into my lap.

"Where's your mama?" I whispered, thinking about Sammy. Did she think we'd abandoned her? Was she afraid?

As if seeking to comfort me, Nebula licked my hand and began to purr, pawing at me to finish scratching behind her ears. I sighed and looked around for the other two. Nigel and Noël were milling through the rooms, exploring the various cupboards and hidey-holes they might be able to squirrel themselves into. Nebula began to groom, purring against my stomach. After a few minutes, I patted her rump and gently deposited her on the blanket by Kip's feet. My night wasn't over quite yet. I slipped into the kitchen and gave Joe a call.

He was in. The station had been free of calls except to help an older lady who had fallen in her bathtub and dislocated a shoulder.

"Kip's sleeping. He'll be okay. He has to wear the splint for six weeks but the doctor said he should heal up quick."

"Take a hot bath, then sleep in tomorrow morning," Joe said. "I'll be off shift around 1:00 P.M., though I have some errands to run. But good news—since I worked through part of my vacation, I'm taking another three days off. You headed back to your place after you wake up?"

"Yeah. I'm going to call Murray as soon as I get off the phone with you. We were supposed to meet Harlow tomorrow morning at my place anyway, so I'm going to ask White Deer to tag along. She and I can work on exorcising the lot."

"I'll meet you around one or so, then. Love you, Em. Sleep tight. *And be careful!*"

I slowly replaced the receiver. Joe was an incredible man. Not every boyfriend would let his girlfriend and her kids and their cats descend on his place with such short notice. Hell, even fewer would be able to handle the baggage that came attached to someone like me—what with kids and cats and the demands of the shop and spirits constantly dropping in. Joe was the gold ring on my carousel, and I wasn't about to let go.

After a quick call to ask Murray to bring White Deer with her the next morning, I flipped on the bathroom light in place of a night-light, then padded into the bedroom and changed into a light chemise that I'd left at Joe's. My mind was mush and I needed sleep. Big time. I slid under the covers and the minute my head touched the pillow, I was down for the count.

HALLOWEEN—AND MY birthday—dawned with a stormy forecast, but Kip was feeling bright and chipper come morning. While I made breakfast, he admired his splint. I knew as soon as the novelty wore off he'd start to complain, so tried to enjoy the peace while it lasted. Randa set the table and I parceled out the oatmeal and bacon. After hailing me with a round of "happy birthdays" and kisses, they settled in to eat breakfast.

"Mom, can I still go to Tony's party today after school?"

Tony, one of Kip's friends, was having a big Halloween party and it seemed far safer than letting Kip run around trick-or-treating. He'd been working on his mummy costume for weeks. Thank God I'd remembered to bring it with me last night. It wouldn't be hard to adjust to his splint.

"Of course you can. I just want you to promise to be careful." I looked at Randa, who was still groggy-eyed. "Do you have anything planned today?"

She nodded. "We're having a harvest dance and food drive at school this afternoon. Gunner was going to take me, but he's too worried about his folks to go. He spends every afternoon at the hospital. So Lori and I are going together. Nobody asked her and she's bummed out."

That figured. Lori was a very caring, smart young woman but she was a little chubby and the ninth-grade boys acted like she didn't exist. Her parents didn't help matters much. Her mother was stick thin and bitched about Lori's weight constantly. I knew because Randa told me, and having met Mrs. Thomas a few times, I had little doubt that Lori received no emotional support at home. It made me mad, but there was little I could do except bolster her self-esteem whenever she came over to visit.

"That's too bad, honey. I'm glad you're being a good friend. And the food drive is a great idea. Do you need money?"

She nodded. "Yeah, I almost forgot. We're holding a raffle and there's going to be a bake sale to raise money for the Bread & Butter House."

I handed her a ten. "Are you guys ready to go? Did you feed the cats?"

Kip nodded, grabbing his backpack. "Yeah, Randa helped me." He listed a little to the left when he slung the heavy book bag over his shoulder. Luckily, he was left-handed like me, so would still be able to write.

After popping the last bite of my toaster pastry into my mouth, I made sure I had everything I needed—keys, purse, money, Nanna's journal—and followed the kids out to the car. I dropped them off at school and headed to the animal shelter, where I was once again disappointed, then dropped down to the shop for a quick check-in.

The windows were gorgeous. Lana and Cinnamon had worked their butts off to make them both spooky and inviting, with pumpkin teapots and spiderwebs dripping like lace and baskets of apples and wheat adorning the displays. They'd even fixed up a miniature tea party diorama—taking the bobble-head jack-o'-lantern, a miniature scarecrow, and a beautiful faerie princess, and arranging them as a Halloween tea party around a giant toadstool. Enchanted, I bustled through the door, only to find Cinnamon in the tearoom, her head in her hands, bawling her eyes out.

"What's wrong? Oh my God, were we robbed again?" I glanced around frantically but nothing seemed out of place.

"No, nothing like that." She sniffed and dabbed at her eyes with a tissue. "I'm sorry, I thought I could handle it, but I don't know if I can."

"What's wrong? Cinnamon, talk to me." I slipped into a chair by her side. "Cinnamon?"

She sucked in a deep breath and, voice quavering, said, "My boyfriend came over last night and he told me the truth. He's found somebody else and doesn't want anything to do with me or the kids! I've spent months trying to cheer him up while he was in jail and now he dumps me!" And with that, she burst into fresh tears and fell into my arms.

I patted her back and smoothed her hair, wondering how many times she'd cried over this loser. She was a smart girl, but she still hadn't learned the hardest lesson of love—you can't change someone unless they want to change.

After a moment, I gently pushed her away and took her hands. "Dry your eyes, chickie, and listen to me. You take him to court and get an order for him to pay child support. And then you make a new life for yourself, without him. There are a lot of good men out there, men who will treat you and your children right. It just takes time and discrimination to find them."

She gulped down her tears. "But I love him—"

"And he treats you like dirt. Is it worth it?"

With a slow shake of the head, she said, "My mother told me the same thing, only she used language I don't think you want repeated in your store. She hates him. Maybe that's why I've stood up for him . . . but now . . ." She hung her head, her cheeks flushed.

"Now he wants somebody else. Fine, let him go. But make sure he fulfills his obligation to his children." I couldn't help but think of my own child-support battles with my ex, and Roy could easily afford the payments. Why did so many men run out on their responsibilities? A lot of men were wonderful fathers and provided for their children, divorced or not, but there were still far too many mothers who scrimped to feed their kids while their ex-husbands lived fancy free.

Lana sashayed into the shop, took one look at Cinnamon, and said, "He dumped you, didn't he? Get rid of the bugger."

I tipped Cinnamon's chin up. "It hurts now, but it's for the best. Lana, can you mind the shop by yourself today? I'm not expecting a flurry of customers given that it's Halloween."

She nodded. "Not a problem. By the way, happy birthday!"

"Oh God, I forgot—" Cinnamon gasped but I motioned for her to be quiet.

"Don't worry about it. Lana, take over while she goes home." I looked at Cinnamon. "Take the day off. Relax, spend time with your kids, soak in a long hot bath, and get in a nap. Promise me you'll be good to yourself today?"

With a final sniff, Cinnamon shrugged. "Okay. Thanks, Emerald. You're really cool, you know?"

I smiled. "I know. Now go on, get a move on." I gathered up my purse and keys. "I'll be back bright and early Monday morning, and trust me, I'll be ready to work."

"How's it going?" Lana asked me as Cinnamon made her way toward the door. "Did they find out who the skeleton was?"

"Yeah, but right now, don't even ask," I said, slipping on my jacket. "I'll tell you all about it next week."

As I headed back out into the blustery day, I realized just how much I loved my work. I glanced back at the Chintz 'n China and smiled softly. Yep, Chiqetaw had been good to me, and I could hardly wait for the holidays.

IT WAS ALMOST eleven by the time I pulled into my driveway. Murray, Harlow, and White Deer were huddled on the front porch, looking more than a little irritated. Knowing I was running late, I had called ahead on my cell and asked them to wait, then stopped off at Starbucks and now proffered peace offerings—a box of cranberry bars, mochas for Murray and myself, a decaf latte for Harlow, and jet black coffee for White Deer.

They held the drinks and food while I unlocked the door and we trooped inside. As I ran a quick check through the house, making sure everything looked okay, I filled them in on the latest.

"Kip's going to be okay?" Harlow asked, warming her hands by one of the heating vents.

"Oh yeah, but today . . . it has to end. We have to cleanse that lot."

As I headed into the kitchen, White Deer stared out the window into the backyard. She turned around, her face unusually solemn. "It won't be easy, but we'll manage it somehow."

"Nanna has a lot of ideas on banishing negative entities

in her journal," I said, going through a few of them. I bit into one of the cranberry bars and closed my eyes. Yum . . . bliss in baked sugar.

"Okay, then. We start the exorcism this afternoon. We may have to do some prep work first, though. If we start early, we can finish in time for your birthday party."

"Providing everything goes as planned," I muttered. I'd had my cocky moments in the past and paid for it, finally learning to hope for the best but plan for the unexpected.

"Speaking of birthdays, I know what Joe bought you!" Harlow grinned, her eyes sparkling. "He's a smart man. He asks for help in selecting gifts when he doesn't know what he's doing."

I'd stuck my birthday on the backburner, but now my curiosity bubbled up. "What did he get me? Perfume? Clothing?"

"You think I'm going to tell?" she said, laughing. "Think again, Miss Nosy. You'll have to wait until tonight to find out. Meanwhile, I'll pick up the cake when I'm shopping for snacks." Harlow had been designated the official refreshments coordinator for the party. She'd ordered the cake, planned out the menu, and was overseeing all of the edibles. Naturally, she'd opted for catered platters and a gourmet cake, which was just fine with me.

"Sounds good," I said. "I hope you've got chocolate in that mix."

"More than you know what to do with," she shot back. "What about guests? Anybody we forgot?"

I thought for a moment. "Horvald and Ida should be back today, and Maeve is coming, and Joe's Aunt Margaret. I invited Cinnamon and Lana, but I doubt that Cinnamon will show." I told them about her predicament.

Murray shook her head. "Man, that girl needs to do

some thinking. He leaves her with three kids and she still puts her heart on the line." She finished her mocha. "Well, I'm off to work. Jimmy won't be able to show up until around eight. He's off checking his trap lines."

"Tell him I could use a mink." Harlow grinned. "So, did you invite Andrew?"

I grimaced. "You really think Joe would appreciate that? Besides Andrew is getting creepier and I don't need any more complications in my life. He's become a pain in the neck. I told you, didn't I, that he's been calling every time he gets drunk and begging me to leave Joe?"

"No! Oh my God, I bet Joe loves that!"

"Yeah, they make quite a pair. Joe would love nothing more than to go over and deck the guy, but I won't let him."

They laughed as they headed out the door, Murray to work and Harlow to shop. White Deer and I set about gathering what we'd need for the exorcism. I pulled out my Florida water, some white sage, lavender, cedar smudge sticks, a piece of amethyst crystal, and a five-pound box of kosher salt.

White Deer was poring over the variation I'd written up with for Nanna's charm. "You know, I think this adaptation you've created will work. It's really quite lovely." She paused, then asked, "Have you seen the Will o' the Wisps lately?"

"A few." I shrugged. "For the most part, they seem to have disappeared when we found Brigit's skeleton." I told her about the journal entry and my theory. "I guess they were there to bring my attention to Brigit's remains. They're nasty buggers, but they did their job."

"A lot of nature spirits aren't very *nice*," White Deer said. "People forget that they aren't human, and don't play by human rules."

Good point.

White Deer showed me the things she'd brought, *just in case*. A rattle, some special incense, blessed river rocks that were taken from a sacred spot—with approval—after much prayer. She also had a bag full of quartz crystals.

"Hold on," I said, dashing to answer the phone as it rang.

"Hey babe, you naked?"

"No I'm not, and when are you coming over?" I asked.

Joe snorted. "I take it you want to be naked. Well, you'll have to wait a little while for that, sweetie. I'm going to be a little late. I need to stop by a store and pick up something for tonight. The store's in Bellingham."

I rolled my eyes. "You're not buying the deed to another empty lot, I hope?"

"Yeah, like I'm going to try that one again. Who knows what you'd manage to find on it? Aliens, probably." Laughing, he hung up after promising to be back around six.

Even though a few last rays of sun had broken through the thick clouds for a rare hello, we bundled tip. The thermometer read forty-seven degrees and evening was on its way. Gear in hand, White Deer and I headed next door, and cautiously entered the lot. It was quiet, almost as if an uneasy truce was under way.

"I'm trying to decide whether it would be better to lay out everything near the yew tree where her body was left, or in her bedroom." Both had their advantages and disadvantages. My main concern with the basement room was that we'd have farther to run if we needed to get out of there in a hurry.

White Deer squinted against a ray of light that splashed across her face, leaving a golden glow in its wake. "My vote is for the bedroom. It probably had better memories than the yew tree, which was essentially her grave."

Good point. I sighed, as we cautiously peered into the basement. I didn't want to go down there again, but if it would put an end to all of this, I wasn't going to back down. The stairs were slick with rain-soaked debris—leaves and twigs and needles from the trees still shedding the last of their summer foliage.

Step-by-step, we descended into the gloom of the basement. I couldn't help but wonder what the layers of mulch were hiding. A movement caught my eye and I flinched as a wolf spider scuttled across the top of the leaves. Where there was one, there were others, and I had no desire to meet his kinfolk. I slogged through the ankle-deep detritus, wincing as my foot met something soft and squishy. Oh God, please let whatever it was be vegetation-related.

By the time we reached the bedroom, the energy was tangible, crackling around us. As the day progressed, the veils between the worlds of spirits and of mortals had started to part. I hurried to open the door.

White Deer set up the high-beam flashlight she'd brought, placing it on the nightstand while I reluctantly sat down on the bed and emptied my tote bag of ingredients onto the ragged covers. We spread out our crystals and incense in a ring on the desk, with the photocopied pages from Brigit's journal in the center, topping them with the copy of the picture of Brigit and Mab. Over the top of everything, I gently scattered Samantha's hair.

White Deer watched while I circled the quartz spikes with salt, taking care to create no break in the thick ring. "Are you going to smudge?"

"Yeah, once I have everything set up. I guess we're about ready."

"What do you want me to do?" she asked.

"Focus on my energy and do what you can to increase it."

"In essence, be your amplifier." She grinned as I flushed, but then I saw she was teasing.

"Yeah, something like that." I lit the smudge stick and smoke began to fill the room. The soothing smell of sage and cedar always reminded me of pot roast and turkey and big dinners around the table. The tension in my shoulder blades began to ease up a little. Come what may, at least I'd go into this clear and calm.

I inhaled slowly and let out my breath in a thin stream. "Winds, mighty winds, hear me. Blow through this space, clear the path for Samantha and Mab to find their way home."

White Deer murmured something that I didn't catch but the energy shifted and grew stronger with her words. I splashed Florida water around the room.

"Waters of life, cleanse and purify. Let our task be exposed, shining before us so we might know what to do."

Again, White Deer's energy echoed my own and heightened it. After a moment, the power began to rise. I lifted my left hand and, using two fingers, drew runes in the air. Runes that Nanna had taught me years ago, runes to attract the attention of the spirits, runes to banish negativity, runes to protect. I seldom used them, preferring a gentler approach to matters, but this situation called for every resource I had.

I drew the rune for summoning, the rune for cleansing, and the rune for protection. A low rumble echoed through the room. Earthquake? Maybe. Astral-quake? Probably. Energy raced through my hand, buzzing like a good jolt of caffeine on a slow morning.

White Deer positioned herself on the bed, cross-legged, and closed her eyes, serene in a way I could never be. She was both peaceful and wise, yet I knew if anything crossed her path, she'd simply take a breath and zap it to hell. I lit a white taper candle and used the flame to keep the smudge stick alight.

Inhaling deeply, I grounded myself as the energy flowed up from the ground to seep through the floor, into my feet, up my legs until it coiled in my belly like a snake around warm hearth embers. I raised my arms and focused on the images of Mab and Samantha, then called out in Nanna's native tongue:

> *"Du, der Du liebesverloren bist,*
> *Komm zurück zu mir.*
> *Von der Welt in der Du schreitest*
> *In die Welt, in welcher ich lebe*
> *Folge meiner Stimme,*
> *Komm zurück an meine Seite."*

> "You who are love lost, return to me.
> From the world in which you walk
> To the world in which I live,
> Follow my voice,
> Return home to my side."

There was a hush, then a rustle. I exhaled. White Deer sat very still and we looked at each other, waiting. Nothing, and yet—everything. Something was stirring, I could feel it even though it hadn't yet manifested. I closed my eyes, focused my attention, and with my right hand reached out for White Deer who clasped it firmly, linking her aura to mine as she magnified the energy.

Again, I held up the dagger and this time envisioned Mab and Samantha and tried to light the path for the two cats to return to their respective homes. I could feel them watching from the periphery—both curious, both lonely. I sent out a tendril on the breeze, beckoning Samantha, begging her to come home and White Deer added her own call. She was working with earth mana, slower than the force of the wind, but deep and resonating with life.

"Let this space be cleared and protected, and made clean once more!"

As we pushed the protective charm out to encompass the entire lot, the energy spiraled, running through the vines, through the blackberry suckers deep within the earth, through the tree roots and rocks, seeking to forge the path for the cats, seeking to link the two worlds so they could trade places. Our force was an arrow, whistling through the air as it attempted to part the veils.

And then, the charm ground to a halt and it felt as if there was a boulder blocking the path. White Deer leapt to her feet and stared into the corner. As I scrambled up, I saw what she was looking at.

Brigit was standing there, Samantha by her side. Tears ran down her face as she held out her hands to Mab, who crouched on the other side of the room. But they could not connect.

"What are we missing?" I shouted, exasperated. "Why won't this work?" As I spoke, a gust swept through and extinguished the candle. The room plunged into darkness. My stomach knotted as I backed up toward the door, White Deer following suit. As we stumbled out into the fading afternoon, the light blinded me, and I moaned, resting my head against the wall.

"I have a splitting headache."

White Deer shook her head. "I can think of only one reason that the spell won't complete. The veils between worlds haven't parted enough. Tonight, when they open fully, we can finish this."

Angry, frustrated, I slogged my way through the

mulch, trying to keep my footing. I forced my way up the stairs, cold and tired.

"Emerald, are you okay?" White Deer put her hand on my shoulder, stopping me.

I shook my head. "I feel horrible. We just left them. Sure, Brigit and Mab are spirits, but they want to be together. And Sammy—how can I just leave her? I can't take this much longer."

White Deer put her hand on my shoulder. "We're doing what needs to be done. Our timing's just off."

I glanced back at the basement. "Tonight, you say?"

"Yes," she said. "Tonight, it will be over and done with." She spoke with such conviction that I almost believed her. She saw me wavering and added, "Trust and keep hope, Emerald."

A distant crash of thunder sent me shivering. I sighed. "So what do we do?"

"Go back to your house," White Deer said. "And tonight, we come back to finish what we started."

With a deep breath, I glanced at the sky. The clouds were gathering thick and fast. "Okay, but there's a storm coming. If we don't get Sammy tonight, I don't think we ever will. She'll be trapped forever."

Fifteen

❖

From Brigit's Journal:

He's gone upstairs to talk to them. No matter what happens, I refuse to cry, or to beg. We O'Reillys have our pride. I think I've forgotten that over the past two years. But never again. Either things work out here, or I return home. I'll know in a few minutes which direction my life is going to take. I'm frightened.

"SO HOW DO we proceed tonight?" I asked. "Do we go through everything again? Or just show up and wait?"

White Deer slid into a chair. She closed her eyes, and after a moment, said, "I think, if we show up and follow our instincts, things will work out. I can't see clearly, except the end—and I can see Samantha home with you."

"I wish Murray could be here." I liked White Deer, but Murray and I were closer, and she offered me more in the way of comfort and support.

White Deer glanced at her watch. "She's planning on

joining us. I wonder what's keeping her?" She pulled out her phone. "I'll give her a call."

I nodded as the front door opened. "I'm going to see who it is," I said, popping down the hall to find Joe coming through the door. He grabbed me up and planted a big kiss on my lips.

"Happy birthday, babe. What are you doing? I know what I want to do."

With a grin, I untangled myself. "White Deer's here, so put that thought on hold for awhile."

He let out a loud sigh. "Okay, but tonight—you and me—your bedroom. After your birthday party."

"Sounds good. Now, come say 'hi' and hear what we've been up to."

White Deer was off the phone. "Anna will be here in a little bit," she said. She waved at Joe. "Has Emerald been filling you in on this afternoon?" He shook his head, and we took turns telling him the latest.

"I wish there was something I could do to help," he said.

I leaned my head against his arm. "Thanks, sweetie, but there's nothing for you to do. It's all up to White Deer, Murray, and me now." I looped my arm through his. "You just take care of the party preparations. We'll do the ghost hunting."

Joe snickered. "Yeah, and get yourselves in trouble, no doubt. But, hey, I'd probably do a lot worse. Okay, I run the show here, and you run the show on the other side. I'm used to it by now." He shrugged. "So put me to work. Harlow told me she's bringing decorations and food. What should I do?"

"Could you pick up the kids from school and keep them away from the house for a couple hours? I don't want them anywhere near this place while we're exorcising those spirits. Unless I know Kip and Randa are okay, I'll be distracted, and distractions can lead to trouble. Please keep them safe for me? I'll take my cell phone and call you if we need help."

Joe looked like he wanted to protest, but finally shoved his hands in his pockets. "Making sure we're not in the line of fire, aren't you? All right. But Emerald, promise me you'll be careful. I want you in one piece when I come home." His voice sounded as shaky as I felt.

I held up my right hand. "If things get too scary, we'll pull back. I give you my word." I reached up on tiptoe and planted a long kiss on his lips.

His arms slid around me and he held me for a moment, not speaking, not moving, pressed against me. I could feel his desire, rock solid against me, gentle and yet insistent. Then he let go and, without another word, took off down the porch steps. I watched him leave, then quietly went to the phone and put in a call to Randa and Kip's teachers to let them know that Joe would be picking them up.

White Deer and I glanced out the window just in time to see Murray pull into the driveway, with Harlow right behind her. The light was fading and I could feel the shift as the veils began to open. After they trooped inside, I showed Harlow where I kept the Halloween candy, should any children come trick-or-treating, and then Murray, White Deer, and I took off for the lot. I glanced at them. "White Deer was right—the timing has shifted. I can feel it."

Murray nodded. "Yep . . . the wind's picked up and the spirits are walking."

As we cautiously entered the lot in the growing dusk, a flicker of apprehension tickled my stomach. The entire area felt like it had torn itself asunder from the rest of the world. Old spirits lived here, and very few of them human. They had slumbered throughout the years until Joe and I decided to expose their secrets to the light. Now, we had to put them to rest for good.

White Deer pulled out her rattle. "Follow me. We'll work our way from the outskirts of the lot this time, down to the basement." I could feel her center, grounding her energy into the soil, letting it run deep into the roots. After a moment, she began to encircle the lot, praying softly in her native tongue as she shook her rattle with every step.

Murray and I followed, shoring up the energy, amplifying it. This was it, the big one. Now or never. A wave of protection began to emanate from our hands, and we pushed it out to roll across the lot, to encompass the shadows and crevices and niches left untouched by time for so many years. Striding as tall as the treetops, we forged our path, mist rising from our steps to swirl around our feet. Onward, we drove the clearing force through the lot, purifying and purging.

As we approached the yew tree, the conflicting forces began to play push-pull, a battle of pain against clarity. Over the years, all the trauma and secrets the land had seen had grown into a cohesive entity—without consciousness, and yet with a will to survive. And I knew, without a doubt, that this entity would act as a beacon for malign spirits, especially tonight. By waking up the lot, we'd opened a portal and now we had to close it.

White Deer continued her prayer as we moved forward. Every step was harder. For every inch we gained, the remaining energy grew more resistant, and yet we pressed on.

I caught my breath as we approached the stairs. There, in the basement, rested the heart and core of whatever had happened to Brigit. We might never know who'd killed her, but maybe we could put the past to rest, and she and Mab to rest along with it.

White Deer glanced at me. "It's time to go down. Time to build the bridge and return everyone to their proper places."

I nodded and started down the stairs. On the bottom step, I almost tripped, and splashed into the muck. One of the mildewing leaves flew into my mouth and the sour tang of decay hit my tongue. Spitting it out, I headed toward Brigit's bedroom, Murray and White Deer behind me. There, inside the room, we could see Brigit, Mab, and Samantha, waiting for us.

"Okay," I said. "Let's go."

As we entered the room, the sound of a car door topside alerted us. "Who the fuck is that?" Frustration swept over me.

Murray patted me on the shoulder. "I'll take a quick look," she said, dashing up the stairs.

White Deer and I waited, poised on the brink between two worlds. Murray's voice came drifting down on the wind. "You'd better come up here, Em . . . I'm not sure what's going down."

I shook my head, glancing back at Brigit. "Damn it. I'll be right back. White Deer, stay here and keep an eye on things, please." I raced up the stairs to Murray's side. "This better be good—" I started to say, then fell silent.

A car had parked by the curb, and wandering through the lot, in our direction, were Brent and Irena. Irena looked nervous, and she was holding a flashlight. I rushed over to her side.

"What are you doing here? What's Brent doing here?"

She flinched a little and I backed away. As irritated as I was, I didn't want to scare her.

"I'm sorry. I didn't want to come, but my brother

begged me to. Dr. Ziegler called me today and said Brent was acting strangely, that he wanted to talk to me. I drove out there, and Brent begged me to bring him here. He was crying, saying he had to come home, and that it had to be tonight."

I glanced at Brent. A luminous glow echoed softly in his eyes and his gaze was darting around the lot, looking for something. Or someone. And then, he saw the yew and broke away from Irena's side as he began to stride toward it, his eyes focused on the tree. As if the present had embraced the past, I could simultaneously see both the Brent who had been a virile young man, and the Brent who was the broken old man I'd met in the institution. Like a double exposure on film.

He began to move forward again and Irena suddenly came to life, her voice stronger than I expected it to be. "Brent, you have to stop. There's nothing left of her— she's gone."

Brent turned, a look of hatred splashed across his face. "Get out of here. I know where you put her! Nobody's stopping me from going to her—do you understand? Nobody."

He stumbled a little and Irena jumped forward to help him, but tripped over a root. She gave a little cry of pain as she fell. Murray raced over to Irena's side and helped her up as I started toward Brent.

"Calm down," I said in the gentlest voice I could muster. "Brigit's not there anymore, Brent. We found her."

He held up his hands, as if to ward me off. "Get out— leave us alone! I don't need you, I don't need any of you. *We* don't need you."

"Brent, that's not true! I'm your sister," Irena called out.

"My sister? Do you think I care? You're just as guilty

as Father was. You left me in that hospital all these years, hoping to keep us apart, but there's nothing you can do now. I won't go back, do you hear me? I'll die before I let you take me back."

Irena turned to me. "I have to get him out of here. This was a huge mistake. The doctor told me it might be, but I thought it would make him happy. But the doctor was right—he's not in his right mind—"

The strength of Brent's laughter echoed through the lot, and I knew, right then, that he had nothing to lose. "You're right," he said. "I *wasn't* in my right mind, but now I am. So all of you get out of here and leave us alone."

Irena straightened her shoulders and began to walk toward him. "Brent, listen to me. You need help. Let me take you back to my house—"

"No. Brigit's here, I know she is. I can't leave her again." He drooped, wearing his anguish like a cloak of feathers. A sparkle of light glistened—a few of the corpse candles had gathered by the yew, but I seemed to be the only one who noticed them.

Irena grimaced. "Stop! Just stop. You know what happened, but you refuse to believe it now, just like you refused to believe it fifty years ago. Why can't you let the past go? Don't dig up ancient history. Brent. Quit blaming me. Quit blaming our parents. Brigit's dead. Mother's dead. Father's dead. It's been half a century. Can't you let her go?"

Brent straightened his shoulders and began a slow march toward Irena. "You want me to let her go? Fifty years or a day, it doesn't matter when you've lost the woman you love! You wouldn't know how that feels, would you? You married your husband for his money. You married prestige and power, but you didn't marry into love. And I paid the price for that, thanks to our beloved parents." He spat out the words, one by one.

"You want to bury what Father did, just like he buried Brigit. Just like he buried all his sins with her body," he continued. Irena began to back away, fear clouding her face. "Why not just sweep it under the rug, sanitize everything and pretend we're still the social elite of the town? Can't let anything soil our reputation, can we? Can't let her blood stain our name. Can't let anybody know what Father's done. Well, it's over!"

I glanced at Murray. Brent thought his father had murdered Brigit? Did that mean he had nothing to do with her death? Absorbed in what was going on, it suddenly occurred to me that he might try to hurt Irena. I jabbed Murray in the side. "We have to do something!"

She shook her head. "I want to hear what he has to say. I'll jump in if he makes any move to harm her, but we're finally getting some answers to a whole lot of questions about Brigit's disappearance and death."

Irena's face crumpled. "Brent, it was an accident. You know that. She wasn't supposed to die, but there wasn't anything we could do back then, and there's nothing that you can do now. She's gone, Brent. She died a long time ago. Sometimes, people leave us. Sometimes, all our plans go crashing to the floor and we're left with nothing but crumbs." She held out her hands to him.

"What would you know about it? You got what you wanted! Queen bee, married to Mr. Moneybags. Cock of the walk, and you the prize peahen. And you begrudged my happiness with Brigit because you were such a god-damned snob. You told him not to let her have the baby," he sobbed. "You're the reason he killed her. You're the reason Brigit died along with my child!"

Baby? I glanced at Murray. Brigit had been pregnant?

By Brent? And then I remembered the journal. The entries about a shameful secret, one she couldn't let the Brunswicks find out about. It was all falling into place. Brent hadn't killed Brigit. He'd been in love with her, and he was the father of her unborn child. And then, either Edward Brunswick had killed her in a fit of rage, or she died in some sort of accident for which Brent blamed his father. Either way, Brigit had been stripped out of his life and her death sent him over the edge.

Irena fell to her knees, crying. "You're right—I didn't love Thomas. He was a good catch and Mother said I should be grateful, so I married him. But none of that matters anymore. Brent, you loved Brigit in a way I can never understand. I've never felt that kind of love. Do you understand? Even for a short time, you had something I'll never have."

I felt someone by my side and jumped, but it was just White Deer. She leaned close to me. "Brigit's awfully stirred up down there. I wasn't feeling altogether safe. And Samantha disappeared."

My heart sank as Brent spoke again, his voice cracking. "Why did you do it? Why did you let Father get away with murder?"

Frustrated, Irena lost her temper. "Damn it, Brent, you know perfectly well that our father didn't murder Brigit. Her death was an accident! You know that. She fell down the stairs and hit her head—you were there! You were the first to reach her side."

"You're lying! He shoved her!" And then, Brent whirled sharply as a voice echoed from the basement.

"Brent? Brent? Brent! Where are you?"

Everyone froze, and then slowly turned toward the stairs. There, clad in a nimbus of pale ivory light, stood Brigit. A living statue, and yet vibrant and beautiful and so terribly aware. She was gazing at Brent, and the look on her face was the happiest I'd ever seen.

"Brigit!" Brent backed away from Irena as the yew tree sighed and the heaviness in the lot began to expand. The Will o' the Wisps went into a dance, darting through the air over to Brigit's side, faerie sparkles against the velvet night.

"Brigit," whispered Irena as she stared with horror at the ghostly image of the red-haired spirit.

And Brigit, she had eyes only for Brent, a look of utter devotion filling her face. The power of their love was tangible, still alive through fifty years of separation, through the veil of death itself. Brent stumbled forward, his longing echoing through the air, through the waves of energy that pulsed like breakers on the shore.

Overwhelmed, I could hear the beating of his heart, the ache of her desire. A terrifyingly fragile link had remained between them despite her long years among the dead, and it shimmered—a thin cord glowing in the night. I understood then that they'd never been truly separated. They'd been bound to one another since the day they met. With a love so strong, how could anyone deny their reunion?

As Brent approached Brigit, Mab fell in by his side, leading him forward. The ghostly calico mewed loudly as they approached the basement where Brigit waited. Then the cat let out a yowl and raced over to coil behind Brigit's skirt, where Brigit caught her up in her arms and buried her face in the cat's fur.

"Brent! Brent? Stay away—she's dangerous!" Irena's voice quavered. Brent ignored her.

"Brigit. Is it really you? Forgive me, please forgive me. I couldn't save you. I tried, but I couldn't stop it from happening. Can you ever forgive me? I love you. It's always been you—only ever been you." His voice cracked and the flicker of tears shimmered on his cheeks.

"I've died a thousand deaths every day, every time I remember your face." He held out his hands, beseeching. "When you looked at me, that moment right before you fell, I knew then that my world had ended."

"Brent! Stop, please stop. She's dead. Leave it alone, let her spirit rest. Come home with me. You can live with me and I'll take care of you." Irena's voice spiraled into the night.

The scene played out like an old movie flickering on a scratched screen in a theater long closed to the public. In my heart, I knew Brent was already dead. He had long been linked to another world and there was nothing we could do to reclaim him, to save him from his destiny.

Brent's eyes flashed, shining as he spoke to Irena. He was poised on the very brink and something had to give. If he went back to the hospital, he'd never again touch the world with a clear mind. "Let me go. Let me be happy."

"No! Brent! Don't!" Irena raced forward.

"Irena! You'll startle him!" Murray shouted, racing after her, but she slipped in the mud and fell face first into a small pile of brambles, letting out a shout as the thorns drove deep. As she struggled to extricate herself, Irena stopped, as if suddenly aware of how close to the edge of the stairs Brent was standing.

She held her hands out to him. "Brent, I'm begging you, come home with me. Everything will be okay. You'll be okay and live with me. We can be brother and sister again."

He gazed at her, then silently turned back to Brigit. She smiled softly and let Mab jump to the ground, holding her arms wide, reaching for him. As he stepped toward her,

she slowly moved back, hovering over the basement, glo-
rious and brilliant, no longer a lost soul.

And then, Brent stumbled toward her almost like a
child toward his mother. In his haste, his foot caught on
one of the brambles rooted by the side of the foundation
and he wavered, flailing for just a moment before he tumbled headfirst down the stairs, a single cry echoing as he
fell. Brigit looked directly at me, relief and peace flooding
her face. Then she, Mab, and the Will o' the Wisps faded
into the night.

Sixteen

❖

Mur IMMEDIATELY TOOK charge. "Emerald, you and White Deer go check on him. I'll call 911."

While she pulled open her cell phone, White Deer and I hit the stairs. Brent's unmoving figure lay below in the muck. A wave of vertigo flooded over me and everything seemed to shift as I found myself staring down at Brigit's body. Then, in the blink of an eye, it was once again Brent at the foot of the steps. My feet slipped and I almost went headfirst down after him but White Deer, who was right on my heels, grabbed me by the arm.

I fell back against the stairs and, breathless, wiped my eyes. "Oh God, I'll be glad when this night is over."

After making sure I hadn't broken anything, I lit off down the stairs again. White Deer was already checking his pulse by the time I joined her. She looked up at me and shook her head. "Dead."

Dead was right. Brent's neck was turned in an unnatural position, but the look on his face was that of a glori-

ously happy man. There was nothing to be done for him—
his long wait was over. I glanced over at the bedroom door
and wandered inside, but it felt empty, as if Brigit was
well and truly gone. There was no sign of Samantha, either. Just an empty room in a burnt-out house on an empty
lot. That about summed it up.

The woo-woo of sirens came whirring up on the street.
White Deer and I looked at each other. There wasn't much
to say. We waited in silence as the paramedics came filing
down the dark stairs, Joe hot on their heels.

"The kids—" I started to say but he cut me off.

"They're okay, I left them with my aunt. I heard on
the scanner that there had been an accident here and
thought . . . I thought . . ." He broke off, unable to finish
his sentence. I saw the terror lurking in his eyes.

"You thought it was me."

He pulled me into his arms so tight I couldn't breathe
and buried his face in my hair. "Don't you ever leave me,
Emerald O'Brien. Don't you ever leave me. Whatever
happens, don't leave me alone."

"Hey, Captain, can we get a hand here?" one of the
medics called over to Joe.

He searched my face, staring deeply into my eyes before he went over to help them. I watched the men work
on Brent for a moment, then headed upstairs. I craved the
light, craved noise and laughter and the joy of having my
family gathered around me.

"*I am half-sick of shadows, said the Lady of Shalott,*" I
whispered to no one in particular. Only the wind heard; it
swept up my words and carried them away.

MURRAY FILLED DEACON and Greg in on what
had happened. She told them that Brent and Irena had

come to visit what had once been their home. Brent lost control, he got loose from Irena's side, tripped and fell down into the basement before any of us could stop him.

White Deer, Irena, and I verified her story—it seemed easiest all the way around. And that, was that. Nobody put up a fuss and I realized that Brent was one of so many people who fell through the cracks of society. Forgotten, mentally ill . . . nobody would pay much attention to the death of an old man. Oh, someone here or there who remembered his name might blink over the obituary notice, but other than that, Brent would fade into history, as obscured by time as Brigit had been.

Irena leaned on White Deer's arm and we made our way over to my house. We gathered around the table, exhausted.

Joe peeked in. "I'm off to round up the kids and cats," he said, then headed out.

I put the kettle on for a pot of peppermint tea. Our spirits needed warming as much as our bodies. White Deer struck up a fire in the fireplace. When the flames were good and crackling, we gathered around the hearth with our tea.

Irena settled into the recliner and stared at the flames. Her eyes were red, but she wasn't crying and I had the feeling the shock of the whole situation hadn't hit home yet. I sat on the ottoman next to her.

"Irena, do you want to tell us about it now? There's no use in keeping quiet anymore."

Her gaze flickered over my face, then to Murray. "I suppose I should. You'll need to know for your report and it will put things to rest. Once and for all." She took a sip of tea while Mur pulled out her notebook and flipped it open.

"Brigit was your maid, correct?" Murray asked.

Irena nodded. "My mother hired her from an employment agency. Brigit was fresh off the boat and so full of hope. Her mother and father were dead, and her sister ran away a few years before that. So Brigit packed her suitcase and came to America, hoping for a new life. She wanted to go to school, to become a teacher. But she didn't have enough money, so she went to work as a housekeeper instead."

"Times were tough," White Deer said.

"For some people," Irena murmured. "Not for my family. I just wish she'd picked another house to work in. Maybe she would have actually been able to live her life all the way through, then." She hung her head for a moment. We didn't pressure her. She would talk when she felt like it.

After a pause, she tried again. "From the start, Brent fell in love with Brigit. They were two of a kind—dreamers, romantics. He'd just returned home from another failed attempt at college and was so emotionally vulnerable. Brent was a poet, an artist. Father wanted him to be a 'real man'—you know, make good on the game, make good in a job. 'Follow in my footsteps, son.' That sort of thing. But Brent wasn't cut out to be a carbon copy of Father."

"Those were the days when men were expected to be strong," Murray said and Irena nodded.

"Yes. When Brent couldn't live up to Father's expectations, it caused a rift in our family. Our mother always tried to stand up for him, but she was drunk a good share of the time. And Father . . . whew, when he got angry, the house shook. I have to admit, I sided with Father. I was such a little snob. All I could think about was how Brent's behavior would reflect on me. And, when he told us that he'd fallen in love with Brigit, it destroyed the family."

I poured more tea all around. It must be terribly difficult for her to dredge up the dirty laundry that had remained hidden for so many years. Secrets that had buried a death for so long. The fire popped and White Deer added another log. Grateful for the warmth, I soaked in the light.

"I had just become engaged to my husband—he was the son of William Finch, one of Chiqetaw's finest lawyers," Irena continued. "Thomas had his degree from Princeton. He was hired to a good job at the Rutherford Savings & Loan. You see, my husband always has had a wonderful nose for business, and it was clear from the start that he'd be heading right up the ranks. Father wanted the match to go through. With the Finch family at the top of the social register, anybody who married Thomas would be set for life, and it would reflect well on our own family."

She blinked, looking lost for a moment. "The day that Brent told us Brigit was pregnant and that he wanted to marry her was horrible. I was there, and remember begging Father to put an end to it. If my brother married a servant, I knew Thomas would find some excuse to break off our engagement. His family wouldn't stand for it. They considered the Irish poor white trash."

I began to have an inkling of the household dynamics that must have raged through the family. Poor Brent. A father ashamed of his son's sensitivities, a sister who put her own desire for prestige above the happiness of her brother.

"What happened?" I asked.

"All hell broke loose."

White Deer broke in. "What did your mother think?"

Irena shrugged. "Honestly, I'm not sure. Nobody ever paid any attention to her. I think she might have taken Brigit under her wing and welcomed her into the family. She liked Brigit, even though she could be harsh on the girl at times. But it wasn't to happen. That morning . . . that horrible morning . . ." She covered her face with her hands. "Do I have to say?"

Murray rested one hand on Irena's arm. "Irena, you need to tell me everything. Please?"

Irena blew her nose and sighed. "Father blew up. So did I. We got into a huge argument with Brent. He insisted that he was going to marry her and legitimize their child. Father threatened to cut him out of the will, and Brent told him to go to hell. Mother was crying and I was screaming at Brent for being so stupid. About that time, Brigit appeared at the top of the stairs—her room was the one in the basement that you found."

She flushed and stared hard at her cup. "I think I called Brigit a slut. Brent shoved me—not hard, but enough to make Father blow up at him. Brigit tried to defend him and Father pushed her away. Not enough to hurt her, but it caught her off guard."

Murray was busy scribbling away, looking impassive as usual. White Deer's eyes were pressed shut.

Irena took a deep breath and let it out slowly. Her voice was almost a whisper. "Brigit stumbled and her shoe caught on a loose board next to the basement steps. I remember she teetered—like a leaf about to fall off a tree. Father tried to catch her but he was all over. She tumbled headfirst down the stairs. Brent was by her side in an instant, but it was too late. Brigit was dead, and her baby with her—she was only a few months along. Her cat padded up and curled on her chest as she lay there."

I took her cup from her and set it on the end table. "Is that why Brent blamed your father for her death?" I asked.

Irena nodded. "Yes."

I mulled over the story. Was anyone really to blame? Maybe, but only in so many indirect ways. Irena and her father had contributed to Brigit's death, but it had clearly been an accident. Circumstance playing out in a tragedy that would come back to haunt those involved. Brigit had tripped on a loose board and died. Brent had tripped over a root and died in the same spot where she had fallen. The sheer sadness of it all was overwhelming.

Murray stopped writing. Her face grim, she asked, "What happened then? Why did you bury her in the tree?"

After a moment, Irena shrugged, looking forlorn and haggard, every year of her age weighing down on her shoulders. "What if the police found out? What would happen to our family name? Thomas would surely call off our engagement." She pressed her lips together, and I had the feeling every image she recounted was as fresh today as it had been fifty years ago. "While Brent mourned over Brigit in the basement, my father told Mother and me that we couldn't breathe a word of what happened to anybody. He might go to jail and then where would we be? Out on the streets. Oh, he probably exaggerated, but at the time we believed him. Brigit was an orphan, from Ireland. Nobody would miss her. He suggested we tell everybody that she ran off with the silverware. Nobody would question us. Servants weren't really human, not in our social circle."

On a roll, her voice grew louder, as if she was anxious to get everything out in the open. "Father gave Brent a couple tranquilizers and put him to bed. He carried Brigit into her room, then headed out back to find a place to bury her. There weren't many homes around back then.

"He decided to bury her in the hole beneath the yew tree. So Mother and I followed him downstairs to get the body . . . Brigit. There, we found little Mab on her chest again, dead. Like she'd crawled up there and just . . . closed her eyes for one last time. We buried them together.

Mother was crying and Father wouldn't speak. I don't even remember what I felt. I guess at that point, I blamed Brent for causing all the trouble in the first place. I didn't even think about Brigit, not really. Not for several weeks to come."

I could picture Irena, young and frightened that all her dreams might shatter. A domineering father and complacent mother. Even though I couldn't imagine myself ever making the same choices or acquiescing as she had, I understood what had enticed her to take part in the cover-up.

"We wrapped Brigit and Mab in a sheet, and buried them beneath the yew tree. The hole was large enough to contain the body, and the woods were thick. We never thought she'd be found. Father sealed off her bedroom and we told everybody she'd disappeared in the night."

"What happened to Brent?" White Deer asked.

"He sank into a state of catatonia. We smuggled him off to the institution and told them he was having delusions. For all intents and purposes, he was nonfunctional for a number of years. Father paid the hospital a pretty penny to keep Brent's presence a secret . . . a couple of months later, we let it be known that he'd run away to Europe. I got married, and everything was fine; then on Halloween night lightning struck the house and burned it to the ground. The timbers fell in on the basement. Everything was destroyed."

"And that's what happened to Brigit O'Reilly." I finished off my tea.

She nodded. "Yes. My parents moved away soon after the house burned. They left Brent in my care, promising me most of the estate if I'd keep tabs on him. I paid for his care out of a trust fund they set up. I didn't go to visit him for a couple of years, then I went every month when I began to realize just what we'd done. I don't think our parents ever saw him again."

She leaned back and stared at Murray. "So that's it. Am I going to jail?"

Murray looked at her and I could read the frustration in her eyes. Sometimes life left everything in a tangled mess. The case was solved, but there was no real happy ending. Except perhaps there was, for Brent and Brigit.

"I can't tell you for sure. I have to file a report. I have no doubt the press will snap it up, so I recommend you tell your husband everything before tomorrow morning. If you're asking for my professional opinion, to me it sounds like an accident. You helped cover up her death, but whatever the judge decides, I doubt if the punishment will be harsh."

Irena nodded. She wiped her nose with her hand. "I can't tell you how good—and how shameful—it feels to get this off my chest after all these years. I don't think a day's gone by when I haven't regretted everything I said or did to the both of them."

She turned to me. "When I found out that your young man meant to buy this lot, I panicked and tried to stop the sale. But I suppose the dead will tell their tales, no matter how much the living try to stop them."

She took my hand. "Emerald, I don't pretend to understand everything that went on out there, and I'm not even going to ask, but I can't help but feel that Brent is easier now. He really did die when Brigit died. Maybe they're together. I'd like to think so."

"One last question," I said. "Who painted the murals? In her bedroom? Was it Brent?"

Irena let out a soft laugh. "I guess the tranquilizers didn't take and he went downstairs while we were outside. He painted all night. The next day when Mother went to take him some breakfast she couldn't find him and we searched the house. He was lying on Brigit's bed and didn't speak again for years. The murals were there, fresh and beautiful. Father said to leave them—even he couldn't bear to paint over them."

Murray asked a few more questions, but I could tell she was tired of the whole mess and just wanted to stamp "closed" on the file. I motioned her into the kitchen while White Deer talked to Irena.

"Are you okay?"

She shook her head. "This one pushes some buttons, Em. Jimmy and I have the same problem, in a different way. And I realized tonight just how much he means to me, and how willing I am to fight for him. If I end up losing my job because of this, so be it. I refuse to sweep my relationship under the rug and I won't let anybody give me—or Jimmy—crap about it."

I grabbed her by the shoulders and pulled her into a long hug. "Don't ever worry you'll be alone, Mur," I whispered to her. "I've got your back on this one, and so does Joe."

IRENA LEFT A few minutes later. She said she was going home to have a long talk with her husband.

Murray, White Deer, and I stretched out in front of the fire and I broke out the Oreos and juice. "Well, happy birthday to me," I said, biting into a cookie. "I have to say, this was not my choice of party plans."

"Eh, at least you're among friends," Mur said, laughing. I tossed a pillow at her and she threw it right back, knocking over my juice and spilling it all over the floor. As I scrambled for a towel, the front door opened and Joe, Jimbo, Maeve, the kids, and the three kittens spilled through. Behind them came Horvald, Ida, Harl, and Harlow's husband James.

"We're still celebrating your birthday, whether or not you feel like it," Joe said, sweeping me up in his arms as the kids joined in for a group hug. He leaned close and whispered, "I had the feeling you needed a pick-me-up. This will have to do for now until I can give you a different kind later, in private."

I snickered and pecked his cheek, then knelt by Kip. "Honey, how's your arm?"

He held up his sling and gave me a broad grin. "Cool. A lot of the kids thought it was really neat and Mrs. Campbell said that we could study broken bones in class next week. Can I get a copy of my x-ray to take to class?" He looked so excited that I didn't have the heart to say no, although I'd had my share of bones for awhile—broken or not.

"We'll call the doctor tomorrow, sweetie," I said.

Randa laughed. "I got an A on my test in Science today."

"Very good, as always. I'm proud of you, honey. How's Gunner doing? Is he back in school yet?" Even though we had spent every day of the past week in the same house, it still felt like a vast gulf separated me from my loved ones. By now, I knew that only time and a little peace and quiet would mend the rift. Working on the astral was lonely business.

"No, but I stopped by his aunt's house and he told me that his folks are out of the woods. They need several surgeries, but they'll live. Gunner's moving out by Miner's Lake for now. He's going to stay with his other cousins. He read my poem and said he liked it, but I think he was being nice." She stopped, blushing. "Sorry. I didn't mean to chatter on like that."

"Hey, I like it when you talk. It makes me feel like you

want me to be part of your life." I gave her shoulder a squeeze. "Now what makes you think he was just being nice about your poem?"

She shook her head, laughing. "Face it, Mom. I'm not cut out to be a poet. I tried, but I'm just not interested. But he asked me to the movies next weekend, if that's okay with you."

"Of course it is." I turned around, thrilled to be surrounded by my close friends and family. Well, almost the whole family. Samantha was still missing. Suddenly feeling overwhelmed, I murmured, "Excuse me, I need a breath of air," and slipped out on the front porch. The clouds were luminous and boiling overhead. Rain would break within minutes.

Joe followed me. "Need a shoulder to cry on?"

I nodded. "Hold on," I said, and dashed inside, where I snagged up a little candle and a lighter before returning to the porch. "Walk with me," I said. "I have some good-byes to make."

We headed next door, through the now darkened lot. I knelt at the base of the yew tree and lit the candle, making sure it was out of the way of any brush or leaves. "Brigit and Brent, be at peace and be happy," I whispered. Joe wrapped his arms around my waist and I felt the tears begin to flow. "And Sammy, wherever you are, we tried—we tried so hard to bring you home. I'm sorry."

Joe let go, and I heard him scuffling around in the brush. "What are you doing?" I asked.

He returned with a handful of wet autumn leaves. As he dropped to one knee, my breath caught in my throat.

"I can't make up for Sammy's loss. But it just seems the right time to do this, and the right place," he said. "Emerald, you are a strange and wonderful woman, and a bouquet of autumn leaves seems so appropriate."

I took them, my stomach fluttering.

"I told you in August that on your birthday I was going to get down on one knee and ask you to be my wife. Well, it's your birthday today."

My birthday, and Joe was proposing. He fumbled in his pocket and pulled out a box. As he opened it, the diffused light from the clouds and streetlights illuminated a gleaming brilliant cut diamond set in a band of Black Hills gold.

"Emerald Rhiannon McGrady O'Brien, will you be my friend, my lover, my companion, my wife? Will you marry me and let me make you and your children happy for the rest of our lives?"

I blinked back the tears and it hit me—this was it, this was real. In the midst of death and pain, joy could grow and life could burgeon forth. I fell to my knees and pulled him into my arms.

"Yes! I love you and the kids adore you. We're good together, Joe. You told me we would be, early on, and you were right. I can't think of anyone in the world I'd rather spend my life with except you."

He broke out in a huge smile and let out a loud whoop as he leapt to his feet, dragging me with him. "The woman said yes! She said yes!" he shouted, so loud everybody in the neighborhood could hear him. He slid the ring on my finger. A perfect fit. "Let's go tell them, shall we? They're all on the edge of their seats waiting for your answer."

"You already told them you were going to ask? What if I'd said no?"

He laughed. "But you didn't! You said yes, and that's all that counts." We turned to head back to the house and stopped in midstep. There, not ten feet away, stood Brent and Brigit.

Seventeen

✢

I GASPED AS JOE pulled me to his side. "Don't come any closer," he warned them.

A tinkle of laughter filled the air. Brent and Brigit looked stunning—young and beautiful and so happy. I slipped out of Joe's embrace to stand by his side. "Don't worry," I said, knowing this was a good-bye visit. "They aren't going to hurt us. They're here to thank us."

We stood there staring at one another, two couples divided by time, by space, by the veil of death itself. They, in their shadowy realm and we, in our own clear and vibrantly alive world. Brent leaned down to kiss Brigit on the forehead. She broke out in a smile that echoed through my heart.

"They're so happy," I said. The week had been harsh and tense, the day so traumatic. And yet, as tears dropped on my cheeks I realized that I wasn't crying for them, but for all the love lost in the world. Love lost to fear and hatred and social mores. I stepped forward with Joe behind me, his hands on my shoulders.

"I hope your love lasts forever," I said to Brigit. "I hope you both find in death what you couldn't have together in life."

They seemed to understand. Then Brigit pointed toward a nearby huckleberry bush and there was a rustle in the leaves. I caught my breath. Not the Will o' the Wisps again? But the brush parted and out raced Samantha! She leapt into my arms, snuggling deep under my chin, her purr reverberating through my body like a hot rum toddy on a cold night.

"Sammy! It's Sammy!" I kissed her on the nose and buried my nose in her fur, holding tight for all I was worth, just breathing in her presence. Brigit and Brent clasped hands, gave us a gentle smile, and began to walk toward the yew tree. Mab followed them, her ghostly tail swishing in the astral breeze. As we watched, they shimmered, then vanished from sight.

The storm broke, startling us from our reverie as a rumble of thunder shook the ground.

"Let's get Sammy home," I shouted over the noise. We raced for the house and had just cleared the lot when a huge bolt of lightning split the air.

"The tree! The lightning hit the tree!" Joe yelled. I didn't look back, but instead took the porch steps two at a time, Samantha digging into my shoulder with the most wonderful pain I'd felt in days. I burst in on an anxious party.

"Sammy!" Randa and Kip rushed me but I ran into the spare bedroom and shut the door. I didn't want her to bolt.

They knocked and I carefully let them in. "She's scared and hungry," I said. "Stay in here with her for now, and whatever you do, don't let her out of this room. Get her some food and water and a cat box."

"Mom, can we keep the cats inside all the time?" Kip asked, his voice muffled as he buried his face in her fur. "I've been reading up on it and . . . they live longer."

I smiled. Just what I'd been thinking. "That's a good idea, hon. We'll figure it all out tomorrow. For now, just keep an eye on her and we'll take her to the vet on Monday to make sure she's okay."

I stood up and headed for the living room but Randa stopped me with a plaintive, "Mom?"

"What is it?"

"Joe said . . . did you . . ."

"She's trying to ask if you said 'yes' when Joe asked you to marry him," Kip broke in, grinning like a crazed jack-o'-lantern.

I threw back my head and laughed. "Yes, I said yes. Is that okay with you guys?" They waved me off like I was a moron and I knew there'd be no objections from their quarter.

Everyone in the living room was talking at once. I skirted the mayhem until I found Joe, who was standing on the front porch. A fire engine had blasted its way up the street to stop next door. After a few minutes, we headed down to the sidewalk to meet a fireman walking our way. He told us that although they were checking for hot spots, it looked like the strike had just split the tree and toppled it. There didn't seem to be any flames.

After he headed back to the lot, I snuggled against Joe, the rain dousing us, plastering our hair and clothes close to our bodies.

"Brigit doesn't need her grave anymore. She and Brent are together. The cycle is over and they're off on whatever adventure awaits them next. Do you mind if we uproot that yew once and for all?"

"It seems as though the lightning had the same idea," he said, sliding his arm around my shoulders. "You know, don't you, that I'll love you forever? That if anything ever happens to me, I'll come back with Nanna and watch over you and the kids."

And right then, I realized—on a gut level—that we were both in this for good. That Joe was the only person I could imagine spending my life with. Life would never be the same, and I welcomed the change. Come ghosts and goblins, harvests filled with old bones, Joe and I would see the adventures through together, days by day, year by year, side by side.

And when the time came, maybe we'd be lucky enough to walk through the veil together. But that day was a long way off, and right now, I felt like celebrating. I looked at my ring and broke into a stupid grin.

"Let's go inside. It's my birthday, and our friends and family are waiting. I want cake and ice cream and lots of espresso and I want to show off this gorgeous hunk of rock!"

Joe laughed. "You caffeine freak, you. Come on, Ms. O'Brien. Your party awaits."

We had a lot to celebrate. Samantha was safe, Brigit and Brent were at peace, and I was going to marry the man of my dreams. I took his hand as we walked up the sidewalk to the house.

"Come on Files," I said. "Let's go home."

And we did.

Charm to Call
a Lost Pet Home

When a valued family pet disappears, many people don't understand that it's one of the most traumatic experiences that you can undergo. But there are many things you can do on a practical level, and I recommend all of them *in addition* to this magical charm—remember, if you don't do the work on the mundane, the magic won't help.

- Make color fliers of your pet and post them all over the neighborhood for several blocks.

- Give fliers to veterinarians in your area just in case someone brings in your cat or dog—vets do pay attention to these.

- Offer a reward, but don't specify how much in the flier. There are people who will try to take advantage of grieving owners.

- Check the local animal shelters to see if your pet is there. Don't rely on a phone call. Check every day that they're open.

- You might also want to call your city's street department to ask if they found any animals on the side of the road—a gruesome thought, but it can at least put to rest some disappearances. Closure is always better than wondering what happened.

- Rent or borrow a humane trap from your local ASPCA or local pet rescue organization and learn how to use it. It may seem heartless to try and trap your own cat, but it does work for a lot of people, and it won't hurt them.

- If you use perfume, spray it around your yard in a trail leading up to your door. This will be a familiar scent for them to follow.

- Engage the neighborhood kids in trying to find your pet. Children are notoriously good at searching out lost animals and understand your worry more than some adults might.

- Search every hidey-hole, no matter how small. Cats are experts at sneaking into tight places.

- Remember: Your pet may be so scared that he or she won't come when you call. Be patient: Sit out in your yard and talk to them as if they were there next to you. Use gentle tones.

- Visit the ASPCA's Web site online for more tips and hints (www.aspca.org).

- And lastly: Don't give up. Two of our indoor-only girls were missing last summer and I fell apart—totally went to pieces. They got out accidentally and Samwise and I were worried sick. Two days later, Luna showed up in the backyard, dazed and hungry. But for a while, it felt like Meerclar had been swallowed up by the faeries—she showed up at the door a couple of times but when I ran to let her in, she vanished back into the night. Two weeks later, our neighbor caught her and brought her home to us. I am forever grateful for his kindness.

For the charm, you will need:

A picture of your pet
A statue or figurine of a cat or dog (match it to your pet's species)
A can of cat or dog food
Six quartz crystal spikes—small or large, but approximately the same size as one another
1 oz. catnip (for both cat and dog)
A piece of blank paper and a red ink pen
A brown or green pouch with a red ribbon

On the piece of paper, write your pet's name in firm, bold letters across the top. Beneath this, print your name, address, and the words:

> *Return you home now, safe from harm,*
> *By the workings of this charm,*
> *Hear my call, come home this day,*
> *Safe the passage, safe the way.*
> *My love protects you while you roam,*
> *And keeps you safe for your trip home.*

Fold the paper and hold it, concentrating on your pet. Visualize your pet walking through the yard, up to the door, and into the house. Send this energy out to your pet, then place the paper in the pouch and add the catnip. Tie the ribbon firmly and place the pouch on top of your pet's picture.

Set the can of food next to the picture, along with the statue, then circle everything with the quartz, pointy ends facing out (like sunbeams). Each day your pet is gone, come to this altar and visualize it coming home, while you repeat the charm.

Hold hope in your heart, and do everything you can on a practical level to find your friend. I wish you well with this—it helped our girls find their way home, I'm positive of it.

Bright Blessings,
the Painted Panther
Yasmine Galenorn